THE ONE WHO HOLDS MY HEART

She could see his frustration in his stance. His muscles bulged through his white tank top. It was grimy, gritty, and dirty with sweat. He released and contracted his fists over and over to calm himself.

She felt that way too, only her anger was justifiable. So what if he didn't know why she was mad? It was better that he didn't.

"I don't want to talk to you," she said, concentrating on his forehead instead of looking him in the eyes. If she dared to stare him down, his eyes would implore her to tell him the truth and the feelings for him she still harbored in her heart would surface. "I don't even want to think about you."

"Then why did you come to my house?"

She didn't answer.

"Okay, if that's the way you feel." He doubted she did, but he was tired of arguing with her. "Then at least tell me why."

"Why?" Chyna asked indignantly. "I left town for not even two days. Two days! You pretend as if everything is supposed to be fine between us. As if we're supposed to pick up where we left off. Well, it doesn't work that way. I don't work that way. Nothing between us can be the same, ever."

She turned to leave when she felt his rough hand on her arm again. With one twist she spun around to face him, but he pulled her off balance with a yank and she fell into his arms. Once in his embrace, Dean crushed her against him.

BOOK YOUR PLACE ON OUR WEBSITE AND MAKE THE ARABESQUE ROMANCE CONNECTION!

We've created a customized website just for our very special Arabesque readers, where you can get the inside scoop on everything that's going on with Arabesque romance novels.

When you come online, you'll have the exciting opportunity to:

- View covers of upcoming books

- Learn about our future publishing schedule (listed by publication month and author)

- Find out when your favorite authors will be visiting a city near you

- Search for and order backlist books

- Check out author bios and background information

- Send e-mail to your favorite authors

- Join us in weekly chats with authors, readers and other guests

- Get writing guidelines

- AND MUCH MORE!

Visit our website at
http://www.arabesquebooks.com

The One Who Holds My Heart

TRACEE LYDIA GARNER

BET Publications, LLC
http://www.bet.com
http://www.arabesquebooks.com

ARABESQUE BOOKS are published by

BET Publications, LLC
c/o BET Books
One BET Plaza
1900 W Place NE
Washington, DC 20018-1211

All Kensington Titles, Imprints, and Distributed Lines are available at special quantity discounts for bulk purchases for sales promotions, premiums, fund-raising, and educational or institutional use. Special book excerpts or customized printings can also be created to fit specific needs. For details, write or phone the office of the Kensington special sales manager: Kensington Publishing Corp., 850 Third Avenue, New York, NY 10022, attn: Special Sales Department, Phone: 1-800-221-2647.

First Printing: February 2004
10 9 8 7 6 5 4 3 2 1

Printed in the United States of America

ACKNOWLEDGMENTS

Via the Internet, the world seems a faceless, toneless invention. It is anything but. There are faceless, toneless persons I've never met personally, but their words, advice, input, encouragement and guidance have made these first few years as a novelist smooth sailing and tremendously exciting. I'm forever indebted to each and every one of you for your faithful spirits, your sincerity and your aid. I thank you so very much. To those who have touched me whom I've yet to meet, I hope to meet you in person one day. Those I see at an event here and there, I look forward to seeing and visiting with you again.

Ruth Bridges at www.atlanticbookpost.com

Rena Finney at www.renafinney.com

LaShaunda Hoffman at www.sormag.com and www.bookcrazy.net

Elaine Hopper at www.elainehopper.com and www.wordmuseum.com

Tonya Howard of Into the Spotlight at www.intothespotlight.com

Wayne Jordan at www.romanceincolor.com

Su Kopil at www.earthlycharms.com

Tyora Moody at www.tywebbin.com and www.doenetwork.com

Tee C. Royal and the ladies at www.RAWSISTAZ.com

Chandra Sparks Taylor at www.chandrasparkstaylor.com

Jacquelin Thomas at www.jacquelinthomas.com

Claudia N. Tynes at http://write4-u.tripod.com

Rebecca Vinyard at www.romance-central.com

Chapter 1

The funerals Chyna Lockhart had attended in the past were long and depressing events. She hated funerals, hated to hear the wailing sobs of grief plaguing those left behind. The last one she attended, for her mother no less, had been simple with barely enough people to fill two pews.

However, this so-called funeral for the eldest Jameson, a patriarch to his family and a cornerstone to the community, was much different. It was more like a home-going ceremony that celebrated the life of a great man, instead of mourning his unfortunate death. People shouted in agreement, their amens and nods confirming the pastor's praise of the man laid out in the casket before them. There were even not-so-stifled giggles when friends and family of the deceased related amusing allegories about his life.

When silence returned, the officiator looked at the family sitting in the first pew and motioned with his hands for everyone in attendance to stand. A noisy shuffling occurred as the massive crowd rose to their feet. Moving from their seats one by one, they formed a long orderly line and waited patiently to view the body.

Loud and deafening music, as old as the woman who sat playing it, drifted from a creaky organ in the front corner. The line moved at an unhurried pace. Chyna was in no rush to get to the front, but her nauseated stomach left her less than steady on her heels. With dread, Chyna managed one foot in front of the other as she approached the open coffin. She soon found herself at the front of the church with only one statement replaying itself in her head: *Joseph Jameson Sr. is dead.*

All of the children of Mr. Jameson were seated at the front. A small crowd of fellow mourners surrounded them, giving their last respects and offering their condolences on the loss. Some shook hands, some just wordlessly passed, lightly touching a shoulder, but whatever they had to say, they did so quickly. Chyna wouldn't speak to them at all. In fact, she didn't want them to see her or to know she was even there.

Clothed in head-to-toe black for the occasion, Chyna had placed large, dark sunglasses over her eyes and had spent almost an hour that morning combing her thick mane of shoulder-length hair around her face. She debated over wearing a veil, but it was too hot. Joseph Jameson Sr. had died during the final days of the notoriously hot summer of Springfield, Virginia.

Still, she was determined to go unnoticed, walking with her head down and holding a crumpled handkerchief to her face at every opportunity. Although they'd known her all her life and could probably pick her out, she hoped the family would be too distracted in their grief to notice her.

She knew she should have said something, offered words of sorrow to the family like the others, but right then she felt like nothing more than a casual acquaintance. Dean Jameson, the youngest male of the clan, had made sure of that.

Mrs. Jameson, of course, would insist she was family. As a girl, she'd practically lived in the home of her well-respected neighbors. Chyna had often sought refuge from her own family, a bunch of socially defunct misfits as far as she was concerned. She was more than a friend, almost a second sister to Jina and Tish. They had often referred to her as such and she always felt as if their inclusion, their outward expression of love that she never received at home, were genuine and true. Their home life was so different than hers. No one ever yelled or raised their voice and they always seemed to have just enough love to embrace one more child: Chyna.

When Mr. Jameson fell ill years earlier, she had become his nurse for a short time. She patiently waited on him, and Mrs. Jameson too, hand and foot.

They had given her so much happiness in her youth, it was only fair to return the favor in their old age. With both her parents dead, the Jamesons were the only family she had left. It didn't matter that she wasn't really related to them. But Dean . . . he'd brought that feeling to a halt, hadn't he?

Chyna shook her head absently. The longer she stood in line waiting to say good-bye, the more she felt a heavy and overbearing numbness trying to swallow her. Unsuccessfully, she struggled to escape the strong arms of grief and sadness that enveloped her.

As she neared the front, Chyna chanced a look at Dean Jameson's still frame. His eyes were blank and expressionless as he stared off into space. His slumped posture and distant gaze tugged at Chyna's heart. She hated Dean for what he'd done to her, but she still cared . . . no, still loved him.

When his eyes seemed to lift and drift toward her, Chyna quickly turned away. Dean Jameson was the second thing she wanted most in her life. The other, he'd caused her to lose.

From an averted view Chyna saw Tish. Her best friend's belly was swollen with twins. Her big husband sat beside her, his left arm around her shoulders for support and his large right hand resting over Tish's stomach as if holding them all together through her grief. They deserved to be happy, Chyna thought. They had been through so much together. Mr. Jameson's Alzheimer's had taxed the family's emotions over the years, especially over the last few months. Then he died. It was so much to bear.

She wished she could tuck herself securely under Dean's shoulder the way Tish sat encased under her husband's arm. Didn't she deserve a happy ending as much as if not more than her best friend? She and Dean would have been perfect together, she thought. But that was not her fate.

Finally, it was her turn to stand before Mr. Jameson's body. She inhaled deeply, suppressing the nauseous angst rising from her stomach to her throat. Bowing her head, she prayed no one in the family would notice her as she quickly stooped and pressed her lips to the forehead of Joe Jameson Sr.

"Rest in peace," she whispered as tears sprang to her eyes. She felt so silly, dumb was a better word, that as a nurse turned freelance writer she couldn't render something more original than *rest in peace*. She erected herself and quickly turned to face the door, catching Dean out of the corner of her left eye.

Damn! He'd recognized her.

Moving as if a large hand pushed her, she walked as fast as she could on leaden legs down the burgundy-carpeted aisle of the church toward the nearest exit. She pretended she hadn't seen Dean when he stood and turned to face her.

Nearing the crowded exit, Chyna successfully pushed her way through the throngs, all the while chastising herself for being identified. She was almost out the door when she bumped an older woman, nearly knocking her to the floor. Instinctively, she reached out with both arms to steady the toppling figure.

"My goodness, honey. Is that you, Chyna?" the elder

woman said to her as she placed her weathered hands on Chyna's arms. "Where you been?"

She watched as the elderly woman's eyes moved slowly up to focus on her dark shades. Was her disguise that bad? she wondered. When the woman peered closer, Chyna fought the urge to rear back, as if doing so could keep her from being recognized. Such an action would only be a dead giveaway. She mumbled an apology for bumping her and gave Loretta Jenkins, a neighbor and a friend of her deceased mother, a puzzling look. She could deny it was her, but once Ms. Jenkins heard her voice, she'd know it was. Chyna could never lie convincingly anyway, so she remained silent and wiggled out of the woman's grasp.

Looking toward the front of the church, she saw Dean following her. He would have reached her if he had not been continually stopped by mourners offering their sincerest regret about his loss. Why he followed her, she didn't know. He'd made it evident he didn't care for her. Plus, this was his father's funeral. Certainly, it wasn't the time or the place to discuss their unsolvable problems. She turned and walked quickly through the exit into the oppressive Virginia heat.

In the parking lot, the numerous cars looked as if they were stacked one on top of the other. She wondered about her own car, as she pushed her glasses higher up on her nose and prayed someone hadn't blocked her in.

Her prayers were answered. As she stuck her key in the ignition, Chyna noticed how the sun shone brightly as if this were a cheery day, as if the past week hadn't been muggy, the rain torrential and depressing, and as if her friend and father figure hadn't just died. She looked around the lot one last time as she worked the key. She hated this car. The engine never turned on the first try.

Chyna surveyed the church one last time until Dean Jameson's tall frame filled the doorway. Chyna ducked.

She saw his hand held to his brow, shielding his eyes from the sun as he searched the dense array of cars for her. He walked down the concrete steps and out of her view. Had he seen her?

She sprang straight up in her seat and turned the key one more. The engine revved. Placing her foot on the gas pedal, she turned the wheel sharply, narrowly missing the tail end of a car parked ridiculously close as she barreled out of the lot. In her rearview mirror, she saw Dean waving his hands rapidly, indicating for her to stop.

Chapter 2

The sky was a master at either concealing what could be a beautiful day or making way for an approaching disaster. Considering the past four weeks, heck, the past six months, Dean Jameson thought despondently, it had to be the latter. First, he found out Chyna was still married when her so-called ex-husband called her his wife on national television. She said she'd been divorced for two years. When he confronted her, she'd promised to explain everything when she came back from California. He didn't even know she was back in town until he saw her at his father's funeral.

He thought his life was back on an upswing when he saw Chyna at the funeral two weeks ago, but that was before she practically ran out of the church and left him standing in the parking lot, the hot dust lifting from the graveled lot and blowing in his face. He tried calling her several times after that, but Chyna stopped taking his phone calls. Now, there was this.

If it did decide to rain, Dean surmised, it was two days too late to make a difference. He stood at the entrance of his former office building, pulling at the yellow police tape loosely secured at each side of the door. Now in shambles, this three-story structure had been the place he called work for the last twelve years. The place where people could find Dr. J six days a week, Monday through Saturday, was now nothing but a pile of charred rubble.

The building was in a nice location, he'd kept it up, and crime wasn't a huge problem, but none of that had mattered when the building went up in flames. When he'd first started his small optometry practice, it hadn't been work at all. He'd loved his job then. In the last few years, the purpose and drive Dean found propelling him to the office each day had dwindled. Recently, he'd thought of selling the place for a nice sum and starting something else entirely. He never did decide what.

There was a time when Dean might have joked that a fire would be a blessing in disguise, but now that it was a blatant reality he didn't know what to make of it. The entire situation was mind-boggling. He still didn't know how the fire started. Was it the wiring? Couldn't have been that the building was too new. But if not, then what?

Picking up a piece of blackened wood, he applied the slightest pressure to it and watched as it crumbled through his fingers into a fine ash that flittered to the ground.

"Yo, Deanie? You in there?" Jojo Jameson called from the entrance. "You all right?"

Dean looked up at his brother who stood at the door looking in. The sun shielded his face, casting a dark shadow over his frame, but he recognized the familiar boom of his brother's voice. "Yeah, what's up?"

"Nothing, just checking . . ." Joseph placed hands in his pockets and looked away.

"Up on me?" Dean finished when his brother hesitated. "I told you I'm all right," Dean said testily, wishing everyone would leave him alone.

"Yeah, well, you know," was all Jojo offered as he shrugged his broad shoulders.

Dean brushed his hand on the leg of his faded jeans and exited the building. In the sun, he shielded his eyes from the bright light.

"Where are Casey and Cassie?" Dean looked around for the van, then at his brother expectantly. The Velenti twins were never far from Jojo's side.

The eldest Jameson, much to everyone's astonishment, had allowed love to take him by storm. Dean smiled, knowing his big brother had fought falling in love 110 percent, but in the end didn't stand a chance.

"There." Jojo pointed and Casey, a lanky boy with bronzy cheeks, waved frantically back at them. "Cassie's with Angie."

Dean nodded and lifted his hand to wave back, astonished. Casey, who didn't seem to talk and barely communicated in any other fashion, had made a considerable progression since Jojo had entered his life less than six months earlier.

"So what you gonna do about your place?" Jojo asked, nodding back to the child as he sat in the van waiting for him. He turned slightly to regard his brother.

"I don't know." Dean shrugged a shoulder as he moved across the street to the van. He hadn't thought much about what he'd do with his life even when he considered ending his practice and finding a new career. Now with his place burned to the ground, it forced him to look at the possibilities quicker than he had wanted to. He'd never been at such a loss of what to do before.

"You can let the insurance rebuild it," Jojo said, "then sell it like you wanted or do something else entirely. Do you know what direction you were headed?"

Dean shrugged again. "I don't care if it's built back up or not. It's not in me anymore."

"Well, you know what I think?" Jojo questioned.

Dean looked at his brother and rolled his eyes. He decided he didn't care, but Jojo would tell him anyway.

"You need a vacation," he continued matter-of-factly. "Rest up, check out your options, see what's what."

"This from the man who hasn't taken a vacation in

twenty years?" Dean replied skeptically. A vacation sounded good to his mind, but his wary body barely rejoiced. The word *vacation* took on a "spring break" connotation. That had been what it was called the last time he'd had anything close to one. "So what exactly did you have in mind for this little find-my-direction trip?"

"Hey, Uncle Dean!" Cassie called out, as the little girl and her aunt exited the building.

"Hey, short stuff," Dean replied enthusiastically.

Casey and his twin sister Cassie's mother was deceased. Dean thought of all that his brother had relayed to him about Angie Valenti, the twins' aunt, who'd stepped up to raise her older sister's kids.

Apparently, the trio had captured his brother's heart. It must have been love, everyone said, for Jojo to take on such a huge commitment. As they reached the van, Dean saw the building they exited had been a popular restaurant, until it was shuttered not long ago. For the first time, he noticed how the entire strip mall was losing its patrons. His building was just the latest to suffer the demise.

"How are you, Dean?" Angie said quietly.

"I'm good," Dean replied as he bent to peck Angie and then Cassie, the more outgoing of the twins, on each of their cheeks.

"How did the place look?" Jojo said, approaching the pair. He placed a firm arm around Angie's shoulder.

"I think it used to be a big seafood buffet or something," Angie said. "It looks promising."

Dean nodded, remembering his brother had told him Angie's dream had been to own and operate her own upscale restaurant. She'd given him a few pointers in the kitchen, and from what Dean could tell, she was an excellent cook.

"So, about that vacation," Jojo said, bringing Dean back to the present.

"I'll think about it," Dean replied noncommittally. He moved to lean his backside against the door of his black Lexus. "I'm really all right. Really."

Noticing the look of disbelief and concern on both Jojo's and Angie's faces, he changed the subject. "What's up, where are you off to?"

Cassie spoke up quickly. "We're going to Kings Dominion!"

"Really? Wow."

"Yeah, we're going to see Aunt Tish and Uncle Chase too."

Dean nodded.

"You should come with us," Angie said. "Tish wants to see you and so does Ms. Alfreah."

Dean nodded again. There was no doubt his sister and his mother wanted to see him. They'd only been calling him every day since the funeral. He'd only spoken to each of them once in the last few weeks.

Dean handled things in his own way. He didn't want to talk about his feelings. He wanted to be alone. That was just how he was. "I'll go down there soon. I will, I promise, but tell them I said hi and that I'm all right."

Dean's sister Tish lived in Georgia, and after his father's death his mother had moved down to help Tish prepare for the birth of her twin girls. The babies weren't due until January, but his mother thought Tish might need her companionship after her father's death. Dean recognized that it was important for Tish to be around positive, upbeat people. Since he didn't fall into that category, he kept his distance. He would visit soon enough.

"I've got to get stuff straight with the place and all." Dean nodded to where his building used to stand, offering that as an excuse not to join them on the trip.

Angie eyed Dean skeptically, but moved to the van and opened the door for Cassie to get in.

"Dean, are you sure?" Jojo asked. "I mean you gotta take a vacation or something."

"Yeah, I'll do that," he lied.

Dean watched as the foursome, buckled securely in the van, drove off.

He turned to his own car and took a seat in the humid interior. He was unsure of what to do or the direction he should go. It wasn't the direction to point his car he was worried about, but his life in general was a question he didn't have answers to anymore.

Jojo suggested he take a vacation to clear his head, and while that sounded nice, it required more effort to arrange than Dean cared to take on. He could always go home, but his small Springfield condominium less than five miles away held absolutely no appeal.

Wherever he went he wanted to be alone. That was important. He wanted to think about everything that seemed to escape him—family, a solid relationship, and love. Those emotional supplements he had always taken for granted as if they'd always be there. People had given him love, of course, and he had a wonderful family and their affection, but he hadn't thought twice about the effort he needed to put forth in order to keep it.

Dean was fooling himself. The last part of his thoughts weren't about his family at all, but a woman: Chyna Lockhart.

Every night since the last time they'd been together the night before he found out she was married, he convinced himself she wasn't for him. She was all he wanted, but he couldn't have her. Someone else still did.

"What happened to us?" Dean asked aloud. Part of him knew the answer, and he knew Chyna was not totally to blame for their downfall. He'd seen the signs, the way she always avoided the topic when he asked her about her marriage and subsequent divorce. He knew something was wrong, but he never would have guessed it was that.

Dean thought of his siblings settling down. Jojo, of all people, seemed committed to a woman with kids. His brother made everything look so easy, but for Dean it was always so much harder.

The girl, literally, next door had fallen into his lap. How much more effortless could it have been? Instead of letting his heart be his guide, he'd shut her out and sent her on her way time and time again. When he finally came around, she came back, but with strings attached.

He'd tried to talk to her. He wanted an explanation, to give her the benefit of the doubt. But she shut him out.

She said she had business to take care of as far as Gary, her so-called ex-husband, was concerned and she'd call Dean when she returned from California. He hadn't pressed her to elaborate. He knew she loved him, but he was so afraid of being rejected. In the back of his mind, he wondered if a fire still burned between Chyna and Senator Gary Williams, a fire that he couldn't extinguish.

He didn't press for answers then, but he needed them now. He wanted, hoped really, that Chyna had gone to California to finalize her divorce.

She's been separated from Gary for over two years, but clearly neither one of them had been inclined to make the dissolution of their marriage complete. That didn't make sense to Dean. Her betrayal would never sit well with him, but he couldn't stop loving her because of it. There had to be an explanation for all this. He was determined to hear the truth.

Dean wondered if it was his jealousy that drove them apart. He had made a big scene when he went to her apartment to confront her. He ranted and raved and used every swear word imaginable. He was that upset. Didn't he have every right to be?

Chyna was still married. Yet, she didn't talk to Gary, much less see him. He lived on the other side of the country. Was it really that big a deal that they remained married? It was just a piece of paper anyway, right? When he was honest with himself he knew it was much more.

Chyna Lockhart belonged with Dean Jameson. And she could never really be his as long as she was Gary's. No matter what she referred to him as, he was still her husband and Dean still wasn't.

The whole scenario made him physically sick. He couldn't put into words the rage he felt when she told him she was going to California to see Gary. What did they have to discuss? Surely she wasn't going to get her divorce after all these years. Certainly not after the fight they'd just had the day before.

He'd debated getting on a plane and going after her. With Gary and Dean standing before her she would have to choose between them once and for all. But then he received the call about his father.

His feelings for Chyna took a backseat to his father's failing health. They'd rushed Joseph Jameson Sr. to an emergency room sixteen days ago. His breathing was sparse and his heartbeat was erratic. Dean knew his father wouldn't be around much longer, but nothing could have prepared him for the rapid deterioration of his health and his quick passing.

He pounded the steering wheel angrily. Thirty-six hours after he got that first phone call, his father was gone. First Chyna, then his father.

Dean couldn't do anything about his father's death. But Chyna's departure was another story. He had it within his power to bring her back. He owed it to himself to at least try. He had to know where he and Chyna stood. He had to make her understand there was no one else for him but her. He'd loved her for nearly twenty years. He had to make her finalize her divorce.

Life was moving on whether Dean decided to move with it or not; he just hoped he wasn't too late. Moments ticked by as Dean took a series of calming breaths. Starting the car, he lowered the window before he suffocated.

She was still in town, of that much Dean was certain. Despite his hangover at the funeral and his fuzzy memory of that entire week, he knew he'd seen her there. She should have been sitting with them, on the first few pews as a member of the Jameson family. She always was a part of their family. He also knew that she'd left without so much as acknowledging him. What did that mean? Were they over for good?

He didn't even know how long she'd been back in town, much less where to find her. She hadn't called whenever she'd returned from California. Maybe she had reconciled with her husband after all.

"Did you see that, son? Did you?" Chauncey Hardig, hard-core business tycoon and lawyer, used one thick stubby finger to press the button to the window of his luxury Sedan. "Look at that, son!"

Chauncey kicked his son's foot. Warren Hardig sat across from his father, glanced out of the window to appease him and sat back against the seat uninterested.

"You remember this scene," Chauncey continued. "It will drive you. It will give you purpose in the morning and fill your bones with fire. Are you listening to me?" Chauncey shouted.

"That's Jameson, sitting in his car." Chauncey checked his expensive two-thousand-dollar watch, "I wish it could have been his old man sitting there, but well, a man's offspring, that's the next best thing."

Chauncey looked back at his son as if remembering he sat across from him. He'd been so consumed with his own rage and the anger he harbored that went back forty-plus years. "Dean Jameson. He'll have to do," he amended. "How's that contact you got? Lisa Stephens, is that her name?"

Warren looked up finally, leaving his own world long enough to pay attention to what his father said.

"Whatever her name is you tell her my contact at the bank is in place. She's to send those papers over, and he'll handle the rest." Chauncey took a deep breath but continued to speak. "You know, son, I said I was going to stay out of your personal affairs, but Lisa Stephens might be the girl who does it for you behind closed doors, but she is not the kind of character you let hang on your arm at respectable functions."

Warren shrugged, not bothering to listen further to his father's wishes. He was right in some respects, Lisa Stephens did serve a man's purpose well, but another woman held Warren Hardig's attention. That was who he really wanted.

"Are you listening to me? I'm getting tired of this silent treatment. Please tell me you are not sleping with this girl!"

"My private life is none of your business!"

"It is when you're flaunting that trash all over town. You cut her loose. She is to serve one purpose only and that is to advance the plot of our ruining the Jamesons, nothing more. You keep your pants zipped. I'll find someone else for you to attend the function with."

"Chyna Lockhart is in town," Warren offered.

"And how do you know this?" Chauncey boomed.

"I hired someone to find her."

"You're not serious! You are wasting your time. You were to contact her ex-husband for an endorsement in the new Hardig buildings, not sniff after his ex."

"I like her," Warren shrugged, sorry he'd revealed his intentions. He liked her a lot.

"You listen to me and you listen good: you relinquish

this stupid crush you have on Chyna Lockhart. She was Gary Williams's wife. You ask Gary for a sound bite for reconstruction of this Springfield area and you scratch his back. He's slipping in the polls. You can give him some cold, hard Hardig cash to help his campaign along. I'll write the check. That's it. And get back on your medication, you're starting to lose it again."

Warren's mouth dropped to the floor.

"That's right," his father said, "I'll have you recommitted. I let you out under the strict belief that you would adhere to the life I'm trying to create for you. We'll take a little trip upstate if you can't seem to get it together." Chauncey raised a finger, ticking off the things he meant for his son to do. "Let go of this Lisa character, or see her out of the state. I don't want the press to get wind of your affair with her. What possessed you to take her in the first place?" Chauncey waved his hand as if he didn't want Warren to answer. "Call off the person you've hired to find Lockhart and, lastly, ask Senator Gary Williams for endorsement on the Springfield transition project.

"Back to Jameson," Chauncey looked out the window again as the black Lexus drove away, "You'll pay him your respects in a bit, let things die down and then you'll ask him to join your team. If he seems resistant, you'll use whatever he cares about. I'll research that in a bit."

Warren nodded like he always did when he was no longer paying attention or no longer cared.

The man sitting across from Warren was his bread and butter, but Warren had a plan of his own. When he inherited his father's fortune, he'd tell the press about this man named Chauncey Hardig. His was a million-dollar story, a best-seller. No one knew Chauncey Hardig was an abusive, mean-spirited and bitter old man. Warren was simply biding his time. He did wonder, however, what the Jamesons had done to cause his father such hatred of them.

He would appease his father for only so long before he planned to cut him out of his life entirely. Warren's only desires were to own a nice piece of the Hardig Empire and to wed Chyna Lockhart.

Warren snapped back to the present when his father barked orders to the driver to return them to their law offices in Alexandria, Virginia.

Chapter 3

"I'm fine, Samson. Yes, I'm sure. I know that painkillers can become habit-forming. I haven't taken them for a week and I've been feeling fine." *Physically,* Chyna thought to herself. Emotionally she was still a wreck. "Thank you for your concern, but I've been through this before."

Chyna fanned her eyes after the last sentence as tears threatened to spill over the edge. "I just don't want to talk . . . to anyone. Or think about it right now," she continued. "I know you're only concerned about me. . . . Yes, thank you. Good-bye."

She placed the receiver back in its cradle. She'd called Samson Godfrey, a good friend of hers, as well as of her ex-husband, in a moment of panic. He'd tried to pursue more than a friendship after she and Gary separated, but she'd politely turned him down. Even still, Samson tried to show the numerous ways he cared for her. He always called to check on her, all the while making it clear that he was interested in her as more than a friend.

Chyna thought she had mastered the ability to put up a strong front, but as soon as she heard his familiar voice on the phone, she nearly lost it. Something inside her wanted to divulge all the messy details of her breakup with Dean and her confrontation with Gary in California. She mentioned her miscarriage, but immediately regretted telling him. She couldn't involve

Samson, or anyone else for that matter, in her affairs. It was the mess she had made.

If she wanted it cleaned up, she'd have to do it herself. Samson offered to come over and cheer her up, whatever that meant. She declined. She needed time alone and refused to use Samson as the recovery man.

For the last week, she'd done absolutely nothing to exert energy, but still felt drained. The sleeping pills had been prescribed by her doctor to help her get through the night, but they weren't working and more often than not, they left her feeling woozy.

She looked at the bottle sitting on the nightstand. Pulling the information sheet from the white prescription bag, she took a moment to read the side effects and then she rolled her eyes when she came across the word *dizziness*. She tossed the bottle aside, disgusted.

She'd been through a miscarriage with Gary too. She dealt with that one the same way she dealt with this one—by shutting herself away.

Technology was a wonderful convenience as far as Chyna was concerned. She didn't have to talk to anyone to get anything in this day and time. Even the deliveryman left packages at the door and didn't need to see her in order to do so. Her only communication was through her phone, on rare occasions, and her computer where she wrote her freelance articles and placed on-line orders for her bare necessities.

Whereas before she'd holed herself up inside the minimansion she shared with her husband, she now hid in the home of her deceased parents. Only one person knew where she was and after she'd called him just a few minutes ago, she was sorry she'd told even him.

She and Samson were a lot alike in the respect that they hung on, hoping and wishing that the object of their affections would suddenly change and one day reciprocate their feelings.

"No more of that!" Chyna laughed aloud. Dean Jameson, the object of her affections, would never love her like she loved him, and Samson Godfrey, her friend, would one day see that she couldn't love him the way he deserved. They'd have to be friends. Just friends.

Absently Chyna rubbed her chest. Dean's rejection still hurt.

Rising from her bed, she moved slowly to the kitchen. Her appetite came and went, but slowly her weight was picking back up. She opened the refrigerator only to find it empty. She would have to go to the grocery store at some point today.

She swore at the thought. Perhaps it was time she left the house anyway.

As she looked out the window over the sink, it seemed for the second time that day that a serious storm would pour out of the sky. If it wasn't raining the last few days of August, adding to the humidity, it was swelteringly hot and uncomfortable.

Chyna looked around the place she was now calling home. It was a dump. She had wished to live anywhere but there as a child, so why, she wondered, as an adult did she continue to stay? She could certainly afford to live in a better place. Finding one just seemed too hard a task to take on. Plus, it was comforting to know the family she'd wanted to be a part of since she was eight years old lived just one house over.

Until she motivated herself, this place would have to do. So it needed some renovations and a ton of repairs— Chyna could do that too. If being married to a senator had taught her anything, it was that she didn't fit in as a high-society wife and that a perfect house didn't necessarily make a home.

This was what she wanted, a quiet life, without all the frills and catering. She'd learned how those things couldn't improve her marriage. She'd learned the hard way that bringing a child into an unhappy marriage wouldn't improve it either. She'd lost her first baby and everything else too.

She wanted a family so badly. She blushed with the memory of the joy she had felt when she first discovered she was carrying Dean's child. Her baby. She liked the sound of those words, but doubted she'd ever be a mother. Her track record was zero-for-two. She could do without her husband, without cocktail parties and fundraising events, without smiling falsely at people with deep pockets just to get them to dig deeper into those pockets and hand over the donations. But she didn't know if she could live without being a mother.

Chyna took a seat at the rickety table to rifle through her mail, most of it junk, before she reached the folded newspaper. It contained a recent article she'd written about loss, grief, and coping. Ironically, she'd written it before she lost her baby and prior to Mr. Jameson's death.

She looked away while tears cascaded down her face. Absently, she put aside the other mail that held no interest for her and swiped at a fly that buzzed around her head. She picked up her most recent weekly paper, which dated back over a week ago, and skimmed the sections when the crime reports caught her eye and she zeroed in on the name Jameson.

> Police officials suspect arson in the devastating fire that completely destroyed the business property of Dr. Dean Jameson. Two other doctors also rented space in the building. There are no suspects. Have information? Call Crime Solvers at . . .

Chyna put down the paper and immediately moved to the living room where her television sat. She checked her watch and realized the midmorning news was just about over. After flipping through the channels, she found a newscaster showing a recap.

"Arson is still suspected in the fire that burned down the offices of Drs. Jameson, Johnston, and Carpenter. Jameson owned the three-story building that sustained over a half million dollars in damage and completely destroyed medical equipment. Officials believe a group of juveniles aged fourteen to seventeen are responsible, but no motive and no suspects have been identified. Jameson is not a suspect. In other news . . ."

Chyna pressed the small red button and the face on the television disappeared. She wanted to call Dean to see if he was okay. She knew he had begun to hate his profession, but she also knew being a doctor still meant a lot to him. How could she comfort him when she was an emotional wreck herself?

He had his family to help him and support him anyway. He didn't need her. Chyna had to get on with her life. He'd get through the ordeal and he'd manage, just as she had. She had another article to write and more clientele to find that needed her experienced patient care.

She decided to place another ad announcing her services in the local paper and then make a few calls to local nursing agencies when she felt better. Until something opened up, she needed to fix up the place she indefinitely planned to call home.

Dean might always be in the back of her mind, but she would have to stop loving him. She doubted that would happen today.

Chyna hated supermarkets. They were cold, drafty, and filled with too many choices. She could never get in and out in a matter of minutes like she preferred. On top of that, she didn't remember where anything was so she had to hunt and search for just about everything she wanted. She should have just ordered a pizza instead.

Moving her cart down the aisle, she squinted at the boxes of cereal and reached for something with the word *bran* on the front in a poor attempt to be health-conscious. She flipped the box to the side to read the nutrition label. It didn't make sense to her, but she put it in the cart anyway. She shut her eyes to block out the Froot Loops, Frosted Flakes, and Sugar Smacks until she got to the end of the aisle, when her cart grazed another shopper reaching for a top shelf.

"I'm so sorry, I—" Chyna looked up, recognizing the woman as the one she'd seen Dean at the restaurant with. Chyna smiled falsely and maneuvered her cart around the woman. Keeping her eyes averted, she felt a large, sharp pang of jealousy kick her in her gut. She wished she hadn't apologized.

"Chyna Williams?"

Why was she always being recognized when she least wanted to be? She turned to face the voice of inquiry. Chyna wanted to shake her head no, denying her own existence, but it was clear the woman recognized her.

"Actually, it's Chyna Lockhart, if you don't mind." She hadn't meant to sound so formal, but what more could this woman expect from her? After all, this woman was sleeping with the man she'd expected to be the father of her children since she was sixteen years old.

"Yes, of course." She smiled. "I'm Lisa Stephens, a friend of Dean's."

Chyna watched as the woman's eyes danced mischievously. The underlying tone of exactly what type of *friend of Dean's* she was wasn't lost. *So this is Dean's type,* she thought, giving Lisa a once-over.

"How is he doing?" Lisa asked. "I heard about his father. What a loving man, a real pillar of this community, I'm told."

Chyna nodded at Lisa's favorable comments. She looked at the woman, scrutinizing her, wondering if by asking how Dean was faring, she wasn't exacting some evil ploy to rub it in that she knew that things hadn't worked out between them. Of course, she knew. She was only inquiring to get under her skin. Her contempt for Chyna was written all over her face.

It bothered Chyna that she didn't know how Dean was doing. But if Ms. Lisa wanted to play games, then she would too.

"He's taking it as best he can," she said, distorting her face into a sympathetic mask.

"I know Dean was very saddened over losing you," Lisa replied. "I assume that since you're back in town, things didn't work out with your husband either. I'm sorry. I mean, Gary Williams is certainly no Dean Jameson . . . but, well, you'll find someone."

"You know Gary? How did you know that things didn't work out with my husband?" Chyna asked. Caught off guard, she'd dropped her nonchalant attitude to reveal her anger.

Who was running their trap about Gary, not to mention Dean?

Chyna watched as Lisa smiled emphatically, showing a mouthful of teeth. Lisa stood straighter and brushed a speck of nonexistent lint from her designer blouse. Shifting her small red carrying cart to the other hand, she placed a hand on her hip.

"Look, whatever is between you all . . ."

Chyna heard the innuendo suggesting that her dealings with Dean and Gary were some type of love triangle. She visibly bristled, but remained silent.

". . . It's really your business. I talked to Dean the night you left town. He had been drinking and he came over to my place. I gave him a place to sleep . . ."

Chyna's eyes rolled to the ceiling, clearly displaying her state of befuddlement. Some people had no shame.

"Unfortunately, I felt sorry for *you*," Lisa emphasized. "Clearly you missed out. Dean's a great man and it looks like you were the loser."

It took every morsel of Chyna's willpower not to haul off and knock Lisa into the Frosted Flakes. She felt utterly foolish arguing over some man. She wanted to take the adult approach, which would be to calmly turn and walk away, but it seemed that her feet were glued to the floor.

She looked Lisa squarely in the eye. Lisa was considerably shorter than she, but Chyna still felt threatened by the woman's appearance. Lisa wore a pair of plaid capri pants that fit snugly around her generously proportioned hips. Her sleeveless fuchsia blouse revealed toned arms, honey-hued skin, and an ample bosom. She carried herself like a woman who made her own hours, like she told everyone else what to do. Chyna tugged at the bottom of the wrinkled, oversized T-shirt she wore, feeling less than adequate.

Lisa's small shopping basket indicated to Chyna she was a woman who knew what she wanted. Chyna figured she could get in and out of a supermarket in twenty minutes. She herself had spent at least that long deciding what cereal to pick out.

Her red basket was filled with greens, peaches, strawberries, and other fruits and vegetables that Chyna never ate on a regular basis.

Chyna had never thought to compare herself to another woman before. Now that she was doing it, she understood why. She felt completely inadequate.

"Dean's a great guy," Lisa rattled on, seemingly oblivious of Chyna's judgment. "I think I could satisfy his needs."

Do I look like I care? Chyna thought to herself. But obviously she did care or she would have walked away by now.

"Miss Stephens," she interrupted, "why should this be of any concern to me? Why should I care about your intentions where Dean is concerned?"

Chyna was ill equipped to handle such a discussion. For one, she had on the frumpiest clothes in her closet. And two, they were blocking the aisle of a grocery store. Assessing the situation, she grew more agitated by the moment.

"I just wanted to let you know, was all. It wouldn't be kosher not to disclose my intentions." Lisa nodded as if she read Chyna's thoughts. She reached up to push her bangs from her eyes. "I just wanted you to know that I get what I want."

Chyna gripped her cart and walked away.

Chapter 4

Finding Chyna Lockhart, as Dean said he would do, would be a difficult task. Dean reasoned that she probably didn't wish to be found. If that was indeed the case, it would make doing so even harder.

"Ah, damn it!" Dean hollered aloud when for the second time that day he hit his thumb with the hammer. He'd dedicated himself to remodeling his parents' home. With his office in ashes, he didn't have anything better to do.

His mother, before she left to visit his sister, had written down a series of ideas for the house in a notebook and given it to him along with a box of glossy pictures she'd clipped from professional decor magazines. From those ideas, Dean was able to put together a basic sketch of how he planned to remodel. But it seemed he was making more mess than progress.

Already he'd accidentally locked himself in a room because he placed the knob with the lock on the wrong side. Then, he'd nearly sent another room crashing to the floor when he hit a vital support beam. After investing almost ten thousand dollars at Home Depot, Dean decided to turn the job over to professionals.

He headed downstairs to retrieve the Yellow Pages from the kitchen drawer. After arranging appointments for work estimates on the extensive project, he realized he hadn't eaten all morning.

Dean preferred a hot meal, but he couldn't cook until the new oven arrived. He'd been dying to try out a new recipe Angie had taught him. He settled for a ham and cheese on wheat bread and sat down at the small breakfast nook to eat.

A thick folded newspaper lying on the counter caught his attention. It was the *Advocate General,* a paper Chyna had written for almost a year ago when she first moved back to Virginia. Dean turned the pages hoping to spot her byline and the small thumbnail, black-and-white picture of her that usually accompanied it.

He smirked when he saw her name. *Chyna M. Lockhart.* He was surprised by how relieved he felt to see her name without the Williams at the end of it. His eyes immediately moved to the top of the page to check the date. It was a recent article. Dean assumed that meant Chyna was still in town.

At the end of the article he found her bio and a small black-and-white picture that couldn't do her justice. It didn't capture Chyna's soft brown eyes, the luster of her jet-black hair, or the pretty pout of her mouth.

Where in the world could you be, Chyna M. Lockhart? Dean wondered sadly as he read the article a second and third time. It was interesting but really he read it over and over again because the words were hers. An article she'd penned gave him the only current connection he had to her.

He looked out the window from where he sat, and wondered aloud, "Where would I go if I were Chyna Lockhart?" He stood abruptly as he snapped his fingers when the idea dawned upon him that Chyna Lockhart was closer than he ever could've imagined. Why, Dean wondered, hadn't he thought of that sooner? Where else *could* she be?

Dean wondered why Chyna continued to stay at that broken-down old house when she could afford something much nicer and much more stable. Her father had saved every last dime and the only thing he did right before he died was leave his money and his house to her. Chyna, stubborn as she was, would probably let the money sit in the bank for another thousand years before she used it to fix up the place. She had to be there.

Rinsing his plate and hands, Dean headed for the back door to the kitchen. Chyna was only two houses away. But before reaching it, he stopped. He didn't have a plan. What would he say to her? What could he say? And how did one review and put to rest almost fifteen years of bickering in the shortest amount of time possible? Millions of questions ran through Dean's mind as he turned from the door to rethink his strategy. He needed a better approach and until he came up with one, he couldn't face her.

Two days passed and Dean's words still hadn't come. Yesterday, he'd decided he didn't need to say anything profound, he would just go to her and let the words pour from his heart. He marched over to her house, knocked on the door, and waited for an answer that never came.

He peeked in the car port and saw that it was empty, but the fresh gasoline on the cement driveway indicated that Chyna, or at least someone, had been there recently. Dean debated waiting on the porch for her or whoever to return, but the blazing Virginia sun made him think twice. He walked home defeated. Where Chyna Lockhart was concerned, he wasn't making any progress.

Back at the Jameson home, Dean sat watching the midmorning news, as he had done every day for the last week. No progress had been made on the culprits who burned down his place either. An insurance representative had promised to call when the police officially had determined the cause of the fire. His lawyer called daily, to ask, "Do you want to rebuild or not?" Dean still had no answer.

The decision hinged on him; his family owned the building and the other two tenants rented. He'd rebuild if the other two wanted to, but for the most part they hadn't acted as if they cared one way or the other. Dean found that strange. One tenant already had joined another group of medical professionals and asked that his money for the equipment be sent to his lawyer. The other doctor was a psychologist with tons of paperwork, recordings of notes, and a truckload of documentation on other people's problems, but no real equipment to speak of. Dean was being given an easy way out. He didn't *have* to rebuild, he didn't *have* to open back up. In a sense he was free from obligation. So why wasn't he happier?

He headed upstairs to retrieve the number of the insurance company. He was tired of waiting for their call.

Passing his parents' bedroom, Dean thought of his father. He stopped and stood in the doorway.

He imagined how it had looked before his father passed. He thought of the pictures he had placed around the mirror to help his father remember the family. At the time, it seemed like a good idea. After all, Joseph Jameson looked in that mirror at least once a day. But instead of seeing the pictures, his father sat and absentmindedly poked at his own face. He was trying to understand why he couldn't remember the image that stared back at him. Dean's mother had told him the pictures wouldn't work.

No one, no book, no *what to expect when a loved one has Alzheimer's* pamphlet could have sufficiently prepared him for coping with his father's mental decline. The only map to understanding what was happening was to experience it firsthand, as Dean did. The doctor part of him sought to get closer, to work with his father like a therapist to try and reverse the devastating trauma, and the damage that would be done.

Dean looked away from the room. Bills needed to be paid, records filed, and issues regarding his father's estate secured. Things that should've been taken care of when the Alzheimer's had first been diagnosed had gone on hold. Dean blindly paid the bills each month, deposited the retirement checks all under the pretense that his father would miraculously heal. Most of the paperwork still sat in his father's old chest and the small secretary he'd kept next to the bed. Dean just couldn't bring himself to open them. Doing so meant he had to deal with his father's death and he really wasn't ready. He might never be.

When the doorbell rang, he went downstairs, glad for an interruption that would keep him from confronting the pain. He hoped it was Chyna even though he knew it wouldn't be.

Opening the door, he was surprised to see Lisa Stephens on the other side.

"Hi, sweetheart," she said cheerily and walked through the door without Dean's invitation. He stepped back and let her proceed. He wasn't in the mood for her.

"Hi," Dean said, shutting the door. He followed her lead to the kitchen.

"Oh, honey." Lisa pouted. "I hate to see you this way."

Dean sat down at the kitchen table. She babbled endlessly and her voice often got on his nerves. This was definitely one of those times.

"I'm doing all right," he said.

"No, you're not!" Lisa placed her hands on her hips and regarded him.

After looking through the cabinets, she moved to the refrigerator and took out two eggs. "I'll make you something to eat," she said as she cracked two eggs over a bowl and began to beat them vigorously. Over a heated skillet she dropped them into the pan and swirled them around.

"I'm really not hungry," he said, but she placed the plate before him anyway. "Listen, Lisa. You haven't by chance seen Chyna, have you?"

Sitting across from him, she drenched a salad with yellow dressing, opened a plastic utensil kit, and began to pierce her food. She looked up and took a forkful of greenery, crunching noisily. "Chyna? Williams, right? No, honey." She shook her head. "I'm sorry, I haven't seen her."

"Look, I'm sorry. I'm really sorry that I keep bringing her name up. I . . ."

"You're just hopelessly in love. I know. I am too," she said and looked away from him.

"Really?" Dean stood, placing a napkin over the soggy eggs. After one bite he knew he wouldn't finish them. "Do I know him?"

"Oh, nah, I don't think so," Lisa said, as she turned around to look at him. She smiled sadly and stood to move closer to him. She wrapped her arms around his waist.

"It's hard loving someone who doesn't really know you exist. I've done that a long time." She looked into his eyes, wondering if he'd ever look at her the way she had seen him look at Chyna. Would he ever know she could love him like he deserved and stop chasing a woman who obviously didn't want him?

"Listen, I've got to get back to the office, I love" —*you*, she thought to herself—"what you've done to the place," she said sarcastically. "Give me a call. If you'd like, I can help you go through your dad's things. If you need help." Lisa backed toward the door.

Dean nodded in appreciation though he found it strange she would offer such a thing. He quickly dismissed any ill thoughts and smiled when he held the door for her.

He was startled and caught off guard when Lisa turned back to face him, leaned in and kissed him firmly on the lips. He backed away when he felt the pressure of her lips increase.

"I'm sorry." She shrugged as if she regretted the kiss, though she knew she hadn't.

"Friends, Dean, can be a great comfort to each other when they're feeling low," she told him, giving him a hungry look.

With that Lisa turned and left quickly.

Chapter 5

Demolition was new to Chyna, but with each swing of the sledgehammer and each piece of wall that helplessly crumbled to the ground, a catharsis took place. She was implementing her own brand of therapy: destruction.

Chyna mentally plastered Lisa Stephens's face onto her walls and swung hard. When the wall finally fell, something inside her eased. She could feel a slight shift, a release in tension.

She had no idea what she wanted to do with the room. She just knew she wanted to make the place as barren and as empty as she felt. When that was done, she'd create something new.

Her parents' home was a mess, but when hadn't it been? Her father was a drunken musician and when he left them, her mother had slipped into a devastating depression that she never rose from. Now that they were both dead, she decided she could make this place livable.

Chyna remembered how she had pretended to do her homework while she waited for Tish Jameson to come by to ask her mom if Chyna could come over to play. The first time Chyna visited the Jameson home, she felt as if she'd stepped through the television into the Cosbys' home.

Alfreah and Joe Jameson Sr. were both teachers. Mrs. Jameson taught English and Mr. Jameson taught wood-shop at the local high school. They complemented each other like no two people Chyna had ever met. She'd prayed every night that they'd adopt her one day. But of course that never happened. As a teenager, she found another way to get into their family. She would marry Dean Jameson.

Now at age thirty, she knew that was nothing more than an unanswered wish as well.

She took another swing at an innocent wall.

A month ago, Chyna had thought she had one last chance to see all her dreams come true. After Dean came to her apartment screaming all over the place about her still being Gary's wife, she'd decided the farce was over. She'd tried to explain the truth to him, but he was too busy yelling, and blaming her to take time to listen to her side of the story.

Did he really think she would be dating him if she was still married? He'd known her virtually all her life, did he think that little of her integrity? There was no sense in trying to explain that night. She promised they could talk when he calmed down and after she returned from California. He forbade her to go. But Chyna left anyway to secure her future and to end the charade Gary Williams insisted on playing.

Her plan had been to make a public announcement in California that she and Gary were divorced. She hadn't told anyone, except Dean, because it had been Gary's one request. During the divorce proceedings, he promised to give her everything she asked for, if she promised to keep it a secret. All he ever cared about was his image, his prominent position in politics. He wanted to make people think everything was fine in his personal life, to increase his chances for reelection. Chyna agreed because it was the only bargaining chip she had to get him to sign the divorce papers.

She could have done as she pleased once he'd signed, but she, despite being married to a liar and manipulator, wasn't one too. She had no idea he would continue to refer to her as his wife. He gave her the freedom behind closed doors to return to Virginia and publicly he kept his position as a beloved senator. His ratings continued to skyrocket.

Chyna could deal with fooling the California's public at large. But she couldn't have Dean believing she was an adulterer or that she didn't love him with all of her heart.

She had only taken the day to go California. She'd arranged to meet a popular reporter at a small California television station. She wore one of the expensive suits a senator's wife would and she conservatively did her makeup.

The interviewer's questions became more and more bold, but she wanted her reputation intact and she didn't shudder from personal questions about her private life with her estranged husband. She told the truth about the six years spent as his wife. She met each question with an air of calmness, giving direct answers and eye movements that met the interviewer head-on. Her voice didn't waver.

Gary would hate her. He'd deny his involvement in the arrangement, but Dean, she hoped, would love her for it. He'd know for certain that she loved him. He'd know that she hadn't betrayed him. The people of California would call her names, but she didn't live there any longer. Virginia was her home.

Things hadn't worked out quite like she'd planned. They never did.

When she'd returned to Virginia, she planned to give Dean the tape of the interview and to make the biggest confession of all—she was carrying his child. She'd called his home, but there was no answer. She left a message for him to come by as soon as possible. She went to their favorite restaurant to pick up a carryout dinner for two and that's when she saw him. And her.

She'd been out of town for a little more than twenty-four hours and there he was wrapped in Lisa Stephens's tight embrace. From the corner, Chyna had watched them walk out of the restaurant together and drive off in Lisa's car.

Chyna took down another chunk of wall with her sledgehammer, pulling the loose pieces of the wood with her bare hands. She discarded them into a bucket not far from where she stood. Dust clouded her eyes and mixed with tears. She could barely catch her breath. Still, she kept hammering away until a knock sounded on the door. Hastily she tried to wipe her eyes, though she surmised that whoever it was wouldn't care that she'd been crying. She wasn't expecting company.

Opening the door, Chyna slowly lifted her eyes to find the reason for her grief staring her in the face.

He came back but this time he checked the car port first. Procrastinator that he was, when Dean Jameson made up his mind, he took charge and didn't back down.

"Uh, hi," he finally said, while his eyes took in seeing her for the first time in many months.

She looked fragile and that shocked him. Chyna Lockhart was tough, strong, and the woman before him was weak and weary. The light that often twinkled in her eye was somewhat dim and if he looked closer he would swear she'd been crying.

Chyna merely nodded. "Hi," she replied.

"You were expecting?"

"I wasn't expecting anyone."

"Oh," Dean said. "Can I come in?"

He watched to his dismay as she crossed her arms over her chest to regard him.

"Now's not really a good time. The place is a mess. I'm

doing some teardown work in the back. Maybe some other time."

She shrugged. The faster she got rid of him the quicker she could put the image of his face on her wall and drive her sledgehammer through it. But he did look good. He always looked good, even when he was dirty. The sun lightly kissed his entire tanned bronze body.

He was a red baby, she knew from the litter of pictures around the Jameson home, and he'd maintained that complexion through the years. Lanky and thin as a reed until his fifteenth birthday, he'd started working out because he had hated being teased and compared to his older, then tremendously bigger brother, Jojo. Now they were nearly the same size.

He was dressed casually in a pair of loose jeans and a pullover shirt. Chyna smelled a mild soap emanating from him. He never wore aftershave. He didn't put anything on his face because it irritated his sensitive skin. At sixteen, he'd been burned in a terrible fire.

Chyna, not knowing what to do with her empty hands, tried to shove them into nonexistent pockets. She then hooked each thumb through the loops of her cutoff jeans. She wanted to touch his face; it looked better and the skin that was sometimes pink and blotchy was now even and smooth. Chyna visibly stiffened as such thoughts she didn't want to have for him kept up their onslaught one after the other. Her fingers continued to itch with want to caress him.

"I, uh, gotta go. I'll see ya," she said quickly and closed the door slowly in his face.

Dean looked at the closed door. He wouldn't have believed it if he hadn't seen it with his own eyes. There was one thing Chyna Lockhart wasn't and that was rude.

Fortunately, Dean wasn't the type to be so easily put off. Turning the knob on the door, he let himself in.

Chyna barely made it down the hall when she turned to find Dean following her.

"That was rude," Dean said, pointing over his shoulder to indicate the slammed door.

She ignored the comment. She hoped her silent treatment would get him to leave sooner than if she engaged in the light banter he seemed to want.

"Mrs. Jenkins said you were making a lot of racket," he said, noting her dismissal. "You should be careful. Our houses are about the same and some of the pipes from the bathroom are right about here.

"They lead to the septic tank," he continued, pointing from the wall to a place on the ceiling.

Chyna nodded, thinking about how tall he was. The ceilings seemed lower and the room smaller with him in it.

Dean lowered his hand. "Where are your goggles?" he asked Chyna expectantly. "The dust making your eyes water?"

She shrugged. "I wear my glasses."

"You're lying. Even if you did wear your glasses, they're not the same. Debris falls, lands on your lashes, and gets into your eyes."

He thought of her long eyelashes. They shielded her eyes like a fluffy, velvety curtain that hid the sunshine. His eyes moved to her high cheekbones, down to beckoning lips that sheltered the slight overbite she had been so self-conscious of as a teenager. Little did she know that the overbite she cursed gave her mouth a sensuous and eternal pout, making her upper lip protrude slightly. Dean loved laving that lush lower lip with his mouth. It made her look as if she always had an attitude.

Right now, though, she really did have one. It was shooting off of her like fire darts meant to aim straight at him. She wanted to make him want to run and hide, but Dean stood his ground. The only thing he seemed to think about was kissing those pouting lips until they parted to receive his tongue.

"I'll remember that, thank you," Chyna replied. "If I want a crash course on proper demolition attire I'll consult the local home store."

"You get some goggles, or you don't demolish anything further," he finished nonchalantly, angered by his tortuous thoughts and the way his body responded just by looking at her.

Removing a hand from his pocket, he quickly grabbed her free hand dangling loosely by her left side. "And some gloves too," he added.

He caressed her hand with his thumb. It was as soft as he remembered. Those hands had cared for his ailing father.

How could you do this to me? Dean looked down at her, silently posing the question, wishing she would read his mind and answer aloud.

He let go abruptly, hating to be reminded of how those hands had stroked him, aroused him, maybe even loved him at one time. Obviously he'd been wrong.

Could it ever be the same between them? Would she leave her husband for him?

Dean remembered the male friend Mrs. Jenkins had so kindly alluded to.

He rarely spoke to Loretta Jenkins. The nosy old woman had lived in the house next door to his parents' home as long as he could remember. If anyone wanted to know the local gossip, all they had to do was ask her. Considering their prominence in the community, the Jamesons rarely associated with her. They were usually the subject on her tongue.

Dean had the unfortunate mishap of being seen by her as he walked to Chyna's house. She'd called him to her porch and asked if he knew the source of the racket that had been coming from Chyna's house. When he revealed that he didn't, Mrs. Jenkins went on to tell him, among other things, about Chyna's most recent visitor—a well-dressed gentleman that came by to see Chyna often.

"So you and Samson Godfrey?" Dean asked. "He visits you every now and then?"

"Sometimes," Chyna acknowledged, resisting the urge to wipe away the hot touch his gentle hand left on her own.

"That's good, I—I'm glad he's been a friend to you."

Dean muttered an expletive under his breath. He hated the thought of her seeing yet another man.

"Sometimes other people aren't available. You take what you can get." She reached to rub her hands on the towel as if they were dirty.

"You settle." Dean raised an eyebrow.

"No!" Chyna said empathically. "You take what you can get! People move on and leave you. Shut you out. Push you away for whatever the going excuse is for the day."

Chyna bit her tongue between her teeth. "Was Lisa Stephens it for you?"

As soon as she asked, she wished she hadn't.

"You've seen Lisa?"

Chyna didn't immediately answer. She didn't like thinking of Dean and Lisa.

She bit her bottom lip to stifle a smart retort. "You better go now."

Dean looked as if he were ready to explode. He was sick of her avoiding the slightest confrontation. He didn't argue this time though.

"Fine! If you need me, I'm down the street. You know where to find me."

"Well, that went really well," Dean muttered as he stomped his way back to his parents' house.

Wasn't this whole thing her fault? Had she told him she

was still married, they could have avoided all the time they wasted together. They could still be friends at least. Now they'd been catapulted into a fake politeness that made him sick.

Lisa Stephens? He recalled Chyna's mentioning her name. What did she have to do with anything? Dean and she were just friends. Had Chyna seen Lisa somewhere? He dismissed the thought. Lisa had already told him they hadn't crossed paths.

Chapter 6

He had some nerve. Here she was facing an onslaught of depression over the loss of their baby and mourning a love affair that had never really begun and he was implicitly accusing her of seeing someone else. He didn't even ask about California and what was so urgent that she'd had to rush off to Dulles International Airport on a moment's notice to resolve.

The pain over the thought of him and Lisa together turned to rage. Her eyes still stung from the tears she'd shed earlier, and here she was on the brink of crying again.

She picked up her keys and a videotape and marched out her front door. This had to be settled once and for all.

She stood on the porch holding her finger on the button for the doorbell. It rang over and over until Dean finally answered the door.

"I didn't think you'd be by so soon. Come in." He was smug. Too smug for her disposition. He was intentionally trying to get under her skin now. She wasn't sure she wanted to talk to him anymore. She rolled her eyes and turned to leave.

He'd had enough of her childish antics. She was a thirty-year-old woman, so why was she acting like a thirteen-year-old girl? Dean wasn't going to let her escape without facing their problem.

"Why can't you look at me for more than ten seconds?

Why can't you be in the same room with me for more than ten minutes? Why the hell can't you grace me with more than five words or remain in a room without running?" With each question his voice became louder. He was releasing all the pent-up frustration she'd caused him over the last month.

"You've never been a runner, Chyna, never." Dean was furious at her and at himself. He couldn't cover it up any longer.

She could see his frustration in his stance. His muscles bulged through his white tank top. It was grimy, gritty, and dirty with sweat. He released and contracted his fists over and over to calm himself, as if he were ready to pound something.

She felt that way too, only her anger was justifiable. So what if he didn't know why she was mad? It was better that he didn't.

"I don't want to talk to you," she said, concentrating on his forehead instead of looking him in the eyes. If she dared to stare him down, his eyes would implore her to tell him the truth and the feelings for him she still harbored in her heart would surface. She couldn't allow herself to do that.

"I don't even want to think about you," she said, her anger rising to meet his.

"Then why did you come to my house?"

She didn't answer.

"Okay, if that's the way you feel." He doubted she did, but he was tired of arguing with her. "Then at least tell me why."

"Why, why?" Chyna asked indignantly. "I left town for not even two days. Two days! You act as if everything is supposed to be fine between us. As if we're supposed to pick up where we left off? Well, it doesn't work that way." She was screaming.

She hooked a thumb at herself. "I don't work that way.

Nothing between us can be the same, ever." Her bosom heaved with the entry and exit of her own breath. Belatedly she wiped a tear from her cheek.

She turned to leave when she felt his rough hand on her arm again. With one twist, she spun around to face him but he pulled her off balance with a yank and she fell into his arms. Once she was in his embrace, Dean crushed her against him.

"Stop it!" she yelled, ready to fight, until his lips smacked down onto hers. He breathed hard against her mouth and with the pressure, every ounce of feeling for him leapt from the corners she'd tucked them into. As those feelings gained momentum, all thoughts of resisting him, of wanting him out of her life, fluttered away.

His lips were hard when they met hers and only when she gave back did they soften. She didn't want this, or at least she'd told herself she didn't. But when his tongue raced in her mouth as she gasped for air, she knew she couldn't be without him. Her hands were fists balled up against him as he continued to kiss her. They flattened to rest on each breastplate of his solid chest.

Dean wanted her. Her fiery temper only ignited his desire. He could tell by her anger that she still cared, that she still loved him. Whatever their problems were, they would solve them.

When Chyna whimpered he softened his lips and used his teeth to take small nips on her mouth, her pouting lower lip. He moved his tongue against hers and softly slipped in and out of her mouth so much like the times he had moved his sex inside her. He wanted it like it used to be.

"Why can't it be like it was?" he managed to ask in between kisses. She'd melted to him, holding him as tightly as he held her, if not tighter. "I want you. Chyna, I need you."

"No," she sobbed out. "It can't work. It can't!"

Chyna pleaded with him even as she kissed him back. Through her confusion, she managed to release the fistful of shirt she had grabbed up in an effort to get closer to him.

Wiping away her assault from his tingling lips, Dean pulled her over the threshold of the house and closed the door. Dean hoped it signaled to her that she wasn't leaving until they discussed the issue neither of them wanted to confront.

Inside, she put a necessary distance between them. She had to make him see they weren't right for each other anymore. Not only that, but she had to convince herself why things wouldn't work between them. She had to stick to her original decision even when his kisses had sent coherent thought from her mind.

Dean eyed her warily. She had never offered him any concrete information about his accusations. She'd never explained why she lied to him about Gary. The night he confronted her, she'd just stood there shaking her head, telling him he wouldn't understand.

"Is this because you're still in love with your ex? Is that why things won't work out between you and me?" he asked.

He hadn't wanted to go that route, but she left him no choice. Her chin jutted to the side and a storm seemed to gather beneath her pretty brown eyes. Dean mistook her expression for regret. To him that meant that his diagnosis was correct. Angrier, he kept running his mouth and dug a deeper hole. "You still have a flame for the senator, do you? That why we could make love and you could fly off to California the next day and leave me for him? You had your fill of me, that it?

"What was I? A convenient roll in the hay? A nice reprieve from your high-society life?"

"I think that—"

"Oh, pray tell, what do you think? Please grace me with

the contemplations of your mind," Dean interrupted
with an air of sarcasm.

Her entire body filled with rage. "I think you should
shut up!" she yelled. "You have no idea what you're talking about. I loved you my whole life. Even while I was
trying to get out of my dead-end marriage I thought of
you, but you were too selfish or too blind . . .

"Whatever problem plagued you through the different parts of your pathetic life, you couldn't see past
your own pain long enough to see me. I was there for
you, whenever you needed me. But you didn't have
time for me.

"At first you said I was too young to know anything
about love. At thirteen years old, I knew I loved you.
When I was seventeen, you said you still saw me as a
child so after I graduated from high school I took a
hint and went on my merry way. Then when your father took ill I was here for you, again. When he was
first diagnosed with Alzheimer's, you couldn't deal
with anything other than your own grief."

Her voice choked on her sobs. "Every time something went wrong you shut me out. Who are you to
question me?

"That night, after we made love, yes, I went to California. Yes, I did. You're right about my actions, but
you're wrong about my intentions. You've always been
too pigheaded to pay attention to anyone but yourself."

Dean had never seen her this angry before. "Chyna,
baby, please just tell me what happened."

"I divorced Gary two years ago. I've *been* divorced from
him!" she screamed. "You don't get it. You don't get anything. I've told you that I'm not with him, but you never
believe me. I'm over trying to prove my love to you."

"Then why does he still call you his wife?" She was
underestimating him now, he thought.

"I told you we were divorced. You were the only person who knew back then." She reached in her bag and thrust the videotape at him.

"I gave him my word that I wouldn't tell anyone so he could keep his popularity in the California polls. It was the only way he would agree to a divorce. I divorced him to be with you. You, Dean. Do you think I would have slept with you if I was married?"

Dean didn't respond. This explanation was more than he bargained for.

She continued, wiping her eye with her sleeve. "I don't feel anything for him. He was abusive, egotistical, a liar, and a complete jerk. I don't love him. I've told you that. Either you're not listening or you believe nothing that comes out of my mouth."

He looked at the tape Chyna thrust into his hand. "What does this have to do with that?"

"I went on TV. I made a public announcement to set the record straight. I wanted you to know the truth. I did it for you, for us."

Dean didn't know what to say. He kept his stoic expression. He wanted to take her in his arms and soothe her sobs. But Chyna wasn't finished. He decided to hear her out.

"But where were you when I was putting myself on the line? Purging my secrets on national television? I took the red-eye back, stayed awake for a day straight to get to you. And for what?" Chyna waved her hands about the space. "To find you at our favorite restaurant all over some woman!"

Dean's eyes dimmed in confusion. "Lisa?" he whispered aloud and realized how that sounded.

"I mean, no. Chyna— Chyna, please just listen," he pleaded.

"Lisa Stephens, that's right! Was she just a quick roll in the hay to you? She made it seem much more than that when she all but laughed at me at the grocery store," Chyna said incredulously. "I went all the way to California to air my dirty laundry and to clean up the stupid farce Gary had insisted on perpetuating and you were with her?"

Dean couldn't process all the information she threw at him. In a few seconds, she'd managed to answer all the questions he'd had about her trip out West. But Lisa Stephens was a friend, nothing more. There had never been and never would be anything between them. He couldn't lose Chyna over a series of misunderstandings.

"Chyna, there was nothing between us, I was thanking her for offering her condolences over my father's passing. That's all."

Chyna threw up her hand. "It doesn't matter, Dean. If things were meant to be between us, we'd have gotten to our destination already. I have to go."

She turned to leave. Chyna ran as fast as she could and nearly broke the kitchen's raggedy side screen door off its hinges as she barreled through it.

There was nothing Dean could say to make her change her mind. Even if she had misinterpreted their embrace, it didn't matter. She didn't think she had. What about what Lisa had alluded to at the grocery store earlier in the week? Seeing them had been the catalyst for a disastrous event.

After she saw them, all cozy and close, she had returned to her home from the restaurant, sulking and depressed over him. Over what she had seen. After what she had been through in California, it was too much. She lost their child. That was the one very important piece of information she had left out in everything she'd just revealed to him.

She thought about telling him. The words nearly escaped her mouth a million times during their heated argument, but she bit them back each time. If she knew him at all, she knew he'd take it hard, he'd feel the loss as much as she did. That announcement wouldn't solve anything between them. In some ways, she wanted him to hurt as much as if not more than she did. In other ways, she kept it from him so he wouldn't hurt.

Years ago, in the same situation with Gary, he hadn't cared at all. He didn't want children. She loved Dean because he was everything her ex wasn't. He cared about others, about her feelings, about family. She would never tell him.

Chyna shook her head. She'd gotten over it as best she could, and reminiscing would only set her back.

Chapter 7

As if nothing had happened, Chyna spent the remainder of the evening working on her demolition project. It was past five o'clock when she returned to her house and it took her another hour to calm her rattled nerves enough to focus on her house again.

She surveyed the destruction of her back room. She needed to contact a roofer to examine the leak in her roof. She stepped her way up the new ladder to inspect a depression in the ceiling. Below her she eyeballed the bucket she'd placed to catch the water. With her foot, she moved it, positioning it in a place that would catch the slow drip.

She watched as the bucket filled quickly. She thought the leak to be a minor problem until the water came faster and the bucket filled to the rim. Chyna rushed to exchange it for an empty one. Taking a deep breath, she relaxed when the water stopped. She stepped up the ladder again, pressed around the hole for more troubled areas, until she heard a crackling above her head. It sounded like water in the upper level ran everywhere. All of a sudden it stopped. Chyna exhaled a deep sigh of relief right before a metal beam crashed through the ceiling. It knocked over the ladder and sent Chyna sprawling onto the floor.

Chyna shook off her disorientation and tried to lift herself, but couldn't. He leg had caught in a ladder rung and twisted awkwardly during her fall. Debris continued to fall around her, and then something heavy fell on her shoulder and she cried out in pain. Dirty, foul-smelling water from everywhere rained down on her and soon what felt like a ton of bricks descended from the upper level to pin her under its weight.

So she had come back. She'd left the senator, come back to town, and thought Dean was seeing someone else. So she called the whole thing off. Just like that? Just that quick? She'd displaced faith in him. Dean wouldn't so easily buy into such ludicrous logic. There had to be more to the story than she was letting on.

She'd run away from him again and Dean was committed to giving her space to deal with whatever it was she was still keeping from him. That's why he waited until the next morning to pay her another visit.

He was there to reconcile what she thought was an irreconcilable difference. He'd given her a night, which, now he thought, was too long. He didn't want to pressure her. The episode last night, the tears she'd shed, made Dean realize that he was responsible for causing her pain. Still, instead of running away, they needed to sit down like two civil adults. She had to remain silent long enough and in the same room with him long enough for him to explain his side of things.

Standing at the door, Dean took a deep breath and knocked. When there was no answer, he reached for the knob and turned. It gave way. He made a mental note to chastise her about leaving her door unlocked. Once inside, Dean called her name and listened for a response or footsteps on the upper level. He didn't hear anything except the faint trickle of water in the distance.

Dean moved down the hall where the running-water sound grew louder. When he stood at the door he looked down and not only saw, but felt a flood of water rush over his feet and inch up his pant leg. The beat of his heart slowed and he quickly sent up a prayer that Chyna wasn't anywhere near this disastrous scene and that she also hadn't been upstairs when the entire floor came crashing down.

The place looked as if a hurricane had struck. Small wood chips floated like globs of what looked like chunky oatmeal. Dust flew through the air like smoke. Dean started to leave the room, heading for whatever was left of the upper level, before he saw the brown skin of Chyna's fingertips covered in dust. They poked through the rubble to grip a piece of wall that rested on top of her body.

It seemed as if it took him days to wade through the water that slowed each footstep. Dean took larger steps, hiking his feet up higher as if he sloshed through two feet of snow, and finally he was there. "Oh God. Chyna," he whispered.

Rubble and large wall pieces completely covered her up to her neck. He felt the pulse of her exposed wrist. It surged lightly under the pad of his middle finger.

Dean began to move more pieces of drywall, chunks of concrete, and soaked wood off of her. He looked over at the porcelain toilet lying on its side and thanked God that it too hadn't fallen and crushed her. He knew if it had, she wouldn't have survived.

When he finally saw her face she looked as if she'd been dousing herself with a bag of flour. She was ghostly white. Thick white flakes hung in her long lashes, in her eyebrows. Dean swore. He'd told her to wear goggles. Her lips were dry and cracked or perhaps it was the film left from the rubbish.

"Chyna, answer me, look at me," he pleaded, and with shaky hands smoothed the chips from her eyes and gently patted her face. It was all he could do not to shake her, to yell at her for being so careless, so stupid, and for not knowing one thing about proper demolition.

"Dean?" she whispered.

"Yes, I'm here. I need you to tell me if you can move."

Her eyes were red rimmed and irritated from the dust.

Quickly, Dean assessed the rest of her buried lower half and knew he couldn't pull her out for fear she'd broken something. Still, he kicked the large pieces off of her and bent to remove the smaller ones. With every piece he lifted or pulled, Dean felt a zillion nicks and scrapes bite into the flesh of his gloveless hands.

"Chyna, can you move your legs at all?" He felt utterly stupid for asking such a silly question, when a large piece of wall he wouldn't be able to move by himself lay across them.

"It hurts."

"Where? Baby, tell me where it hurts."

"My shoulder," she whispered. "And my leg."

Her face distorted when she twisted her body to move her leg. She bit her lower lip and stilled as the pain increased.

"Don't try to move it," Dean said alarmingly. "Just one of your legs or both of them?"

"My right one."

Dean reached for his cell phone and dialed 911. After telling them the location of the house he hung up. He pushed away as much of the rubble as he could, cursing his stupid pride for not coming to see her sooner. Silently he cursed her for not being more careful. Lifting the last piece, Dean ensured that Chyna's head was supported and that she didn't drown in the water covering the floor.

Dean paused when he heard a man's voice call for Chyna from the front of the house.

"Chyna?" the voice called again.

Dean heard the footsteps quicken down the hall until

they encountered the water and the stomps turned into a sloshing sound. When Samson Godfrey stood at the door, Dean looked up only slightly irritated. He turned his focus back to Chyna.

"What the hell are you doing?" Samson asked as he moved inside the door. He bent down by Chyna and tried to shove Dean away. "Haven't you caused enough trouble already?

"Chyna, dear heart, I'll call the ambulance," Samson said.

"I already called them," Dean said heatedly. Samson Godfrey's proprietary manner where Chyna was concerned made Dean reaffirm his dislike of him.

"What the hell happened?" Samson inquired, shooting an evil look in Dean's direction.

"It's not his fault, Samson," Chyna whispered in Dean's defense. She had enough coherence to sense the tension between Dean and Samson. She almost wished they both would just leave her alone to figure herself out of her own mess.

They both looked at Chyna when she spoke. Dean kept his eyes averted and silently summed up Samson Godfrey. He wondered if he had any muscle under the abundance of expensive attire he wore. Strong or not, Dean dismissed Samson as a complete fool when Samson stood, reached under Chyna's arms, and attempted to pull her from the rubble.

Dean was on his feet immediately. With a shove against Samson's chest, he pushed him away from her. "Are you crazy? Don't pull her, her leg is stuck and she said it hurts."

Samson looked down, belatedly seeing the thickness of the wall that covered most if not all of her lower body. "What would you have me do? Sit here and twiddle my thumbs?" Samson said heatedly.

"I said don't pull on her and I meant it. Her legs are

stuck under a truckload of rubble and if you'd taken a moment to observe, you'd have seen that."

Dean looked down at Chyna and changed his tone. "Chyna, sweetheart, I need you to stay awake, okay? I need you to look at me. You're going to be okay, I promise."

"She already knows your promises don't mean anything," Samson cut in.

Dean looked away, chagrined. Chyna had probably shared a lot with this man when Dean himself was unavailable. He agreed that whatever Samson thought of him was probably true, but he was on a mission to change all that.

Taking her cold hand in his, Dean pretended Samson wasn't in the room at all. He focused on trying to think of a way to get Chyna out of the mess he, sadly, had helped create. Where the hell was the ambulance?

He stood abruptly. "Chyna, stay awake! I know you're tired."

To Samson he said, "Keep her head supported! I'll be right back."

"Where in God's name are you going?" Samson's voice rose an octave, but Dean was already to the door.

In a matter of seconds, Dean rushed from Chyna's house down the street to his own. On the way back, he heard the sirens of the ambulance in the distance. A second time, he waded through the water of Chyna's back room. He took a moment to pull the cord from the machine.

"Put the goggles over her eyes and cover yours with your hand," he ordered Samson, though he didn't care what the man did to protect himself so long as he listened to the instructions he gave for protecting Chyna.

"What?" Samson yelled over the loud sound of the power machine. He searched for the goggles while Chyna reached above her head to locate them for herself. Holding them over her eyes, Samson shielded his own while the whirring of the chain saw motor and the quick blade sliced through the fallen wood. It sent chips flying everywhere, but expertly Dean carved each piece into something smaller and more manageable. He then moved the rest of the pieces with his hands until he could see Chyna's legs twisted painfully inward and intertwined with one of the ladder's rungs.

When the ambulance finally arrived, Dean had set her leg as best he could. In doing so, he felt each of her painful whimpers pierce his heart. He didn't say anything when Samson helped the paramedics carefully lift her and secure her to the gurney. And he could only look on as Samson got into the ambulance with her before it sped away. This wasn't the end, he thought as he carried the chain saw back to his own house. There he left the machine in the garage, grabbed the keys to his car, and headed for the hospital.

Chapter 8

Chyna blinked her eyes rapidly and tried to bring herself into a sitting position. She noticed her leg first; the white cast started just below her knee and stopped at allowing a peek at her toes. Her shoulder ached, but otherwise seemed okay. Her wrist was wrapped in a brown bandage. She didn't realize she'd hurt it at all. "At least it's not broken too," she said aloud, flexing it tentatively.

What a fool she had been. The revelations Dean had made meant Chyna misunderstood what happened between him and Lisa. Chyna had let her own grief shut out the man she loved, and to top off her situation she'd nearly killed herself. Of all the places to be, she managed to put herself in the hospital.

She looked up at the ceiling with its brown-stained boards. The room had ugly curtains that made it seem like the most unfeeling, sterile institution she had ever been inside. Being there brought back memories of her last visit.

"Hey, you're awake," Dean said, as he entered the room cheerily.

She gave him an exasperated sigh. Had it not been for him she'd probably still be lying under the weight of her second floor.

She looked toward the window, away from him. She needed to get out of there. Before she could do that, however, she'd need to find a way to get Dean to leave. It would prove difficult, but everything concerning Dean Jameson was.

"How are you, Chyna?" Dean moved closer to the bed and placed his hands on the bed's safety railing.

"Fine," she replied.

"Don't lie," Dean said.

"If you know so much about my state, why bother to ask?" Chyna returned, swinging her head around angrily to face him. She hated his deep-set eyes, the way his brows knitted together, showing her his sincere concern.

"'Cause for once, I'd like you to tell me the truth about your feelings." He changed subjects. "I brought you a gift, a plant."

Dean reached for the fern on her bedside tray table. He picked it up and held it for her to see. He placed it back on the table.

"Thank you," she whispered. She did like plants and the fact that he remembered counted in his favor.

"Chyna, dear heart, are you decent?" a voice called from the door.

Chyna pounded her head on the pillow in utter frustration. Her plan to exit the facility just gained one more deterrent. She could tack on another whole two hours.

"Yes, Samson, I'm decent," she said exasperatingly.

Samson waltzed into the room as if he owned the place. He set down the two vases. One was filled with red roses and the other with yellow ones.

"How are you, dear?" He leaned down to touch his lips to her cheek and belatedly noticed Dean just on the other side of her bed.

"I'm all right, Samson. Thank you for the flowers, they're beautiful." The flowers were beautiful, but she knew he only brought two bouquets so he wouldn't be outdone by anyone, especially not Dean.

"Listen," Samson said, "I just came by to say hey. See how you were doing this morning. I'll pick you up whenever Charlie says you can be released. Just page me. I imagine you'll be here a few more days for observation?" he questioned.

Chyna started to shake her head in protest. *Not if I can help it.* Instead, she kept thoughts of her plot to herself.

"By the way, you owe me two hundred dollars for the new shoes I ruined."

He was joking, Chyna knew. She merely smiled to acknowledge his attempt at humor while thinking he shouldn't joke at all. He was a good friend and she was thankful for his attention, but never in the years she had known him would she have called him funny.

"I'd say you were ripped off," Dean muttered.

"What?" Samson looked up spitefully at Dean, and Chyna might have laughed at the expression if she weren't experiencing her own bout of misery.

"Two hundred dollars at Payless? I'd say you were ripped off."

Samson looked back at Chyna, ignoring Dean. "Okay, well, sis has my pager number in case you need it. I'll see ya." Samson leaned in again, touching his lips to Chyna's cheek. Cordially he nodded at Dean before exiting the room.

"Now that he's gone, what do you want to do? Watch *The Young and the Restless*? I think Victor is about to go nuts over Vicki again, for the umpteenth time, no doubt."

"Dean?" Chyna said with exasperation. The day Dean Jameson watched a soap opera would be the day hell had frozen over. "Please tell me you're not into soap operas nowadays." She regarded him skeptically.

"Not really. I've just had a lot of time on my hands and I was a little bored. During the summer, Tish and Jina used to watch them, said it helped pass the time. I just turned it on and there it was," Dean said. He shrugged his shoulders as he flipped through the channels.

"It's either that or talk shows." He shrugged a shoulder. "I guess I've gotten into this analytical thing with some television shows. I mean some of it you can actually apply to your own life. You sit there thinking how stupid these people come off. But some of the stupidity they exhibit is the same kind we as people do in our own lives. It's just illustrated in a rather dramatic form on television. The moral is there just the same.

"These two people, for example," Dean said, pointing to the television.

Chyna listened and watched as a couple roughly embraced each other. Their lips brutally met again and again. It wasn't like that, she thought silently, but still she listened to what Dean said. She looked down from the TV to pull the strings of her sheet and hoped Dean got to the point quickly. She wished he'd leave and take his *how a soap opera applies to my life* philosophy with him.

". . . one person is always chasing another," Dean continued, "and then when one of them stops chasing, the other turns around and does the chasing. You know, this guy. His life is perfect. He has a woman who adores him, money in the bank, smart kids . . . it gets old for some reason, greed, his taste buds change, and he no longer wants what he has."

Chyna pretended she didn't know what Dean was talking about. She wasn't chasing him anymore and if he was implying that he now chased her, she couldn't believe such a thing.

Dean kept talking. "Anyway, you're going to be here awhile so I thought you might as well make the best of it. We could play some cards. I'll get you some board games from the gift shop downstairs. Would you like that?"

"No, Dean. Thank you," Chyna said hastily. Then as if an escape plan came to mind, she casually pretended she'd changed her mind. "On second thought"—she brightened—"I would like something. I, uh, I'm hungry."

She had to get him out of here, and for effect she

yawned dramatically. She could talk her friend who was a nurse there into implementing whatever was necessary to release her. If she worked quickly enough, she could be released before Dean got back. "Some crab Rangoon, uh, sweet-and-sour chicken," Chyna said quickly. She rattled off the things she knew would take at least fifteen minutes in advance ordering.

"How about a light, late breakfast? I know how much you like scones from the bakery," Dean offered.

Chyna rolled her eyes. Her plan wasn't working and her frustration increased. "I broke my leg, hurt my shoulder, and sprained my wrist! I am not recovering from gastric bypass surgery."

She wanted him to agree and leave. "But thank you, that would be great." Having him gone for any time at all was better than having him stay another minute. She watched amazed as Dean nodded and, without further comment, left.

Chyna immediately turned her head, twisting herself until she could reach the nurse's call button. Ten minutes later when someone came to check on her, she asked for her friend, Samson's sister, Nurse Charlize Godfrey.

Charlize Godfrey was late for work. Again. She loved her brother, Samson, but would be glad when his visit was over. He was a great lawyer but he left a mess in her apartment. By the time she cleaned up the place and fought Springfield's growing transit nightmare, she was almost an hour late for work.

She stormed to the nurses' station, storing her purse in the cabinet and her lunch in the small fridge. Reaching for a handful of latex gloves, she stuffed them into her pocket and mentally tossed aside her life's personal annoyances in exchange for work-related ones. She had charts to review, patients to greet, and the night's issues to go over with the staff.

"Your friend is back."

Charlize looked up when she heard her coworker's voice over her shoulder.

"What?" Charlize said. She stopped what she was doing to locate the voice. "What'd you say?"

"I said your friend is back," said the nurse. "Lockhart, she's in room three-oh-one."

Charlize looked down at the chart she was preparing and, sure enough, it just happened to be that of her friend, Chyna Lockhart. Without further comment, she marched down the hall, hands on her hips, to room 301, preparing her mind to do battle with a woman more stubborn than she was.

"What do you think you're doing?" Charlize boomed when she entered the room. She found Chyna managing her legs over the side of the bed.

"Oh." Chyna blew her hair from her forehead and turned her body to get a good look at her friend. "You scared me. How are you? What's the matter?"

"What's the matter? You're in the hospital, not me."

"Oh." Chyna waved her hand dismissively. "I just had a small disaster." She didn't bother to elaborate on what happened. "Didn't Samson tell you what happened?"

"No! He said you'd hurt your leg was all."

"Well, yeah, that's all," Chyna said, falsely wishing that were the extent of the damage she'd done not only to herself, but to her house as well. She hated to see what awaited her there.

She hoped her friend wouldn't get any more upset and mad but would agree to help her out of the mess.

"Listen, Charlie, my friend," Chyna said sweetly, using her friend's nickname. If she could just drag her leg to the floor without banging it, she'd show Charlie she could walk or hop her way out of there. How difficult could it be? "I need help, please. I can't stay here."

"I don't know anything. I don't have any idea what you're talking about, Chyna. Even if I did understand what you were saying, I'm going to pretend I don't."

Chyna frowned. She felt the right and determination she once had to get out of the hospital slowly being zapped from her bones. "I can't stay here, I just can't. Please help me, please."

"Okay," Charlie said. "But tell me, if you go home, who's going to help you? How will you get around?"

"Well, I could stay with you," Chyna pointed out.

"You could, Chyna, you could, and I would help you. You know that, but guess what? Samson is staying with me, sleeping on my couch, because he's not quite Johnnie Cochran just yet. Really, he's too cheap to pay for a hotel. I live in a one-bedroom apartment, remember? Where is the room in that, Chyna?"

Chyna chewed her lip. "My house is such a mess, I sent the place crashing about my head, I don't even remember what it looks like. I could manage there. But there's one thing I'm certain of." She looked at her friend again, laughing falsely to keep from crying. "Charlie, I'll die if I have to stay here one more day, one more hour, one more minute! I can't stay in this hospital, I can't!"

"You could stay at the house. I would take care of you, Chyna," came Dean's reply.

Both Chyna and Charlize looked to the door when Dean appeared. Chyna's nightmare worsened. She knew not enough time had passed for Dean to have gone to the restaurant and returned already. She also didn't see any sign of food. Nor did she smell anything to feed her starving stomach. She sat against the bed, her good leg resting on the cold floor and her heavy casted leg still under the covers. If she could chop it off without too much pain, she'd do just that and leave it there.

Chyna looked up. What he said finally registered in her ears. For a moment, a resounding "yes" was ready to leave her lips, but she clamped down on her own tongue to prevent herself from saying anything. For a few insane minutes, she'd thought she would go anywhere and agree to anything if it meant her release from the hospital. Whether she wanted out badly enough to stay at the Jameson home was another matter entirely.

Her fight was gone. When Charlie shoved Chyna's dangling leg under the covers, Chyna acquiesced. Charlie proceeded to tightly tuck in the covers around her as if a barrier might keep her from getting out of bed.

"You aren't leaving right now," Charlie said. She straightened from her task and set heated eyes on Dean. "And she's not going anywhere with the likes of you!"

Before Charlie could lash out at Dean again, Chyna placed a hand on her stomach. "Where's the food, Dean? I'm really hungry." She had to get one of them to leave or they might physically battle before her very eyes.

"Lunch will be here in a few minutes," Charlie responded. "And I'll see to it that you have something healthy, not some high-cholesterol, high-fried fritter. She doesn't need that junk," Charlize said, looking up at Dean.

She wrote furiously on the tablet, then noisily dragged a slim cart on wheels closer to Chyna's bedside. Once there, she stuck a thermometer into a plastic sheath and put it into Chyna's mouth. "Why in God's name would she stay with you of all the people in the world? What are you doing here anyway? Haven't you done enough?"

"You know, Charlize, this is an A"—Dean pointed to Chyna and then hooked two fingers at his chest—"and B conversation. You can see your way out. This doesn't concern you."

"The hell it doesn't concern me. She won't tell you about your selfish self, but I can."

When the beep thankfully sounded, Chyna took a deep breath. "Please just stop it. You guys, just quit it!"

"Don't tell me you'd consider staying at that house, Chyna? The proximity you live in now is too close."

"Did I say I would stay there, Charlie?"

"No, but I can tell when a thought of pure nonsense crosses your mind. I can just see the wheels turning in that thick head of yours."

"When can I be released? I just want to get out of here."

Staying at the Jameson home crossed her mind, but the realization that Dean might be living there and not just dropping in to do some minor renovations made the offer less appealing. Chyna shook her head, erasing the idea from her mind. She would manage at her own house. It was a disaster, so what? She'd stay in the front room while repairs were made. She'd adjust, somehow.

"When can you be released? When can you be released?" Charlize's voice raised to a high pitch with each repeat of the question. "You're asking me when you can be released? You have a slight temperature, your blood pressure is up, and you're lying on your back with a sprained wrist and a broken leg."

Charlize took a deep audible breath and shook her head with unbelief. "I'll see what the doctor can do. I'm not promising anything and if you come up with another place to stay that includes someone to help you, then I'm all for it, but I will not let you stay with him!"

"Please, Charlie, just try," Chyna pleaded, "just tell them that you'll visit me like you did when I . . ." Chyna cursed under her breath and placed her tongue between her teeth. She looked over at Dean, who stood casually as if he hadn't planned on leaving any time soon.

"You can come see me, check on me?" Chyna finished hurriedly. She'd almost let it slip that her friend had come by to check on her during the week following her miscarriage. If Dean found out, she'd never recover. She couldn't bear it. Chyna watched as her friend rolled her eyes but otherwise didn't say anything. She averted her eyes from Dean's unknowing gaze.

Charlie hung the chart in its slot at the end of the bed and moved to the door. Chyna took a deep breath after her friend left. She settled her back against the pillow and pinched her eyes with her good hand.

"An inspector will be by to check out your place, Chyna," Dean said. "Half the roof is caved in and most of it's flooded. It's barely livable. I'm sorry, Chyna, I'm sorry that I yelled and that we argued. I never meant . . ." Dean stopped talking when Chyna waved her hand to request that he be quiet.

"Inspectors are going to come look at my home?" she asked. Dean nodded but she didn't want to hear any more.

"Yeah." Dean cleared his throat. "Yes. But, I could get Bubba to do it. He can write it up, make a report to them if you'd like."

She nodded.

"Chyna," Dean whispered.

"What! What? What?" she yelled.

Placing his hands on the railing of the hospital bed, he regarded Chyna. "Why's it so hard for you to ask for help? We're family."

Dean didn't understand any of it. They were acting like strangers.

Chyna shook her head in protest. They weren't family. They wouldn't ever be family. She looked at him accusingly. "Maybe I don't want your help. Maybe I don't want you to care, or help me, or do anything other than be quiet!"

Chyna crossed her arms one over the other, forgetting momentarily about her bandaged wrist, and then unfolded them.

"Well, I will help you. I do care and I'll do anything, give you anything you need," Dean said easily. He brushed the hair away from her brow, and Chyna annoyingly smacked his hand away.

"If you're going to stay, at least be quiet, please," she said as she turned to look at him. Her eyes drooped with fatigue. Dean nodded and without further comment, he sat down in the metal chair next to her bed. He rested his ankle on the edge of his knee when he crossed his legs and reached to grab a raggedy magazine from the tray table.

"I'll take care of everything," he whispered just loudly enough for Chyna to hear. "I'll take care of you."

She didn't want to hear him, but she did and knew Dean's last statements were exactly what she was afraid of.

Chapter 9

"Yep, I'd say she's got some serious water damage up there. See this?" Pulling a piece from what remained of Chyna's roof, Bubba Sparks of Sparks Carpentry held it down for Dean to look closer.

He shook it and Dean had to move back to keep the gross-looking fungus stuff from landing on his head. In his gloved hand, Bubba brought it closer to his face, turning it as if it were some type of intricate design he wanted to duplicate. "Wood's rotten, cheap roofing don't last long," Bubba said.

Dean nodded. He knew there were a host of problems hidden in the Lockharts' home. Feeling somewhat responsible for its present shape, Dean stood in Chyna's destroyed, uninhabitable place to see what an old friend of both the Jamesons and the Lockharts had to say about its repair and reconstruction.

Bubba was thoughtful a moment. In his waterproof boots, he looked around the place and shook his head in disgust. "That sorry daddy of hers, musician, wasn't he? Whatever he was singing, the blues didn't pay no bills, you understand? He didn't keep up the house like a man with a family should."

Dean nodded in agreement. Having known and met Mr. Lockhart only a few times, he remembered him as a man who stayed out all night in the clubs and barely came home long enough to rest before he was gone again. Sometimes for weeks, even months at a time. Dean often wondered why Chyna never mentioned him and realized that was because she probably didn't know much about him.

Bubba took a deep breath. "They weren't nothing like your family, Dean. That daddy of hers was the cheapest man around. If he could get someone to buy air, he'd have it bottled up in a heartbeat and sell it on the corner.

"This place is a death trap!" Bubba said disgustedly. "It's a wonder she wasn't killed. I'll get some folks I know to fix up the place, won't take but a few months. I'll light a fire under some people. Least I can do. She took care of my Georgia before she died, you know. Owe her real good for that," he said, looking around the place, then shrugging his shoulders. "Took care of your daddy too, didn't she?"

Dean nodded.

"She didn't ask for nothing much. My Georgia got that blasted cancer in 'er bones. Chyna would come home from school, give Georgia her baths, kept the house tidy, made dinner, burnt up my food."

Bubba laughed with a saddened air. He coughed a few times to cover the grief. "Yeah, she tried. Did better'n I could. Don't worry 'bout a thing and tell her not to worry. Just help her to get better. Keep her out of this place, ain't fit for her to live in it right now."

Dean watched Bubba move his aging body carefully down the ladder. Tipping a hat he wasn't wearing, he gave Dean a courteous nod before he left.

Dean made a mental note to help Bubba put the place back together again. He'd offer physical labor and the finances to see that it was restored. Bubba wasn't the only one indebted to Chyna Lockhart.

* * *

Dean helped Chyna through the door of the Jameson home. The smell of paint, wood chips, and primer wafted past her nose, but the smell of home, baking bread, apple cinnamon lingered. Even though Mrs. Jameson wasn't there baking like she used to, Chyna could still smell remnants of all that she might have made if she were.

"I brought a bed down to the den and set things up for you in there," Dean offered.

"I could have made it up the stairs . . . uh, thank you."

"I got some of the stuff you like. Part of the roof that caved in, water had nowhere else to run so it trickled into the kitchen cabinets. I had to throw out most of the food."

Chyna nodded, repeating her thanks as she hopped her way into the kitchen.

Not knowing what else to do, she sat down at the table. "How about a sandwich?" Dean offered.

Chyna nodded. Suddenly the hunger returned full throttle. She couldn't believe she'd agreed to stay at the Jameson home, and after only five minutes of being there she was thankful to be out of the hospital, but agreeing to stay there after some persuasion from Dean might not have been the best decision after all. *What other choice did I have?* she thought silently.

"I can make it." Chyna broke from her thoughts and stood from the chair. She washed her one good hand and managed to get the mayonnaise, turkey, and cheese from the fridge. Holding the jar against her chest, she managed to twist the top off the jar.

Dean stood back to watch her. When it was time to cut the sandwich, Chyna realized she had a problem. Searching for a plastic bag to cover her bandaged hand, she found the box but it was empty.

Dean turned to watch her and Chyna pretended she was about to do something else like get a glass for something to drink.

"What?" she huffed when he continued to stare at her back.

"Want me to cut that?"

"No! I'm looking for sandwich bags," Chyna replied tersely.

"Planning to wrap everything up and take it on a picnic?" he asked.

"Nope," she said, not bothering to look at him. "I can wrap my stupid bandaged hand in the plastic bag and hold one end of the sandwich while I cut it." She didn't know if it would work but she had to try.

Dean washed his hands and grabbed a larger knife from the drawer. It probably cut better than the butter knife she held in her good hand. He proceeded to cut her sandwich for her. She all but exploded.

"Don't you have some place to be?" she asked impatiently and noticed the clean glass and the juice he'd placed on the table. It was obviously for her.

"Yeah, I've got to meet with the adjuster," Dean said in a low voice.

Chyna immediately winced. She hadn't asked about his place of business. He loved his job. And owning such a building as the Jamesons did was a big deal.

Chyna silently chastised herself for acting as if she didn't care, when she did. She told herself that staying out of Dean's affairs and that not asking or pretending not to care was for the best. But she was concerned that he wouldn't know how or what to do next.

His life seemed to have fallen down around him starting with the death of his father. She knew what it felt like when it seemed as if you'd lost it all, but she didn't wish that same despondency on him, ever. Then, if she'd been able to share it with someone, it would've been easier to bear.

Chyna wondered if Dean shared his sorrow with Lisa Stephens. To think about them hurt like hell. Chyna and

Dean's inability to open up to each other like they did before hurt too. They were being cordial, but there was still an invisible wall between them.

They were once close; Chyna convinced herself that time was over and they'd never go back to what they once had. She was truly apologetic for so much more than his place burning down and for whatever hand she played in their relationship's ultimate demise.

Dean nodded. Snatching a paper towel from the wooden rack, he folded it neatly into fours and placed it beside her plate. "Do you want some grapes?"

"Yes." Chyna shook her head and Dean got out a bowl for the fruit. He rinsed the green grapes and set them on the table before her.

"Thank you."

He was becoming the most thoughtful person she had ever met. The bed he moved downstairs, the room he set up, was all to help her, make her stay as mobile and accessible as possible. Chyna even noticed that a couple of boxes of her clothes had been brought over.

If she was going to tolerate his presence, she was going to have to tolerate his insistence upon helping her as well. Resisting wasn't doing anyone any good. "May I have some potato chips?" Chyna asked and Dean immediately moved to the cupboard, opened the new bag of her favorite brand of barbecue potato chips, and placed those in a small amount in a bowl next to the grapes.

"Do the authorities have any idea who destroyed your place?" she asked. Dean shook his head as Chyna crunched noisily on a chip. "I read about it in the paper. I'm sorry."

"Thanks," he said. "Will you be all right by yourself for a few hours?"

Chyna nodded without argument this time. It would be nice if she could put aside her independent-woman attitude for just a few minutes and let his sincerity and helpfulness wash over her.

"I'm all right. Thank you, Dean, for inviting me to stay."

"You're always welcome here," Dean said quickly and before Chyna could protest, he bent to kiss her on the cheek and left.

"Mama, you covering your smoking again?" Lisa smiled, knowing the answer before she asked.

"What's it to you?" her mother called back.

"Well, I think considering what the doctor said, you shouldn't do that."

"Come to see about me, did you?" Sheila Stephens said once her daughter entered the room. "What have you been up to?"

Lisa looked away. "Nothing," she said, guiltily.

"Of course, nothing. After all, down at that Hardig building, you're just playing the role of a lawyer. You're what? A legal assistant? Secretary?

"I came over here to see about you and this is all you ever give me. You dump on me all the time! I'm sorry your life is so miserable, but mine ain't a bed of roses either."

"Come to see about me? What'd you bring? See? Not even a pack of Marlboro Lights."

"Do you think you're lugging around an oxygen tank because you're an Olympic swimmer?"

Lisa prepared for some smart retort, braced herself for a cutting comeback, but the only thing returned was the same incessant wheezing cough her mother would issue when she'd gotten herself worked up. Her mean, smart, and hurtful responses wouldn't come fast enough. The inability to reply as she wanted left her breathless and gasping for air.

Rushing over to her mother, Lisa roughly clapped her hands in quick succession across her mother's back until the phlegm clogging her airways cleared.

"You trying to kill me?" her mother said when it was evident the patting had worked.

Lisa stood quickly, nonplussed. That line, at least, she had been expecting. A *thank you for your help* would've been nice, but no such luck.

"You still sniffing after that Jameson boy?"

Lisa didn't bother answering. She left the room for the kitchen to fix her mother a sandwich. Removing a pill from each of the six medicine bottles that lined the countertop, she placed the pills in a small plastic cup beside the sandwich plate on the tray. She reached for a large bottle of juice, twisted the top, and poured it in a cup.

"You know, Jameson? That youngest boy don't pay you no never mind? Don't play dumb with me, and don't play like you deaf either."

Lisa held the tray on one hand, carrying it to the living room where her mother sat for at least ten hours of the day. Without answering, she moved the playing cards, the *Soap Opera Digest,* the *Inquirer,* and a heap of other magazines her mother used to keep her company from the table and placed the tray on it.

Her mother looked up at her, then back disgustedly at the food. "I hate this junk, you know that."

Lisa shrugged, taking a deep breath. "So you tell me all the time," she finished nonchalantly and turned to straighten the living room as if the words her mother constantly spewed upon her hadn't hurt. They did—they stung as deep as they always had, but there was nothing she could do. Her mother had turned into a bitter old woman, looking almost thirty years older than her present age of fifty-two. With a bad heart and failing lungs, Sheila Stephens had nicotined herself as close to death as she could get.

"You need anything else, Mama?" Lisa said as politely as their conversation thus far would allow.

"Anything else? Do I need anything else?" Sheila harrumphed. "How about a grandchild with the last name Jameson? They got more money than the law allows any black men I ever seen. Why didn't nothing happen when you was over there playing financial adviser?" Sheila asked incredulously.

"Two years in accounting school and you a financial adviser? Lord, if that wasn't funny to me! Girl, you should be on comedy something or other. I should've snagged the elder Joseph Jameson for myself, before he went batty, that is. Look at you, I can't even live vicariously through my daughter. By the way, Chauncey Hardig was over here again looking for you."

Lisa looked over at her mother alarmingly. "What'd you say?"

"What could I say? You only come over every few days, when you're feeling guilty, no doubt." Sheila shrugged and bit into her sandwich. Transferring a wad of food to the corner of her mouth, she looked at her daughter. "Said you was supposed to do something for him. Said Warren ain't been by because he wasn't feeling well.

"The Hardigs ain't nice. They got houses and tons of land, but the cops are probably after them. That young Hardig, he ain't too stable. The Jamesons, see, daughter o' mine, got a little bit of money, them kids got that. If I was you, I'd bet on Dean Jameson, the doctor. Jojo fine too, but the doctor seems a bit more gullible. Easily duped. That's what you been doing over there, isn't it? Duping them? You know anything about the office burning down? Been all over the news, you know."

Lisa shook her head. She was shocked that her mother would know so much about a project she had tried to keep secret. She realized her plan was falling apart at the seams. But ruining the Jamesons wasn't her ploy alone.

She worked with Warren. Only Lisa hadn't seen him in weeks.

Sheila shrugged a shoulder as she let out a snort that suggested she didn't believe her daughter, before she continued.

"Sure. I tried to dupe a Jameson in my day. Didn't work," she yelled as her daughter ran from the room.

Once in her car, Lisa pulled the cell phone from her purse and dialed the last number that had called her. "I'm coming to see you now. Now!" she yelled into the phone. "Right now!"

The things her mother had told her were no surprise. She already knew all that stuff about the Hardigs and the Jamesons. She knew who was the better man to go after. Where her mother had failed, Lisa planned to succeed. She pressed the button to end the call, tossed the phone back in her purse, and sped away to the Hardig building.

Chyna was getting better at maneuvering herself about the house. The pain from the sprain sustained to her wrist was a distant memory. She was using Dean's computer and able to type at a pretty good speed to complete her articles. Her leg was still in a cast, but at least it didn't feel like a ton when she needed to move. She had even managed a sponge bath, though she longed for a real one where she could submerse her entire body, and let hot, hot water cascade over her, reaching into every crevice. Until then, a soapy sponge while standing at the sink would have to do until the cast came off. She counted the days.

Getting the cast taken off was not a big deal. What worried Chyna most was leaving the Jameson home once her own home was finished. She and Dean, once Chyna had set aside her attitude, had been able to develop an easy camaraderie. They'd been civil to one another once she let his easygoing nature calm instead of rattle her.

Chyna had let down her guard, and if she wasn't careful she'd get her heart into a mess.

That's what Dean was counting on, that she would relax. He was charming her, at least that's what he hoped he was doing. With his back to her, he felt Chyna's presence in the kitchen and smiled. He was taking things slow, but any minute—just a bit longer—he planned to increase the speed limit.

Chyna found herself at the entrance to the kitchen and something with a spicy odor wafted past her nose, causing her stomach to churn with hunger.

"Dinner's almost ready," Dean said over his shoulder, surprising Chyna, who hadn't thought he'd noticed her entrance. Especially since she'd been standing there for some time lost in her own thoughts.

Moving farther into the kitchen, she dismissed all thoughts of her life's future direction and took time to notice one of the dishes already on a plate beside a stove. Dean ladled some crimson sauce over it.

"What is that? It looks like something out of a magazine and much too good to eat. I don't remember your cooking skills being all that great. Dean, who taught you how to cook?"

Dean stood back from the counter as if he too needed a moment to admire his culinary skills. Everything he'd created thus far in the past several days had surpassed his expectations. Then he shrugged his shoulders, containing his pleasure until after they'd taken the first bite. One thing he'd learned about cooking was that it could look good, but taste awful. A couple of failed dishes still lingered in his mind. He looked over at Chyna.

"Angie. She gives Saturday morning classes for people who want to learn to cook. Extra money until she starts her catering business, or the restaurant."

"Angie and Jojo?" Chyna asked.

Dean shrugged his shoulders. "They're moving pretty

fast. Guess some people just know what they want and go for it."

"Yeah," was all Chyna said. If she counted correctly, it seemed that over the course of six months, Dean's older brother, Jojo, had met the type of woman he swore he'd never date. Things seemed simplest, she was reminded, for everyone but her. Chyna nodded again, watching Dean as he tossed greens in a wooden bowl. She nodded at the food. "You could take a picture of it. It looks like something out of *Bon Appétit*," Chyna said in awe, nearly smacking her lips with want.

"That's a good idea," Dean piped up. "Angie mentioned wanting to start a collection of photos to write for some food magazine. Accompanying photos help sell articles?"

Chyna nodded. "They do. I have some photos I try to get to go along with the *General Advocate* articles, but in a food magazine, there's no doubt it would help readers to visualize the dish and increase their desire to make it. But I think those photos are pretty professional."

She looked up and realized Dean had left the room. When he returned, he handed her the camera.

"The photos you've taken look professional to me. You're quite the photographer."

"What? Why do you say that?" she asked even as she took the machine he extended to her.

Dean cleared his throat. He reached to remove the salt and pepper shakers, and cleaned up a spill with the dishrag. He didn't want the background of the picture to look too cluttered. He turned the dish from side to side, trying to capture its best angle.

"The pictures of us. I saw them along with some of your mom and dad while I was packing up your stuff from the house."

Chyna nearly dropped the camera directly into the pretty chicken dish, but she recovered quickly, maintaining her composure and her grasp on the camera. She loved to take pictures but something else alarmed her. What else had Dean uncovered while packing up her things? Most everything except clothes and personal items were packed away in boxes. She hadn't really tackled the task of unpacking them since she'd had the majority of her things shipped from California.

She was startled at the thought of Dean noticing the ton of books she'd once purchased on pregnancy and babies. The explanation she formed quickly on her tongue, that she and Gary were considering having kids, would've been true. But there were some newer books she'd purchased not long ago. Books about how to better prepare herself and her body not to meet the same fate she did the first time she'd gotten pregnant. Those books still graced the shelves of her living room bookcase. She'd meant to pack up the books, donate them to a local birthing center. Now, however, they were lying somewhere like a virtual time bomb waiting to be discovered.

"I see," Chyna said finally, not knowing what she saw or even what Dean said since the panicked thoughts had raced through her. She scratched her head, looking down at the food. Holding the camera to her face, she prayed for steadier hands, closed one eye, and looked through the viewfinder with the other. Leaning closer, she focused and pressed the button.

"I, uh, also saw the books on having a baby. I guess you were thinking about starting a family when you were married to Gary?"

"Yes. Yes, we thought about it," she said hurriedly, feeling flustered. Chyna rushed through a few more shots, turning the camera, unsure whether she got a focused shot or not. She just wanted to be done with the entire thing. She placed the camera on the counter, glad for the emptiness now filling her hands before she had a chance to drop everything.

"Seems like a lot of books just to be thinking about something you're not actually doing yet."

"Nothing like pretending you're doing something to get you ready for the reality when or if it should come."

"How'd Gary feel about kids?"

"I really don't want to talk about it, okay?"

"Seems like a self-conceited jerk! I couldn't imagine throwing a kid into the mix, causing Mr. Senator to pay attention to the needs of someone else. He'd actually have to care about and nurture someone other than himself," Dean said matter-of-factly.

"He didn't want them," Chyna said aloud. She looked at Dean, wondering how he could make such a perfect assessment about someone he'd never known or met. At least, she didn't remember them actually meeting in person.

"I always wanted a family," she said. She didn't want him to know, and thinking about this entire conversation brought her attitude back.

"You'll have one," Dean said. *We will have one,* he thought. He had several promises he'd made about their future stored up in his mind. Chyna shook her head but Dean didn't say anything to reassure her. It wasn't time yet, but soon enough he'd planned to let her know all that he envisioned for them, their future. But not now; he knew he'd only scare her away.

"Should we eat?" Chyna heard Dean say and before she could nod her head in response, the chime of the doorbell rang.

Somewhat startled, she turned her head from Dean. "I can get it," she said and to her surprise he nodded, allowing her to move to the door. "Do you have some croutons?" she asked, looking down at the salad. Dean nodded and went to the cupboard while Chyna answered the door.

She surprised herself when she made it to the door in just a few seconds. Her leg was close to being healed and she'd been able to move faster by putting more weight on it. What surprised Chyna even more was Dean's quiet acquiescence that allowed her to get to the door without his insistence that she sit down while he did everything for her.

With a smile, Chyna opened the door, prepared to give a hearty greeting to whoever was visiting the Jamesons. But when she looked up, the smile left her face and words of cordialness left her mind. She stared into the cold eyes of a man that represented times spent in a part of her life she'd rather forget. She didn't have any nice words for her ex-husband's supposed friend, Warren Hardig.

Chapter 10

"Chyna, what a lovely surprise. I didn't know you were friends of the Jamesons."

At that instance it seemed the sky just over Warren's shoulder darkened with the threat of rain. More importantly, Chyna couldn't shake the sense of impending danger with Warren's visit. Nothing good came of the man standing before her. What was he doing here? Her stomach immediately began to ache with a profound sense of dread and loathing.

"Warren," Chyna managed as courteously as she could. "I, uh, I . . ."

"May I come in? Is Dean around?"

"Yes, yes, he's in the . . ."

Relieved that he wasn't there to bother her, she relaxed visibly. Were Dean and Warren Hardig friends? Dismissing such thoughts, she realized that even if they were, it was none of her business. She just hoped the Jamesons never had the unfortunate occurrence of befriending or doing business with Warren Hardig.

She pointed in the direction she had come from and when she moved back from his stifling height, her good foot caught the edge of the straw welcome mat at the door. Before she could stop herself with her injured leg's waning support, she felt Warren's arms reaching out to assist her.

"I'm fine, I'm fine, I . . . Thanks," she said once she

was standing upright. It took a force of sheer will not to run screaming from his embrace. She had plenty of reasons not to like him. She could never forget the night that Warren, even if in a drunken stupor, forgot that she was married then to Gary, supposedly his friend. She never forgot one minute of that haunting night.

"You've always had lovely, long dancer legs. With some practice, I'm sure we could exact the loveliest arabesque."

Chyna ignored him completely. His comments meant to flatter did nothing but repulse her. An arabesque, though she only knew it to be a term in ballet, somehow didn't conjure up an image of a dancer's derriere flat on the floor. That was the only dance move she'd be able to exact. Chyna nodded for lack of anything else to do.

He always seemed to open his mouth with something inappropriate to say, reminding her of why she neither liked nor trusted him. Comments like what he'd just made, and ones of a much more intimate and vulgar nature made in her and Gary's California home, would never be forgotten.

"You okay?" Dean said, exiting the kitchen and making his way down the hall. He reached for Chyna's hand.

Willingly taking it, she used his support to gain better footing and moved down the hall. Over her shoulder she said, "I'll leave you."

She smiled tightly at Dean before turning in the opposite direction. When Warren said a courteous good-bye she didn't bother to acknowledge him.

"What's happening, man?" Warren said. He made his way into the kitchen as if he'd visited often.

Dean shut the door and followed Warren. He made his unhappiness at the interruption evident when he crossed his arms over his chest in a menacing stance.

He'd hoped to have a nice quiet dinner with Chyna and he wouldn't put that notion off for Hardig business.

"Oh, man," Warren said, eyeing the cozy table set for two. "Sorry, I interrupted. You're making moves here?" Warren spread his hands to encompass the space before him. The set table was filled with delicious-looking food.

"What can I do for you?" Dean said, nonplussed, and made a mental note to find out how Chyna and Warren knew each other. After Chyna had turned to leave, Warren's eyes seemed to linger on her derriere a little too long. That wasn't lost on Dean for a second.

"What can I do for you?" Dean repeated.

"Man, really a bad time, huh? Listen, I just came to talk to you about my struggles with the county zoning ordinances. See if you were in the market for a new career in the business scene."

"I'm not interested," Dean said flatly.

"You haven't even heard me out, bro."

"I'm not your bro, Warren."

"Damn, tough crowd," Warren said, looking around the room. He turned to lean against the refrigerator door and crossed a foot over the other in a stance that suggested he planned to stay awhile.

"So what's up? Heard about your place. Shame. But now that you know that area is full of crime, seems you'll be looking for some real estate to work in. Remember I was telling you about my dad and me, our next venture . . ."

"Yeah, Warren. You asked me about this property stuff before and I told you then I wasn't interested in advocating for the construction of a second Hardig empire. Nor am I looking to rent space a Hardig owns. I'm an optometrist, that's it. My parents were into that stuff, they got involved in county politics. Not me, I don't do politics."

"Really?" Warren replied. "So your daddy dies and you've decided what's important in life."

"Even if he hadn't died, I'd still know what and who I did and didn't want to associate myself with. Now drop the discussion of my father and I'll continue to talk to you. If not, you know where the door is."

Thoughtful for a minute, Dean continued. "Media says majority of the county residents don't want another Hardig building in their backyard."

He watched as Warren stiffened and shrugged a shoulder.

"County never knows what they want until it comes. Building goes up, people stand in line to shop."

"Probably because other businesses that were there first had to close up shop and then there isn't much place else to go. Isn't that the philosophy of most of the conglomerations you and your dad own? Buy up the space, jack up the rent, move in. You leave people little choice and they'll have to come back to buy Hardigs' products?"

Warren nodded, and Dean saw he'd shut down the man's argument.

Good, Dean thought to himself, maybe Warren had finally taken the hint and would request the help of someone else. Getting through to the Hardigs wasn't easy though. They didn't take no for an answer.

"Man, you Jamesons are hard on us. Say," Warren changed the subject, "how's that Gary Williams like his wife over here with the good doctor?"

"They're divorced." Dean's jaw twitched, knowing that Warren should have known that fact by now, as it had been all over the news after Chyna did the interview. Perhaps, if he wasn't grieving his father's death so hard, he would have noticed before Chyna told him.

Then again, he probably knew it but pretended he didn't just to push Dean's buttons. Warren was headed down the wrong path.

"I'm not getting into your personal life, so leave mine

be, Warren. We were discussing your business. Rather I was telling you that I wanted no part of helping you or Chauncey Hardig with your business ventures. Now is there anything else? I am honestly swamped with the issues surrounding my establishment. I wish you luck but I can't get on board. It's not my thing right now."

Dean had wanted to say something more but circumstances surrounding why he didn't like Warren Hardig or any Hardig went beyond their proprietary manner. It was something Dean couldn't place his finger on, but he'd always had a feeling in his gut that the entire family was bad news. He knew it was wrong to take on the feelings of his father where the Hardigs were concerned, but he did anyway. If Joe Jameson Sr. had had reason to dislike anyone, it must have been a good one.

The dislike wasn't one-sided. The Hardigs didn't like the Jamesons either, except when they seemed to need something. That's when they came knocking on a Jameson door, because they needed someone to do their bidding.

Alfreah Jameson had given her time to their functions and charities endlessly in the past years, but it seemed a mere thank-you had never left their lips. Warren lost his mother at a young age and Dean's mother had probably felt sorry for him. At least, that's what Dean had deduced. For the most part, the Hardigs were users, abusers who happened to own a lot of property in Old Town, Alexandria. They bought up space like one would hotels and houses in a Monopoly game. That they owned so much seemed to give them the right to walk on everyone else. Small shops and specialty boutiques had been forced to close. Mom-and-pop shops couldn't survive either when a Hardig came to town.

"I hear you," Warren said. "But, uh, what if I said I could get you some happening office space in Old Town? Heck, we've got some buildings we're buying in

Georgetown if you want. Get you some clientele to pay big bucks, put you in a better spot, and cut up some of that rent for ya."

"Why would you do that, Warren? I mean you can't blame me for being a little suspicious."

"I just need you on my team, D! You're intelligent, and logically minded. People would listen to you!"

Dean shook his head in denial. He wouldn't be a part of something he couldn't get passionate about. More than that, however, there was some kind of pleading desperation in Warren's voice. The family's dealings weren't on the up-and-up and Dean wouldn't associate himself with crooks. "I can't, but I appreciate your asking me," he said falsely.

"I'm not really asking, Dean. I'm telling you to help me. The longer I look, the more I see you don't get it at all. I haven't been asking you to help me for some time now because I like hearing the word no. Want to know what else? I think that Chyna Lockhart is the most beautiful, breathtaking woman I've ever seen. I'd hate to see her run into any kind of trouble, or you. I'd hate to see that solid family name tarnished in any way."

Dean shook his head and his nose wrinkled as if he didn't understand any of what Warren had just said.

"You want to repeat that? Because if you're threatening me, you should know I'm not the kind to take orders. Make your business plain. And if you continue to look at or speak about Chyna in any negative way, you'll wonder what happened to your vision."

Dean had never threatened anyone before. He'd never had to and he was confused about this new hostility he was receiving. Did the man want his help that badly or was he just playing games? He couldn't figure it out, but the charade was making him angrier by the moment. He'd get to the bottom of it in due time.

Warren carelessly shrugged and shook his head

before backing away to the door. "I thought I did make my business plain.

"Oh." Warren raised a finger, pointing to the door. "Be sure to ask Chyna how she and I know each other. Man, those parties in California, Gary Williams." Warren shook his head, grinning as if he had private thoughts about what went on in California while Chyna and Gary had been married. "Quite the senator. On second thought, maybe you shouldn't ask. Chyna was something herself! Quite the hostess she was.

"About helping me, I think you understood me the first time." Warren turned and saw Chyna standing at the door. He smiled and moved past her.

"I'll be seeing you two. Wish you the best, and remember to vote for a Hardig when you get that county building proposal in the mail." Warren reached for Chyna's hand, but when Dean moved beside her he obviously thought better of it and put his hand back in his pocket.

"Tell your mom," he directed toward Dean, "I said hello. My dad keeps asking about her. Wondered how she was doing. Chyna, it's wonderful to see you again. I'll be sure to tell Gary you're doing well."

Warren turned and continued out the door, but not before winking at Chyna.

Chyna watched him leave and visibly shook her shoulders. She was repulsed by his very presence. She wished Dean would have knocked him out simply for those past transgressions. It would have been more than her own husband at that time had done. From Dean's look of outrage it was clear their encounter hadn't been good.

Moving farther into the kitchen, Chyna took a seat at the table where Dean released his anger by slamming pots and pans. He heaped now-cold portions of food from the various serving dishes onto a plate and shoved it into the microwave. After slamming the door, he punched numbers angrily with his thumb before jabbing the start button.

Chyna took the silent opportunity to question Dean about what Warren had alluded to.

"You're getting into the business—real estate, retail?"

"Hell no," Dean returned heatedly. He didn't bother looking at her. What angered him wasn't what Warren suggested but the manner in which the man talked in circles. He didn't know what their issue was with him and he had no plans to help him with anything, despite how he had made it look. "How do you know him anyway?"

"What?" Chyna stammered. "I, I, uh, he's a friend of Gary's is all." She did tell part of the truth, though any friend of another man wouldn't climb into bed with his wife. She looked away, ashamed. Dean in his own state of anger didn't notice, or at least wouldn't call her on it this time. The mood was shot, she realized. She'd been looking forward to their dinner and sadly it had lost its ambience with Warren Hardig's interruption.

"Go ahead and eat," Dean said to Chyna. When she slid into the seat, he said a quick grace over the food and repeated his earlier routine of heaping another plate with food and slamming the microwave door. In seconds the beep rang. Dean put his own plate of food on the table and sat down heavily. They ate together in silence.

Chapter 11

For once Chyna awoke on her own accord, not jolted by the power saw the construction workers were using to renovate the master bedroom. Chyna thanked God they'd taken the morning off.

The encounter with Warren Hardig hadn't improved Dean's mood, and while he didn't or wouldn't tell her what had occurred to make him so mad, she didn't need to know in order to see and feel that somewhere in the distance there was an ax about to fall with her name on one side and Dean's on the other. Chyna wasn't psychic but she had feelings about things. Uneasiness sometimes ate at her gut and seeing Warren Hardig again had brought back the physical pain she kept when she'd been married to Gary. The feeling lingered and a sense of dread cloaked her like a heavy winter coat.

"Food," Chyna said aloud as she moved from the bathroom and down the hall to the kitchen. She doubted it would ease her ache, but it would at least soothe her hunger. Before she reached for a box of cereal, however, the paper bag on the counter diverted her attention. The bag had the logo of her favorite arts and crafts store. Tubes of paint, paintbrushes, and a pallet for mixing colors were laid on the counter.

Some of the tubes it seemed had been opened, as if someone was beginning to paint. Chyna lifted the newspapers scattered about and saw the remnants of brushstrokes. She couldn't resist following the lines with her finger but her hand strayed in a different direction. She picked up the brush, no paint on its tip, and followed a line just with the edge. She looked up and over at the backsplash above the stove.

For a few moments she wondered what would go there, what Mrs. Jameson would like. Looking further, she found the white plastic cut out of stencils. She nearly laughed and the painter inside her became insulted. At one point in time, she drew and painted flowers and full-color landscapes without help. She hadn't lifted a muscle since her first miscarriage.

Tearing off a piece of the paper, she wrote down a list of art supplies: acrylic gloss medium, acrylic gel, charcoal pencils, a notebook, types of brushes she had used. Reviewing her list, Chyna looked over at the colors Dean had already bought. He had purchased the most expensive brands of paint he could find. She had all the primary colors and from these she could make everything else by mixing them together.

One of her smaller joys had been mixing the colors. She often labeled the new color she'd made with something silly she'd thought up herself. Chyna looked down at the paper again and crumbled it angrily. With a halfhearted throw she sent the paper sailing into the air against the wall in front of her. It bounced back to meet her.

When the doorbell rang, Chyna jumped. On her good leg, she hopped to the front to see who it was at the door. She heard the jingle of keys, and instantly backed away, thinking it was Dean's way of getting her to greet him. She thought he'd given up on trying to pamper her. Ready to greet him with a mean glare, Chyna softened immediately when Dean's sister Jina opened the door.

"Hey," Jina said.

"Hi," Chyna replied.

Over her shoulder, Jina carried a blanketed bundle. Over the other, a strap that led to a blue diaper bag.

"Let me take that for you." Chyna reached for the tote when its strap hooked on the doorknob. She moved to the door, about to close it, but turned to Jina and asked, "Isn't Tony with you?"

Jina shook her head. "We saw Dean at the store. Tony stayed to help him get some stuff . . . for the deck or whatever Dean's planning to have fixed next. They should be a while. The only place I could spend the entire day in is a shop that has size-nine shoes and size-eight clothes." Jina smiled. "But enough about them. How are you?"

Walking slowly into the kitchen, Jina pulled a chair from the table and sat down. She removed the thin blanket covering the baby and settled him over her lap.

"Oh, I'm great, I guess. I feel a little awkward being here without . . . your mom," Chyna said hurriedly, realizing she was about to mention Mr. Jameson.

"And Dad?" Jina finished, reading Chyna's thoughts.

Chyna shook her head. "Yes," she whispered. "It's just different, you know. Having been his caretaker and all, I had something to do, some way to help."

"Girl, please, before you were his caretaker, you didn't have to do anything or find any way to help. We're practically sisters. What's the matter with you?"

"Nothing." Chyna looked down at her fingers, realizing she'd gotten paint on them. She rubbed them together, the slick, oily feel stirring something inside her. Taking a napkin from the table, she tried to wipe it off.

Jina looked at Chyna's fingers and asked alarmingly, "Are you bleeding?"

"Oh no, it's just crimson-red . . . paint," Chyna corrected when Jina looked at her. "It's just paint."

"So you're painting again? That's wonderful," Jina said happily.

"No, I . . . No." Chyna wanted to protest but couldn't find a reason to say otherwise. At least there was no reason that would get them off the subject entirely. She admitted to herself, at least, that it wasn't that her desire hadn't been to paint, it was just that she didn't want to be forced into something. She didn't want to play a silly game that was designed to get her back into it. Chyna took a deep breath and smiled sadly at Jina.

"Is Dean treating you badly?" Jina asked. "You know he's only mean to you because he loves you."

"Ha!" Chyna laughed falsely and her loud outburst caused the baby to stir briefly.

"You know," Jina continued, "I said that I was going to mind my own business, to stay out of this, but damn it, I really can't, Chyna. That no-good, foolish brother of mine needs some help, mentally."

"It's so much more than that, J," Chyna whispered, looking out the window.

"Do tell? But one thing is clear, he's a fool, my own brother, temporarily insane, and Joe and Free Jameson didn't raise any fools. I don't understand any of it, I don't understand why it's taking almost fifteen years to admit what's obvious to everyone else."

"It's not the same as it was then. It won't be the same. As soon as my house is built back up, I'm leaving, J. I'm selling the place and I'm moving to another town, another state, as far away from here as I can get, and he can get on with his life and I can get on with mine."

Chyna hadn't meant to say she was moving, she had only thought about it recently. Moving wasn't exactly what she wanted to do, it just happened to come out. "It hasn't worked out between us in all these years. I have stopped believing that it will. We weren't meant to be anything other than friends."

Jina shook her head as if confused. "Nonsense!" she said. "I could get Jojo to beat him up!" she added seriously.

"What?" Chyna smiled and managed a small laugh for the first time.

"He'll do it. He won't hurt him, just knock some sense into him, that's all. I'll give him a call."

Chyna laughed out loud, covering her mouth. "No, but thanks, J. I'll probably beat him up myself before I move."

Jina sighed loudly, throwing up her hand. "So with nothing solved, you're leaving. Again? Chyna, just like when you went to California? Just like after you quit working with Dad? Where in the world did you go?"

"Now that, that was different," Chyna began, but realized she couldn't elaborate on the reasons why the situation was so *different* without mentioning the miscarriage.

"I had to," she said when Jina continued to look at her expectantly. "I wanted to take care of your father. I enjoyed it but I just, I just couldn't anymore."

"Tell me why," Jina pleaded. "See, that's the thing no one understands, is why you felt you had to leave. You didn't have to be his caretaker anymore, if you didn't want to. Didn't you know that? But to leave altogether, we don't get it. Did it get too hard? Was he too close to home?"

Chyna shook her head. "No, Jina, most of the people I've taken care of live in this neighborhood. Most of them I've known since I was little."

"So what was it then?"

"I was just, I just couldn't, okay? Please, just try to understand." Then Chyna began to get angry thinking of Lisa Stephens. Was the entire family so clueless about Dean's relationship with her? "I . . . It's not like he's going to miss me, J. Lisa Stephens will come back around and that will be the end of it. He'll forget about me, he'll go back to her."

Jina blinked rapidly. "What?" she said, confused. "Lisa

Stephens? Don't tell me she's been sniffing around here. Again?" Her eyes grew wide with outrage. "And hello? There is no *go back to her*, Chyna. They were never together, and if they were, I'd give her a piece of my mind and tell her to stay the heck away from our family!"

Chyna looked at her friend, confused. Silently she prodded Jina to go on.

Taking a deep breath, Jina continued, "Look, when Daddy got sick, that heifer was around here poking her nose into our business. She offered to help Mama with Daddy's paperwork, offer financial advice about what to do with his estate. I didn't say nothing, and Mama was too nice to say anything. That woman came in here telling everyone what to do like we were a bunch of illiterates. None of us had the word *stupid* stamped on our foreheads. We all have college degrees, but she took advantage of Mama and the rest of us when we were all grieving. She used that time to worm her way in here, making it seem as if none of us had time to see about Mama's needs . . . and you know? Tony and I were having issues. . . ." Jina looked away and then down at the baby. "I never told anyone but T.T. this, Chyna. When Tony and I had some problems, Lisa Stephens took it upon herself to try and console him."

"What?" Chyna gasped.

Jina shook her head in confirmation. "She didn't get very far. You know Tony and I had hit a rough patch but we love each other. We maintained that we would always be able to work things out. It hadn't been twenty-four hours since our fight. Tony was here fixing up something for Mama, and Lisa was over here pretending to do God knows what. I walked in to find her coming on to him. You should have heard the things she said about me. She told him how she could help him get over me. I almost leaped across the couch. I was so furious, I could've beat her down."

Jina leaned back in her chair. Blowing out a loud sigh, she shifted the baby onto her shoulder. "Don't let her come anywhere near him, Chyna. He doesn't like her like that. Mama, me, Jojo, this whole family, we feel sorry for her."

"That's it! She tries too hard and more importantly she's a damned liar."

"Dean does not love her. You hear what I'm saying?"

Chyna nodded.

"I thought she and Warren Hardig were an item anyway," Jina finished.

Chapter 12

Chyna blinked rapidly. "Wait, back up. What did you say about Warren Hardig?"

Jina looked up. "Lisa Stephens and Warren Hardig, a couple weeks ago, they were on the business page of the paper. Talked about this new building he wants to put up in the area. Lisa was hanging on Warren's arm in the picture and the paper alluded that she and him were an item."

Chyna shook her head, trying to dismiss all this. "That's not a big deal, they are both lawyers."

"What?" Jina said incredulously. "Lisa Stephens is no lawyer, she's a legal secretary. Big difference. She might even be a receptionist, she lies so much. She answers phones over there at the Hardig building. Not only that, she lied telling Mama she was a certified public accountant. I did some checking and she was in school, but she didn't finish. She told Mama she could invest some of our money, so then I guess she was a financial planner. My God, I'm glad Mama didn't give her a dime. I told her to get the heck out of our house and to stop bothering us. She'd probably have taken us for a pretty penny."

Reaching across the table, Jina took her friend's hand. "Hear me, Chyna, please hear me when I say that Dean doesn't love her, he pacifies her. That's all. You fight for what you want. Do you want Dean?"

Chyna didn't answer.

"I'm sorry, honey. Just, uh, don't answer that, okay?" Jina shook her head and smiled. "I know you love him."

Chyna kept her head still, her eyes the only thing she let move. She wouldn't answer questions about how she felt about Dean, not even to one of her closest friends. Revelations about Lisa Stephens, however, were news to her. Seemed as if Jina had dropped so much on her, she needed time to sort through it all. She smiled falsely at her friend, and tried to look nonchalant while her mind flipped through, categorized, and filed all the information Jina had just dumped on her. After a few moments of thought, still nothing was clear.

"One more question, Chyna."

"What is it?" Chyna said, though she didn't want one more question posed about issues she couldn't and didn't want to answer—let alone discuss.

"Gary, your ex? He's been in the paper a lot, he's slipping in the polls. The next election doesn't look good for him."

Chyna shrugged, unconcerned. Gary Williams had nothing to do with her, not anymore. She didn't care one way or the other what became of his political candidacy. "So what? That doesn't concern me," she said.

"I see," Jina replied. "I mean you aren't in any further contact with him, are you?"

Chyna shook her head.

"My brother," Jina continued. "Chyna, he's stubborn, and when it comes to you, even as confident as he is, there's one person he feels he can't compete with. That's your ex-husband. I know you may not believe that. When you got married, Chyna, his whole world crashed. Dean's not poor. If anyone could manage his money, could set away some serious funds and do without, it's my little brother. But a *senator?*" Jina emphasized. "Senator Gary Williams—his title says it all. Not just money, but power, status. Dean felt as if he could never compete with that.

"Think about it, okay?" Jina stood. "Listen, I've got to go potty, can you hold him for a second?"

Chyna didn't have a moment to adjust her thoughts. Her friend's mouth seemed to run a mile a minute, leaving the listener absolutely no time for processing. But when she looked up, her eyes widened. *What?* Could she hold him? *No!* her mind screamed in protest. She didn't want to. In fact when they'd entered, she told herself she wouldn't even ask. But now, her friend standing over her, poised to give her the baby, she wondered what she could possibly have said to get out it. *I'm allergic* came to her mind, but instead she said, "Uh . . . why don't you lay him down in the bedroom? I'll keep an eye on him. . . ."

"Oh, please, Chyna, you'll be fine. He won't raise a fuss, he hasn't been sleeping long, he's eaten, had his diaper changed, passed gas, he's good for a bit. You take care of frail people, for goodness' sake, babies are the same only cuter." Jina laughed and without further comment, leaned down and practically dumped her son into Chyna's arms.

Chyna's reflexes kicked in and she had no choice but to open her arms to support the baby's form. She situated the child into a more comfortable position, ensuring that she supported his head, while Jina moved to the door, keeping her eyes on them as she backed away. "See, you're a natural," Jina said and disappeared.

Chyna looked down at the child. "No, not a natural . . . huh, Robby?" She was thoughtful a minute. "Are they going to call you Robby or Bobby?

"Robby or Bobby, they're both great. I like them both! Robert Joseph, after your grandfather, he would've loved you. There is so much love here in this house, in this family," Chyna said, taking a deep breath. "Just, uh, don't let them call you Bob. You don't look like a Bob.

"See?" Chyna breathed loudly. "I'm no natural," she said more softly when Robby's face grew tight as if he was about to cry. "I'm just your regular fool. How does that song go?" Chyna sang an off-key rendition to the child.

She purposely stood when Robert began to fuss louder and she stopped singing, thinking that her cracking rendition would make an adult cry. She began to walk, or rather swayed, considering her broken leg, and tried to soothe the baby with a gentle beat. "You look a lot like your mama," she whispered, "and you got a little bit of . . . Dean, I guess. The lips and your nose and you're bronzy red like Dean was. How is it that offspring can skip around and miss their parents to look like their aunties and uncles?"

Chyna looked at the child, his face relaxed and close to sleep. Her eyebrow dipped in confusion. "You don't talk much, do you? Well, let me tell you, you got to learn how to talk and really quick, because your mama ain't gonna let you get a word in edgewise."

Chyna looked at Robert, examining his cute pie-shaped face, his little pug nose and large eyes. She gasped when he opened them briefly to stare at her and closed them just as quick as if what he saw wasn't what he wanted.

Chyna continued to trace his features, knowing that in days, mere weeks, he'd grow and change rapidly. But now, his breath when he yawned smelled like warm milk and his tiny pink tongue had a faint white strip down the center. His cute little pink lips tooted upward to the sky, moving at times as if they were still suckling the nipple of a bottle.

Seconds passed and Chyna felt the sting in her eyes and burning in her heart. She swore under her breath. "I mean, shoot, shoot, sweetheart. Don't ever say bad words like your auntie."

Taking a deep calming breath, Chyna was determined not to cry. Determined not to get depressed that it was someone else's child she was holding and not her own. "Life is so unfair, but I'm not going to cry, no, sirree.

"Oh, man, I mean what do I have to cry about?" Chyna laughed. "I just made a mess, that's all. I made a big boo-boo . . . all by myself," she said, thinking back to all that Jina had revealed about Lisa Stephens.

"Was there truly nothing between her and Dean?" she asked the baby, wondering if she misread everything she thought she had witnessed, shut Dean out when she was hurting, and lost him and everything she wanted in the end. "Your aunt's a fool, Robby, a complete and utter fool."

Babbling her endless questions to the child, Chyna didn't notice that Dean had returned until she looked at the door, startled that he'd been able to enter the house and move down the hall as quietly as he did.

"You're going to be a great mother," Dean said, pushing himself away from the door and moving toward her.

That did it, Chyna thought to herself. "I've got to go," she said quickly as she limped her way to the door. As had been done to her earlier, Chyna filled Dean's arms with his nephew.

Dean watched her panicked exit as he supported his nephew's form expertly, continuing to eye Chyna. "What did I say? Chyna, are you tired? Does your leg hurt?" he went on when she didn't answer. "You haven't been up long. You were sleeping when I left."

"Who are you?" She turned to look at him. "The hall monitor? St. Nick? Even Santa isn't due for another few months. I'd appreciate it if you wouldn't see me when I'm sleeping and know when I'm awake!" Chyna said heatedly. "Just because I wasn't up moving around doesn't mean I was asleep, you know."

"I checked on you," Dean said quietly, looking down at his nephew.

Chyna looked away. "Well, I don't need you to check on me, okay!"

"And if you break your other damn leg, or need help?" Dean said, his temper rising to meet hers.

"Just like I have found a way to deal with everything else in my life," she said, thinking of the recent months, "I'll deal with it. I won't be in your hair much longer so there's no need to keep worrying about me."

"I will worry about you, Chyna! Always."

Chyna threw up her hands in frustration. What could she possibly say to that? She turned on her heel to leave, bumping into Jina as she limped closer to the door. "Sorry," she muttered in her hasty exit.

"I was, uh, going to compliment you on the house, Dean. The improvements you have made look wonderful," Jina said as she moved farther into the kitchen.

"Thanks," Dean mumbled.

"But I think what I should be doing is clocking you over the head with a two-by-four. Where is one, anyway?" Jina said as she pretended to look around the room for a piece of wood.

"This ain't none of your business," Dean said.

"That may be true, but when has that ever stopped me before? I just don't understand you two."

"Welcome to my world," Dean offered.

"A world you made for yourself, big brother."

"I had help, you know."

"Please! Give me a break. So Chyna helped you make a mess of both your lives. Clean the damn thing up."

"Hey, uh, want me to take him?" Both Jina and Dean looked to the door when Jina's husband, Tony, entered and pointed to their son.

"Yes, honey, thank you. We'll just be a few more minutes," Jina said as she took her child from Dean's arms and placed him in her husband's.

With nothing to do with his hands, Dean gripped the edge of the counter.

"Whatever," he said to his sister's expectant gaze. "I suppose Ms. Lockhart talks to you, tells you every cotton-picking thing? I think she's sick."

"What? What are you talking about?"

Dean lowered his voice and looked toward the door, before placing his eyes back on his sister. "I said I think she's sick."

"Sick? As in ill?"

Dean nodded. "She's lost a lot of weight." He shook his head. He hadn't voiced his thoughts aloud until now. Thoughts that reminded him how Charlie, Chyna's friend and a nurse at the hospital, had tried to cover up mentioning the fact that she had been in the hospital recently. Dean had deduced it hadn't been that long ago.

"Oh, Dean, come on, she's not sick. That I'm fairly certain of."

"*Fairly* doesn't cut it, Jina. She was in the hospital right around or after the time she stopped working for Dad. Did she tell you that?" In his mind, Dean had worked out the order of events from the time Chyna had told his mom she couldn't continue to take care of their father. Everything from there was sketchy but he knew that time encompassed a visit to the hospital. What plagued Dean and made him fearful was that whatever the issue she was going through just might've been something he couldn't fix. Much like the time his mother had first told him his father had Alzheimer's. That time, thinking about some life-threatening illness he had no cure for had paralyzed Dean with grief, and as of late he thought it just might be happening all over again.

"How do you know? She could've been getting a checkup. Did you ask her?"

"And you think just by asking she's going to up and tell me?" There was a lot he had wanted to ask her, including whether or not they stood a chance at love. Was she sick? Did she love him? But thoughts of their night together before Chyna returned to California, and a consuming, raging jealousy against her ex-husband, reared up in Dean so strong he left all the matters that needed to be handled between them unresolved. He settled for their spontaneous conversation, their politeness as if they were strangers. Even their arguing, as far as Dean was concerned, was better than knowing she no longer had a place for him in her heart. He didn't want to know that.

"I don't know," Jina said, "and neither will you unless you try. Stop playing these stupid games and get some answers. She won't just up and volunteer information.

"Another thing, she thinks you're seeing Lisa Stephens, so where did she get that idea from?" Jina said and didn't wait for an answer. "Chyna isn't sick, she's hurt, and you've got to find out what, who hurt her and make it right. Poke and prod until the truth comes out."

Dean stared at his sister a moment, knowing everything she said was right. He didn't want to deal with the things she'd told him he needed to confront. He took a deep breath and smiled down at her. "You actually made sense, for once."

"Thanks. Having a kid will do that to you. Really mellows you out. If you ever get it together, I guess you and Chyna can have a couple."

Dean sobered at that statement. Thoughts and revelations slammed into his mind so quick he felt out of breath. Then there was pain. Pain he remembered seeing in Chyna's eyes. The baby books in her home. Just moments ago as Chyna had held his nephew, when Dean had told her she'd make a great mother, the look of loneliness, of losing something filled her eyes. Everything was painfully clear. Nothing was physically wrong with Chyna and the final piece was that the last time they'd made love they hadn't used any protection. It all fit now, just that quickly did the pieces seem to fall into place.

"Hey, hey now." Jina patted her brother on the shoulder, and pulled him into her arms. "Don't get winded on me now. I gotta go. I'll see you."

Absently Dean bent to embrace his sister. Fleetingly he remembered her hugging him, she and Tony saying their good-byes. But when they'd left, Dean remained standing there in front of the sink seeing and hearing nothing but feeling everything. The past pain and the hurt. And now that he knew the truth he had to try to fix his future, work hard to confront the past, and put it away. He moved down the hall to get to Chyna.

Chapter 13

Chyna did all she could to keep from crying but in the end it was no use. Burying her face in the pillow, she cried as quietly as she could. When the door swung open she turned on her stomach to keep the intruder from seeing her tearstained face and prayed it was Jina.

She could handle Jina. Chalk it up to seeing her beautiful baby, becoming emotionally sentimental over her friend's angelic child, and holding him in her arms. But Chyna couldn't handle Dean. Not now.

"Are you all right?" Dean said as he moved farther into the room and sat at the foot of the bed.

"Fine," Chyna said falsely.

"What's the matter?"

"Nothing!"

"Then why are you crying?"

"Because I feel like it."

"Well, I, uh, I figured something out." There was absolutely no way to approach this. "I'm not leaving until you tell me what's wrong."

"Suit yourself." Chyna dug farther into the covers. He would get tired, she thought, at least she hoped he would. After what seemed like the longest few minutes in her life, however, he was still there.

He wasn't going anywhere. He had too many questions that needed answering, and he thought with his latest revelations, he had all the answers he needed.

Chyna spoke when it seemed like he wasn't going to leave. "I've made a mess of my life, Dean."

"Okay."

Chyna laughed. Leave it to him to be so unfettered. "Did you hear what I said? I made a mess, an irreparable, messy mess!"

"I helped you make the mess." The silence grew thick when Dean started talking again. "They say that it comes in threes: the loss." This was the only way he would eventually get to it. There was so much on his mind, but in order to get to the present, he had to backtrack for just a minute. "You know, I was waiting for just one more thing, Chyna, and now I know." He couldn't bring it up just yet. The more he thought about it, the more the weight set in, the more sorry and devastated he felt. He was sorry. So very sorry he'd shut her out.

"First"—Dean cleared his throat—"I thought it was Dad, next my business. I was waiting for one more event, that's all I needed, and the cycle would be complete. I didn't know what it was until Jina said something just now. That something knocked the wind right out of me."

"Loss doesn't always come in threes, Dean, that's just a saying. It doesn't happen like that all the time," Chyna offered weakly, though she knew that the first loss had been their child. His father and his business had been second and third.

Dean nodded. "When Mom first told me that something was wrong with Dad, I was like, well, whatever it is it's fixable. I was certain I could fix it. That no matter what, *I* could handle it. Not the doctor, not Jojo, Jina, or Tish, just me. And then over time, it would turn out that I'd be the worst possible person for the job. I could barely handle the news let alone fix a damn thing.

"I went to this seminar at GMU one night. Just by myself. There was a handful of people there, mostly older people, wives and daughters. At the door, they give you this little pamphlet, *What to Expect When Your Loved One Has Alzheimer's: A Caregiver's Guide.*

"The lecturer was up at the front. He starts off with a picture of the brain, a little pointer, 'Alzheimer's is a disease . . . this disease causes the brain to decline in memory,'" Dean mocked, his voice taking on a professional and stiff tone. He folded his hands and made a stern face, probably like the person at the lectern had looked to him and the other seminar attendees. "'This results in dementia, loss of intellectual functions, such as thinking, remembering, and reasoning.' They have a top-ten-symptoms list, Web page after Web page link, support groups, phone numbers; one place even had a hot line. What the hell do you say when you call a perfect stranger? When Mom told me exactly, my only reply was, "You mean like Charlton Heston?"

"I was thinking about everyone, how they handled their grief, how we all coped, and Mama got through and only one other person I can think of was strong enough from the get-go till the end . . . to cope with whatever happened. Only one person had taken care of other people in the same situation, watched them die, and helped them and their family through it. That person served as so much more than just a home health aide, nurse's aid, whatever the title is these days. That one person, that other person, was you." Dean looked over at Chyna only a moment.

"You held it all together, held it and took care of him like you were some kind of supernurse, developed a schedule, handled his incontinence, his tantrums and his orneriness, and no one thanked you or thought you'd had any other purpose than to do that *duty*." Dean shrugged. "For lack of a better word.

"You've been there and I've treated you so bad and I haven't been there, mindfully present. You stayed here when I didn't want you to and you've been here for as long as I can remember. When I was sixteen, you were here calling the ambulance and helping Tish and me, after I nearly burnt down the house and myself to a crisp. For the life of me, I couldn't figure out why you left, why you stopped caring for Dad. Now that you're back, I . . . I don't want you to ever leave again. Jina told me just in the kitchen there, a few minutes ago, that if you and I ever got it together, maybe we could have a couple of kids. She didn't know it but those few words sent something sharp straight through me. They gave me the key to all my questions. You stopped taking care of Dad because you were pregnant with our baby."

Chyna looked away. If she could have floated away into outer space, she would have. But no such luck would befall her. Instead she sat up, ready to leave the room, when she felt Dean's hand on her shoulder.

"Don't leave."

"Please let me go," she managed, her voice cracking.

"No," he said flatly.

He pulled her back onto the bed, and when she lay flat, he moved to straddle her hips. "You're going to talk to me. You're not going to run, you're going to look at me." He waited a beat for her to look at him. "When were you going to tell me? Didn't you think I had a right to know?" He was upset but he couldn't go on being mad at her. "I'm sorry, baby, I'm so, so sorry, but I didn't know. I would have helped you, I swear to God, Chyna, I would have been there, if I just knew . . . if you just told me."

She hadn't wanted to hurt him, so she had kept the secret to herself. She really had. It wasn't to punish him, but silently over the last few weeks, punishing him for something he knew nothing about had felt good for just a little while. Right now, however, she felt terrible. She could see the hurt so vividly in his eyes and she was so sorry she'd kept it.

"I made a mistake, okay?" What else could she say? It was too late for any kind of reasoning behind her decision.

Dean shook his head as if that wasn't good enough. "When we made love, I told you that I loved you. I showed you that I loved you the most intimate way I knew how. So you came to the restaurant, saw me hug Lisa—that's all I did, hug her, and I pecked her on the cheek. Did you think that I could so quickly, so easily dismiss our love in a few hours?" Bit by bit, he was remembering the restaurant scene. He'd been drunk, he couldn't remember much of that entire week. It'd been the night after his father died. He had drunk himself silly.

"Then you just happened to get into her car and go home with her?" Chyna asked.

"No," Dean said easily. "She drove me home, saw me inside, and let me pour my heart out about you." Dean tapped his index finger against the center of her chest. "After I nearly drank myself to death, she was there getting food. I saw her and she told me she saw you back in town.

"She made it seem like you slept together."

"When?" Dean demanded.

"When I ran into her at the grocery store."

Dean nodded. He'd get to that in a minute. Lisa had obviously lied about knowing Chyna was in town. "You believed her over me. You didn't come to ask me?"

His fingers gently took her chin, forcing her to look at him.

"Still," Dean continued, "no matter what, Chyna, to me, all that doesn't matter, 'cause I still love you. I still love you, Chyna. I had a ring."

Chyna had struggled to keep her eyes from his until he said the last four words. This time she willingly looked at him. "What?" she questioned, daring to believe her ears.

"To ask you to marry me."

"What?" Chyna heard him but this turn of events left her baffled. She now knew for certain that she was the one who had turned her back, not just on him but on everything she wanted most.

"You turned your back," Dean said as if reading her mind and the progression of her tortured thoughts. "I love you, and you turned your back on us.

"I still love you, Chyna. Instead of coming to me, you didn't even try to ask me what happened. I wanted to be there to help you and you cheated me of that. We'll have children, someday," he said and placed a hand on her stomach.

"No. I can't. I mustn't be any good that way. I had a miscarriage when I was married. I can't."

Dean didn't know what to say, but if she thought it would change his mind, she was wrong. "Well, it doesn't matter—you're perfect, to me. You still are what I want. I don't care about that!"

This entire mess was unreal. Didn't he want a family? Didn't he want kids of his own? She had to maintain that it wouldn't work between them. He'd get over it. She had told herself a million times it wouldn't work, and now here he was saying, telling her that it would. "It won't work."

"I want to make love to you, now."

"What?" she said again even as she felt his hardened length pressing at the juncture of her thighs. Subconsciously she opened to receive more of him. She wanted him too. Since the last time they'd been together, she wanted to be with him again and again, but she couldn't think straight.

When he bent down to kiss her, her heart pounded to a thundered roar in her ears.

"I've always loved you."

"No," Chyna cried, trying to turn away from him. It seemed too easy, or just then it did. All of her life she'd wanted his love, wanted it willingly, and now she had it, or it seemed she'd never lost it. But now she didn't know what to do with it. "You don't."

"Yes, I do," Dean said. "Kiss me."

"What?" Chyna replied. She licked her lips.

"You heard me," he said as he pressed his lips to hers. "It's been a long time."

Chyna forced her lips closed when he kissed them again and again.

"I can't live without you. I need you in my life just as much as you are in my heart. We'll fix this, we will, we'll get past it, please, Chyna," he said, nipping her lips again.

Her hips undulated against his and he proceeded to rub himself against her, stretching his legs out to center himself between her legs. She gasped and his tongue gained entrance inside.

"I love everything about you. I love making love with you. I love it when you hold me inside your body. You used to bite me, right here on my shoulder, when you were about to . . ." Dean smiled mischievously. "It drove me wild, it made me so hard, I can't get you, your habits when we do it, out of my mind. I haven't been the best communicator, Chyna, I know. It's more than sex, it always has been, it always will be. Your mind, your spirit, you are kind and compassionate, and I'm sorry it's taken me so long to tell you. I'm sorry you ever doubted how I felt, how I feel now. Just let me show you, now. God, now, Chyna."

Chyna gasped when his hands moved up her shirt. Expertly he lifted her bra and found her nipples, tender and erect. She physically ached for him. His hand massaged her breasts and the buttons of her shirt were loosened one by one.

Chyna tried to cross her legs across his back to embrace him. Her breasts felt heavy and she felt her resolve slip a bit further with each touch of his lips. "Stop, not yet!" She was on the edge, but she had to be sure and she wasn't yet.

"Do you really want me to?" he said even as he moved

over her as if he were already deep inside her, as if they were one, slipping back into the familiar rhythm only the two of them knew. She tried to lift her leg but the heaviness of the cast prevented her from doing so. When she dropped her leg in defeat, the cast clanked loudly against the metal bed railing and the sound shot her quickly back to reality.

"I need time, Dean. I just need some more time, please," she said, stilling his hands. When he snatched his hand away, she reached to grab each side of her shirt and pull it closed.

Without another word Dean rolled over and proceeded to stand. Looking down at her, he said, "Time, huh? Is that it or are you just punishing me?"

"I wouldn't do that," Chyna said, anger and frustration battling each other. "I need some time to sort this out. Okay?" She had to be sure that this was it and with a little more time she would be certain. Her mind reminded her heart of the hurt and the pain Dean had caused her. "I'm sorry, I can't just jump back to where we were. I need to take some time."

"You do that!" Dean replied. "But while you're thinking and taking a time-out, I'm going to be planning, because I'm not giving up. Not this time. I won't give up on us. I won't because I love you."

Chyna looked away. She heard the slam of the door behind her. Moments later, she heard the car's engine rev and when its roar grew distant, she fell against the covers, buried her face in the pillow, and burst into tears again.

Chapter 14

Their relationship now could only be classified as weird, Chyna thought to herself as she picked up the renovation diary Alfreah Jameson had left. The more she looked at the book, the more it seemed she yearned for her own creativity.

Without her consent, Dean completed the list of crafting supplies she had made some time ago. Chyna diligently sketched the ideas as they came to her. She smiled, thinking how Dean had given that back to her. The skill never left her and once she sought to do it on her own, he hadn't pressed her further. They were dealing with everything in their own way and as much as she didn't want to analyze every single part of their even keel, she felt optimistic about their future.

In the midst of helping her, Dean gave her the time she requested while subtly he wooed her deeper in love with him. Dean Jameson cooked, he hated going to the video store so he ordered movies on Pay-Per-View, he went for takeout, and in the middle of all that, he charmed her with gentle kindness, showing her exactly how much he loved her, like he said.

When Chyna woke, sometimes, to the sound of music, she was ecstatic to find Dean playing piano. He'd said that since his dad's death his fingers had felt numb if not paralyzed and the music just wouldn't come. One of the reasons he hadn't played at Joe Jameson's funeral was the fact that he had a hangover and wouldn't know where the piano was let alone play it. But his beautiful music drifted against the walls of the house once more, and to Chyna that meant some of the pain had eased. It would never go away but it subsided enough to let that wonderful talent back into his life. It was weird how painting was to her what piano playing was to him and with tragedy, they'd each abandoned those things that had brought them so much joy. Slowly though, they'd both found a way to let it back in and slowly they were finding their way back to one another.

In October, the days got shorter. Chyna wrote and submitted ads to advertise her services as a private nurse. She was moving on, she thought as she stretched her castless leg.

Thanksgiving was less than a month away and Chyna saw herself seated with all of the Jamesons, the awkwardness and the tension long gone, as a member of the family. Chyna looked over at the phone, thinking of Bubba. The Lockharts' and the Jamesons' longtime friend should be calling any day now with news about the progress of her house. He'd said a few months and it had been that, though the heavy rains had probably set their schedule back a week or two. Not to mention, Chyna never thought about the hidden problems that lay within her house increasing the cost to fix it.

Tossing those worries aside, Chyna concentrated on the present. She took a deep breath as she reentered an upstairs room where Joseph Jameson Sr.'s things had been moved after his death. When that room was empty Chyna backtracked into Mrs. Jameson's room where the scent of talcum powder and freesia sachets she kept in her drawer seemed to linger for so many years. Underneath Alfreah Jameson's signature scents also lingered the cologne Mr. Jameson had worn. It was amazing, Chyna thought, how his scent hadn't dried up and dissipated. With opening the door, the subtle shift of air seemed to reawaken it and stir it up into her nostrils.

When she moved past the corner wall, she saw Dean sitting on the floor. She turned, leaving the door ajar as she knelt on the floor. Wiping her dusty hands on the legs of her jeans, she said, "I dumped that last box," by way of explanation.

"Oh, good. Thank you," Dean said, taking a moment to look at her. He hadn't heard her return. He stood abruptly, trying to shake the loneliness that descended over him. He tucked his father's old watch in his pocket, and moved over to the mirror. He reached his hand out, grabbing the numerous Polaroid snapshots that lined the edge of his mother's large, dresser-top mirror. Each picture snapped with the tape Dean had placed on the back. He carefully pulled each one. But when one tore he stopped. He snatched away his hand as if he'd committed a heinous crime. "I did this"—Dean gestured before him—"to help him remember. I wrote the names on them, not that he could remember how to read them let alone remember who we were just by our pictures. You're here too," Dean said, pointing to the picture of Chyna. His thumb touched the picture and ran lovingly over her face.

He stopped, created a small stack of the pictures he'd managed to remove without damaging them, and shoved them away gently as if he were tired of doing that simple task. Turning to face Chyna, he took a deep breath, and said, "There's some paperwork I gotta go through. I've called most of the creditors to tell them, but there might be some places I forgot."

Chyna only nodded. Taking a space upon the floor, she let Dean roll out a two-drawer metal filing cabinet before her. Getting on his knees, he began to remove the numerous file folders containing Joe Jameson's life on paper.

* * *

While only a few hours had passed, it seemed like they'd spent the majority of the day in that one room on their knees. Chyna shifted and stretched her legs before her. She and Dean were knee deep in Joseph Jameson's paperwork. The more they uncovered, the more they discovered that what they read didn't make sense.

Chyna had insisted they take a break and eat something, and to her dismay Dean heard none of her suggestions. She watched as he tore through papers, scrutinizing them, turning them every which way as if that would help him to better understand the information contained on each one. Chyna began to realize that the numbers didn't seem to add up. The house mortgage said *paid* in one folder and in another it said it wasn't. There were tax papers, bank accounts, and hastily scribbled checks; Dean couldn't make sense of what didn't add up.

"Dean? Dean, listen," Chyna tried again, knowing his inability to make sense of everything only fired his temper, and she waited with patience for his frustrated outburst.

"Something is wrong with this." Dean scratched his head as he continued to scrutinize the paper. He didn't bother to look up at Chyna. "Why the hell is this dated almost two years ago and this is dated forever ago?" he asked aloud.

"I . . . I don't know," Chyna said, though she knew he wasn't really even asking her to begin with. "I do know that we should take a break, take a step back from this, and see what's what, right? I mean you're getting tired and then you get cross-eyed, and the numbers, well, for me they just jumble together. I hate numbers anyways." Chyna attempted humor, but wished she hadn't when Dean looked up at her as if she'd said the dumbest thing he'd ever heard.

"I'm not so tired, Chyna, that I can't see two plus two

is not supposed to equal six, all right?" Dean snapped, muttering an expletive under his breath. "I'm sorry, Chyna."

"It's all right," she said to reassure him.

"It's not," Dean replied more calmly this time. "My dad fixed up that building with his own hands. He bought it when I was a teenager, and when I finished medical school, he turned it over to my name when I got the practice up and running.

"This"—Dean waved his handful of the erroneous papers—"makes it seem like he or I still owe a significant amount in materials, service, electricians, plumbing, all kinds of crap that he already had the know-how for, or knew someone who knew how to do it. This"—Dean picked up a stack of papers in his other hand—"makes it seem like everything is legit and that we're in the black."

"Right," Chyna agreed, "but we can't figure it out if we have two different data sheets. We need to see the bank manager, an accounts specialist, even see what the IRS has to say."

When the phone rang Dean looked up as if he'd never heard anything like it. "You want me to get that?" he heard Chyna ask and shook his head. He moved a few feet away to his mother's nightstand, reached for the receiver, and picked it up. "Hello? Hello?" he repeated when he heard someone breathing, but no voice returned. "Hello?" he said again and the line clicked. Dean hung up. At Chyna's questioning glare, he shrugged his shoulders.

Chyna stood, dismissing the call as nothing more than someone with the wrong number. "I'll make us something to eat," she said, knowing that if she attempted to cook, Dean would out of politeness pretend to eat. That was the only way to get him out of that room. They'd been in it all day and while Dean would never admit it, revisiting his father's things would always be very hard to do. Obviously, he hadn't wanted to come up there, because he'd avoided it for so long. Chyna knew from many years of helping others in the same situation, one shouldn't immerse oneself in something for the entire day, but tackle such tasks in stages at various intervals. Whether he admitted it or not, he needed a break. "I'm going to make something in the kitchen and you're going to eat it."

"Will it kill me?" Dean asked, then ran a hand over his face and smiled.

Chyna sighed audibly. That he was making a joke was a good sign, and right now she'd settle for anything to ease the tension. Shaking her head, she returned his smile. "How about if I burn it, I'll order pizza; if I don't burn it, which means it's edible, you eat it?"

Dean nodded. "Fair enough." Before she could reach the door, he stepped over the pile of papers scattered about. He grabbed her hand, pulling her toward him. "I'm sorry for snapping at you and, Chyna"—he looked away from her piercing eyes—"I really appreciate your being here, I need you to . . . to help me. Can I kiss you?"

Chyna nodded, and his lips met hers. She wanted to tell him that everything would be all right. That she would be there, always, to help him, but she didn't. Not just yet.

Despite what she'd been expecting, his kiss was brief, cordial, a thank-you kiss and very sweet. She looked at him again, longing for so much more. But she'd started this I-need-time bit and until she told him she was ready to move a little faster, he respected her wishes. *It won't be long,* Chyna thought as she moved to the stairs, a bit of pep in her step.

In the kitchen she washed her hands, and searched the fridge for something she knew how to make without burning it. When the phone rang, she absently picked it up, forgetting that Dean would answer it upstairs. "Hello, Jameson residence," she said.

"Hello, Chyna, it's Gary, your ex-husband. Remember me?"

Chapter 15

"You can't seem to do anything right, can you, Ms. Stephens? Once you altered the records, you were to take them to the bank, speak with the man I personally put in place, and he would do the rest. How hard was that? Tell me. What my son sees in you I've no inkling at all."

"You son doesn't see anything in me, Mr. Hardig, we're mere conveniences to one another. Isn't that what you wanted? We have different wants in mind. He wants Chyna Lockhart and I want Dean Jameson."

Chauncey Hardig nodded. "My son thinks he wants Chyna Lockhart, but he'll get that notion out of his head."

"Where the heck is he? I want to deal with him, not you," Lisa shot back.

"He's not feeling well. He will be available in a few more days."

"What the hell is the matter with him? Did you have him committed or something?"

"Of course not. I said, he'll be along and he will. Please go back to your office, thank you. If I have need of you, I'll page you."

Lisa stood. "You're a pig, Mr. Hardig!"

"Be careful what you say. I sign your paychecks, and don't forget it."

With that, Lisa Stephens left the large office and moved down the hall where her smaller one was located.

* * *

Alfreah Jameson left what she thought was a financial mess back home in Virginia. What seemed even more devastating than dealing with that, however, was that she left the place she called home and after forty-six years of a wonderful marriage she was now a widow. The last two years hadn't been the best. They were filled with downright pain and loathing against a higher being she felt had taken her husband's mind, then in a short span of time took her husband in the flesh. That was why she had left. The finances she believed her sons would tackle, and it would work out, but she had left to save her own sanity.

After the funeral was over, after thank-you cards had been sent and calls made, she'd packed up what few pieces of luggage the plane's officials would allow her to carry and sadly said good-bye to her other children and moved to be with her youngest daughter who now resided in Macon, Georgia. She kept using the word *temporarily*. But the longer she stayed, the longer *temporarily* lost its application to the situation.

She could make Macon permanent but Alfreah maintained for her children's sake that she would, one day, return to Virginia.

She could hear the collective gasps if she were to relay to them her desire to stay. Any kind of change, especially one so drastic, would spark a great debate among all of them. After Jina, the loudest, Alfreah thought, smiling, would be Jojo, the director. Dean and Tish, her more quiet children, would visit with their mother alone, poking and prodding with questions. *Mama, are you sure? Mama, you could move in with me.*

Nope. Alfreah kept reviewing her home, reliving the memories she kept near. Getting her youngest son to do some renovations had an underlying purpose. Sure the house needed fixing up, Dean needed something to do with his time. It was evident in the way he bumped around the house after Joe had died. The way the house was now, it was too painful, and too many memories lingered there for her to be all right with returning alone. Alfreah Jameson had her memories in her heart and in the journals she kept. She could read over her passages no matter where she was and be transported to that time when the memory was originally created.

The things she had picked out from the ton of magazines, *House Beautiful, Better Homes and Gardens, Homes of Color,* were so different from what she truly liked. Modern, upscale, and elegant, while she and her husband were country, traditional, and rustic.

Alfreah shook her head as one last thought of Virginia and all that it stood for came to flood her mind. The time in her life before she decided to marry her husband, the one mistake that had left her indebted to Chauncey Hardig. Chauncey Hardig would never leave Virginia, of that Alfreah had been comfortably certain. He would never, could never leave all that he'd established, which meant if Alfreah stayed in Macon, Georgia, he would never be by to bother her, ever again.

Chauncey Hardig was an unscrupulous man. In his pursuit of her he hadn't taken the word *no* to mean anything. Her husband had been diagnosed with Alzheimer's not many years ago, and Chauncey Hardig took it upon himself to visit her, to ask if she needed anything, to try to console her. And after Joe died, Chauncey had come back again. Her blatant refusal of his advances hadn't gotten through his head in all these years. He was smart, he visited her when she was alone, when her children had left for the day. She left Virginia and hoped Chauncey Hardig planned to stay there until his death. In Macon, Georgia, Alfreah believed she'd finally be free of him. There was only one man in her life and he was gone. She would forever respect him, his memory, and never would she take up with his nemesis. She hoped that her move would lay to rest his vendetta against her and her deceased husband.

The hang-up calls had become more incessant. Only they weren't for Dean or any one of the Jamesons. They were for Chyna. When Gary Williams was able to reach who he was looking for, he decided to speak and unfortunately Chyna listened on the other end. For an entire week she was at a loss of what to do with her ex-husband's requests to see her. Finally she knew not seeing him would spark more phone calls, and in order to find out what he wanted she had agreed to see him. Against her better judgment Chyna stood at the door marked SENATOR GARY WILLIAMS.

It was a poor move on her part—nagging guilt, her desire to at least be friends with him outweighing the more logical mind-set that told her she could never be friends with him. Gary Williams took up more than five years of her life, because she let him, because he was unhappy with himself and his only way to cope with a job his deceased father had thrust upon him was to use her as a verbal punching bag.

She stood at his office, staring at the closed door. It didn't surprise her that there was no secretary around—it was almost after five o'clock that Friday evening. No one but her, standing in the long empty corridor of the D.C. senate building that housed his office.

Why would she come at all? she'd asked herself on the drive there. *Why? Things with you and Dean have a chance. You're playing with fire. Why mess it all up?* Chyna knew she had to know why her ex-husband insisted upon calling her at the Jameson home. Why, when they'd said all they needed to say, did he decide he had one more thing to ask of her? She prayed whatever her ex-husband had to share wouldn't dash the future she and Dean were trying to build. Doubt crept in and laughed at her. It never worked out like she wanted. She was reminded how when it seemed everything was in her grasp, someone or something waited to pry happiness from her hands.

Chyna formed her hand into a tight fist and before she pressed it against the door, it swung open. Filling the space, however, was the man who resembled her husband, only ten years down the road. Surely, this man before her now wasn't the eternally confident, debonair Gary Williams. He'd aged so much.

"Gary?" She said his name with such shock that Gary hung his head as if agreeing with her disbelieving assessment.

"I'm, uh, I'm surprised you came, but, I . . . thank you, Chyna. I appreciate it." He dragged a hand over his receding hairline and back down again over his face as if weary, beat. His clothes were terribly wrinkled, his face sagged, jaws hollow and loose, and it looked as if he hadn't shaved in days. Chyna couldn't in that instant remember what had drawn her to him. Perhaps his political fire and his drive for a seat among the bigwigs. That was a long time ago.

"Please come in and have a seat, I—" he started, then motioned for Chyna to sit down after closing the door and moving back to his desk. He took a seat behind it.

Chyna didn't sit down and quickly she put aside any empathy for his present look that tried to creep in. She wouldn't feel sorry for him, he'd created his plight. "I didn't come to stay long, Gary," she said as she adjusted the strap to her purse over her shoulder. Calmly, she placed her hands on the back of the chair Gary had suggested she take.

"I hope you are doing well," Gary said.

"I'm fine," Chyna replied quickly. "Thank you."

"I'm having some troubles, with my new campaign . . . the election, next year, a bit of a snafu . . ."

Chyna nodded, waiting for the ax. His stuttering, stammering verbiage was getting them nowhere.

"I was wondering," Gary went on, "if you might give me the names of some people you know who've done similar stories about senators in the local media, much like that charade you put together in California to denounce me. I should at least be able to make my own plea."

Chyna smiled. It had done the trick. Telling the truth, coming out publicly as she had done had cast doubt in the minds of those who thought he was untouchable and the victim of her adulterous lifestyle. People knew the truth now and she had only done it then for Dean and for herself.

The interview she had done had affected him probably much more than he thought it would.

"Charade, Gary? I told the truth." She wasn't even mad that he considered her acts more lies. She knew the truth.

"Your own distorted version of it."

Chyna shook her head. "Is there anything else?" She shouldn't have come. Chyna realized that now. But for a few moments, it was good to see him looking down and out. "I think I wasted my time coming here. There is nothing I can do for you."

"You're afraid."

"What?"

"You came because you're afraid."

"No, Gary, I'm not afraid of you, I won't ever be afraid of you again."

"Right, you've got that Jameson clan behind you now. You're free to shack up with him now. Even during our marriage you lusted after him, didn't you?"

"I never allowed Dean to come between us!" Chyna said heatedly and hated herself for getting worked up. He was only trying to rile her and she let him.

"Didn't you?" Gary raised an eyebrow. "Five minutes

you sign the divorce papers and you're with him. Many people still believe me, you know. I mean, I'm alone, you're with him. Who should they believe?"

Years ago, perhaps, Chyna had been duped about the kinds of dealings that went on in his chosen profession. Naive, then, about love and life as she had been, this man before her had painfully woken her up to how brutal life and supposed love could be. Chyna shook her head. She didn't care what Californians believed. She wasn't up for reelection in any popularity contest.

Chyna turned on her heel. She had to get home, back across the Woodrow Wilson Bridge that separated her from Virginia, and away from this man that kept her from Dean far too long.

"Do you know if he's planning to rebuild his practice, your boyfriend?" Gary said to her retreating back.

"What?" Chyna turned around to face him only when the words *rebuild* and *practice* set off the alarm bells in her head.

"Your, uh, boyfriend? Is he planning to rebuild the office? I heard a lot of people were looking into the property. Hardig has proposed a building on that land."

"Your point?" Chyna asked, realizing that everything prior to their present subject wasn't the issue at all, but meaningless chatter until he could inquire about the real matter he wanted information on.

"Point is, Hardigs want. They seem to get what they want and I hear they want that run-down plaza, and Jameson's corner property is part of it. Jameson's father left him with some financial troubles, didn't he?"

"And this is your business because what, Gary? I'm not stupid. Don't attempt to play games with me," Chyna replied heatedly.

"No, of course not, Chyna. You're one of the smartest women I know. My career will be over unless I can exact a serious PR campaign. With a series of favorable articles and marketing tactics I can bring up my numbers in the polls. You know a lot of people, that family you insist on lusting after knows a lot of people. Or we could just forget them altogether; you could say you and I have reconciled."

Chyna watched as Gary swiveled in his chair before proceeding to pick up a newspaper on his desk, effectively dismissing her and her presence in his office. It was as if he'd dropped his bomb and there was nothing more he cared to discuss. He must have thought she would just run out and do his bidding.

Or what? What could he possibly do to her? Chyna wondered. "Or what, Gary?" She was afraid to know, but she had to find out what she was up against, what he planned, and just how far he would go to get even for the mess he blamed her for creating in his political life. She could handle just about anything, more defamation in the public's eye, more references and people who followed California politics calling her all types of names. That had lessened since she moved. The public confrontations were while she had tried to make her residence in California. In Virginia, it was as if no one knew her and no one cared. Nothing came to mind that she couldn't handle.

"Or I make your boyfriend's life a living hell."

Chyna looked up as Gary continued.

"Small city doctor, how hard could it be to ruin his pathetic existence? You don't even have to come back to California, just leave him. I'll see to it that the media finds out and all is well with me. The rest, as they say, is history."

Chapter 16

Chyna was livid, but a bit of reasoning crept into her mind. She moved down the hall on leaden legs that carried her to the security terminal. Once there, she sent her purse through the scanner and let the security guard wave a wand over her body. As she exited the door, she stood still a moment letting her breathing calm and her pulse settle down. This was some sick game from one twisted individual. She didn't believe one word that came from Gary Williams's lying mouth. She thought only of Dean. Ruin him? How? The Jamesons, Dean, were untouchable. Not one letter was out of place regarding his building. The news, investigators, the media had said arsonists, a group of unruly teenagers, or thugs had brought that building down. And reconcile? Leave Dean? *No. No.* Chyna shook her head with disbelief at Gary's request. He was rattling her. There was nothing Gary Williams could do to her, not anymore. But he could hire someone to do his dirty work for him. He had money and power. Despite his political connections, he could dispatch things without being implicated in any wrongdoing.

Chyna waited for the oppressive traffic to clear so she could get her car out of the cramped space of the D.C. streets. Finally a car stopped, and she waved with a courteousness she didn't feel. She looked back at Gary's building in disgust from her rearview mirror.

She shouldn't have come there and when she got home, she'd tell Dean all that had transpired. They were on an open and honest keel, now. There were no secrets between them and despite what Gary Williams thought, Chyna had changed over the years and she wasn't giving Dean Jameson up without a fight.

Gary Williams locked his senate office door. Took quick strides back to his desk, where he picked up the phone. After he punched a series of numbers, the line cleared and he said, "I'm sure you were able to get her leaving the building. When the news airs in a bit, I'll expect a deposit into my account. And by the way, thank you for your financial contribution to my reelection campaign, Mr. Hardig."

The long drive to Virginia, stuck in bumper-to-bumper traffic, gave Chyna a bigger headache from the constant thoughts that ran through her head. Parts of the puzzle needed putting together and she was missing vital pieces. Chyna searched frantically for her cell phone to call and tell Dean she'd been running some errands, which was partly true. The rest, the absolute truth, would have to wait until she got to the house to tell him all that she'd learned, and together they could make sense out of it.

She had wanted to know why her ex-husband had been calling her, and now she did—to ask, to plead for her help, and to use her to help him with his own political welfare. Chyna would never, could never do such a thing, not for anyone and certainly not for him.

She pulled up in the Jamesons' driveway and exited the car. Moving to the backseat, she retrieved the grocery bags. She had to make things right, ease her conscience about visiting her ex-husband. If she knew Dean Jameson, he'd be mad about that tidbit of information alone.

Setting one of the bags on the ground, she reached to turn the knob, pushed the door open, and retrieved the bag again as she moved inside. She shut the door closed with her back.

She wasn't much of a cook. Anyone who knew her knew that, but the peach cobbler she pulled first from the bag, care of Sara Lee, would have to smooth whatever became of her meal. Pasta was more her thing; she could manage the simplicity of stuffing shells with the ready-made cheese and meat mixture, turning on an oven, and baking for the time specified. Heat and eat, that was her style. Yep, Chyna thought, dinner wasn't hard at all with such modern-day conveniences.

"Why all the fuss?" Chyna asked herself aloud, then ran over the many ways she could respond as Dean posed the same question. *Well,* Chyna practiced silently, tonight was the night she finally told Dean she was ready to move forward with their relationship, but before that she wanted to tell him about her visit with Gary and about how she believed both he and Warren Hardig were conspiring to do him in. As far as Gary was concerned, she couldn't decide if he was just fooling around with her or if he actually had something to gain with the destruction of Dean's property.

Those revelations had come to her quickly after leaving D.C. If that wasn't the case, why would Gary ask about the rebuilding? Gary had made it clear that Hardig was interested in that property, but having burnt it down to implicate Dean seemed far-fetched. Did that tie in with ruining Dean's life? Was that what Gary meant? Chyna couldn't be sure but she'd put nothing past her ex-husband, and while one incident had forever marred Warren Hardig's character, she had to lump him in there as well until she had cause to rule him out.

She'd also planned to tell Dean that she was sorry she'd kept things from him for so long. For almost two weeks Gary had called her cell phone. Then when she'd not returned his calls, he resorted to calling the house only to hang up when Dean answered. Dean wouldn't allow Chyna to help him do anything if he felt she had to have any dealings whatsoever with Gary. But that was the only reason she'd sat atop her secrets, until she knew more.

She had thoughts of what Dean's sister Jina had said, about Dean's insecurities where Gary was concerned. Still Chyna countered that Dean was so much smarter than Gary, so much more confident, kind, gentle, and that the air of deep-seated jealousy Jina had alluded to was exaggerated. In Chyna's mind, there was no reason for him to be jealous. The two were different in every possible way. *There is no comparison,* Chyna thought to herself. And Dean had to know that she wanted him and not a return to a life of misery with her ex-husband.

Comfortable with her plan, Chyna put the bowls of premade salad into the fridge. She took a deep breath and a moment to focus. After salting the water that would boil the noodles, she turned, leaving the kitchen in search of Dean. When she neared the end of the hall, she heard a loud voice and hoped Dean wasn't fighting again with the adjuster or any other insurance representative. Instead when she opened the door, she found Dean placid as he sat on the couch staring at the news reporter who graced the television screen.

"Continuing with a story our newscast first brought you, we are here with an exclusive. This is what remains of Dr. Jameson's building, and finally after almost three months it looks like the case is closed! Weeks ago, what we first told you was that this heinous crime was thought to be the work of an arsonist, but our newscast has learned Dean Jameson, whose family owns the building, is the guilty party behind its destruction.

"Undisclosed sources say that this office building, in a prime retail location, is apparently worth much less than records claim. The Jamesons own the entire three-story unit on Commerce Street, but business has suffered greatly in the last few years due to the increase of crime and the mixing bowl, better known as the Springfield Interchange Project. The billion-dollar construction operation has driven many residents out of the area. What makes this story so complex is that Jameson, who has not yet been arrested, has been linked to single-handedly orchestrating the fire that burned down and completely destroyed his own place of business. Sources say that he leaked information to his girlfriend, Chyna Lockhart, the former wife of Senator Gary Williams, telling Lockhart that he'd joked about burning his place down, and it seems in the next few days he'd done exactly that.

"Today, just hours ago, Lockhart was seen leaving the D.C. area senate office building, where Williams's office is located. There is no word whether Williams and Lockhart have reconciled. Courtesy of our sister station, California TV aired an interview Ms. Lockhart did earlier this year. She portrayed her husband as an unhappy and bitter man. While she did not blame her husband, she maintains that she is the one who ended their six-year marriage.

"We'll have more for you on this developing story at our eleven o'clock news hour."

Chyna watched the television in disbelief. The last footage she saw was of her trekking down the steps of the building and moving quickly to her car. She looked at Dean and started to speak up when Dean started laughing mirthlessly.

"That was something, huh?" Dean said, as he reached

for the remote control to turn off the television. Chyna immediately relaxed, thinking that if he believed any of what he had seen, surely he wouldn't laugh. She would've joined in had not what the media concocted been made so believable. But apparently from his humorous outburst, he trusted her, he believed her even when the woman on the tape truly looked like her. She had to tell him that in that aspect, the reporters had been right. It was she who exited the building, and she had ended her marriage to a bitter and unhappy man, but in every other instance what they were portraying was a hideous and terrible lie.

"I'm laughing, Chyna, but I guess the joke is on me, huh?"

Chyna immediately sobered.

"Reconciled? Don't leave me hanging. Is that what you did? The only thing you've been telling me is that it's too late. I love you, it's too late, I'll take care of you, it's too late. You tell me that's not you. Sure as hell looks like you, but if you said it wasn't you, I'd believe you. Tell me right now!" Dean shouted, causing Chyna to jump with every assault of his words.

"Oh, wait a minute, can't forget this." Dean held up Chyna's cell phone in one hand for her to see. Then turned it so he could view the lighted screen. It beeped as he scrolled through her calls.

"Got a lot of messages here, a 202 area code, Gary Williams, his name even shows up. There it is right there." Dean tapped the display screen with his index finger. "You got a total of, let's see, one, two, three, damn, you got twenty-eight messages over the last few days, all from your ex-husband! Well? Say something, don't just stand there. You knew your husband had it out for me?"

Chyna quickly blinked back the tears that threatened to spill down her cheeks. "Dean, listen, I went to see Gary, that was me, but—"

"You were there?"

"Yes, but I needed answers."

"Answers to what? You tell reporters I thought abou burning my place down? I didn't tell you that," he accused.

"Now wait a minute—"

"No, you wait a minute, I trusted you!"

"And I never betrayed that trust," Chyna insisted.

"You didn't?" Dean accused.

"No I, I . . ."

"You what, what can you possibly say . . . if you'd have just told me what's going on."

"I didn't know what was going on. I still don't know. I had no idea until today that . . ." She did have some idea, but it wasn't enough to do anything with. She just speculated. Her mind just conjured up things she had eventually later dismissed.

He wouldn't let her get a word in edgewise because he was afraid. Afraid of the rejection. Chyna could see it, practically read it in his eyes. He would never admit it but she knew him. She knew firsthand how it hurt to be rejected, because not only had she done it, but it had been done to her. They'd rejected each other countless times over the years. Chyna surmised it was his turn again now to reject her before she could do it to him. Only she hadn't planned to. She couldn't let that happen. Not this time.

Dean looked away as if reading the many emotions that tramped across her face. The only way to save himself was to pretend that by her visit to see her ex, she was giving him a hint he didn't seem to want to take. "Is this your way of telling me that that's it? You want to reconcile with him?" Dean spat out words, knowing many of them served only as a way to distance himself from something that just wasn't meant to be. They weren't meant to be no matter how much his heart still told him otherwise, he thought.

He moved to the door to grab her when she turned to leave. "Don't forget this," he said, placing the cellular contraption into her palm and closing her fingers around it.

"I know you don't mean those things," Chyna said. "I know you don't have an unkind bone in your body when it comes to me. I believe that you would never intentionally hurt me, but words, Dean, words? They hurt just as much as a physical strike. They cause pain like physical blows."

Chyna looked away, searching her mind for reasons why he couldn't be more accurate about her intentions. Why he didn't seem to know, or recognize that anything she could do to defame him and the people she considered her only family would hurt herself. What did he think she could possibly gain from their demise?

"Chyna, Chyna, I'm . . ." he began to apologize. He was ready to tell her how much and how hard he wanted to love her. How much he did love her and ask her to just lie down on the floor, the bed, anywhere she was willing to with him. Lastly to ask her permission to love her, make love with her until everything else, the chaos, and the drama, the rest of both their crazed worlds with their problems drifted away. "Chyna, I—"

"No, no, save that!" she said and resisted the urge to lay a hand on his chest to stop him from coming closer and ultimately melting her resolve to say what was on her mind. It was apparent that he needed time. She had made up her mind about them and had been ready to move forward. Maybe he was now experiencing that same fear that once kept her from letting go of the past. Together they were a mess. They seemed somehow to keep missing each other's signals. "You've said enough, the great orator has said so much, already.

"But, um . . ." she continued, "maybe, just maybe you could listen for just a few seconds." She'd say her piece, and then she was out of there. She spoke calmly, her tone barely above a whisper. "You know, I don't have to take this. I really don't. You want to create more excuses to push me away. Just one more, huh? Why not? It can go with your ever-increasing displays of pure stupidity. Yes." She shook her head as if agreeing with herself. "More of your dumb and insane responses. I've had it, I've so had it, I can't see straight. I'm outta here." She let one foot move her away from him.

"The news says I told you that I thought about burning down my business. I never said that. Why would they say that if you hadn't told a reporter? What am I supposed to think? What am I supposed to do, Chyna?"

"Trust me!" Chyna's voice was now near screaming pitch. "Trust in us, that I would never hurt you, that I'd never do or say anything you've told me, in the strictest confidence or otherwise. When would I have talked to a reporter? When would I? God, Dean, why would I? Me, Chyna Lockhart, remember me? Why would I have continued to live here in your house and disrespect you like that? Did I change that much, am I that unrecognizable to you?"

Before he could answer, Chyna was moving, quickly and desperately, to the door, and in her haste to exit she looked down to step over the threshold when she rammed her shoulder against Bubba Sparks's wiry frame. Startled for a moment, Chyna looked up into his face and instantly she knew he'd come to tell her about the progress he'd made on her house.

"Hi, honey," Bubba said, smiling. "Been calling you on that cellular gadget, don't work none."

Chyna nodded but slowed down in her haste to get away. "I just wanted to let you know that the house—"

"Yes, Bubba, yes, thank you," Chyna said quickly. Her house was ready. There was no need for him to go on, she could figure out the rest for herself. If only the news could have been one week sooner. Just a day sooner and she could have saved herself from so much pain, from the last few minutes even. She thanked Bubba again and moved to her car feeling so much more than regret for being rude to her friend, but she knew Bubba would understand. Her hands shook so much she could barely get the key in its tiny hole to unlock the door and the same problem occurred again when she tried to insert it into the ignition. Somehow she managed, and within seconds she was speeding far, far away from the entire episode.

When Dean came to the door to watch her leave, Bubba looked over at him, his gray, bushy brow dipped in confusion as to what had just taken place. Finally, he said to Dean, "You need a swift kick in the pants, do ya, son?"

No, he thought to himself as he paced the living room floor. He didn't need a swift kick in the pants, and thankfully Bubba had said his piece and left Dean alone with his thoughts. His many, many thoughts ran amuck. Moving to the kitchen, Dean looked around the room in disgust. Pots and pans were everywhere. He turned off the double broiler and took a moment to look at the counter space. He noticed the makings of dinner, the pie, the leftover chopped vegetables and pasta shells, and the plastic bag holding two rented videos. "Dinner and a movie? Is this the work of a woman who lies?" he asked himself aloud, knowing the answer.

"I need some damn answers!" Dean boomed as he picked up the knife and stabbed it into the wooden cutting board. Before he could think about what he would do or say, he grabbed his keys from the small entrance table. Exiting the house, he slid into the seat of his black Lexus and pointed his car to I-95 having absolutely no idea what he would ask Gary Williams when he met him.

Chapter 17

Holding her protruding belly, Tish Jameson-Alton waddled hurriedly to the phone and picked it up on the third ring. "Hello?"

"Hi, Tish," Chyna returned.

"Chyna? Are you all right?" Tish asked, concerned, wondering why her friend sounded as she did. The last Tish had heard from Jina was that Dean and Chyna were having a rough time. That was no surprise. She always thought they would work out their differences, eventually.

"Sure, fine, thank you," Chyna lied and knew as soon as she called Dean's sister she should have left her alone. "How are you, T.T.?" Chyna asked, using her friend's childhood name.

"Something is wrong," Tish told her friend. "You sound horrible, and what is all that noise in the background?"

"Oh, it's thundering, it's just going to rain soon," Chyna replied.

"Chyna? Please tell me you told Dean about the baby by now?"

"Yes, well, he knows about it."

"So you told him or he found out some other way?"

"It's a long story, T.T. I have to go, I'm so sorry I bothered you."

"Chyna, you're not bothering me," Tish protested. "Are you still there?"

Chyna nodded silently, then realizing she was on the phone and her friend couldn't see her movements, she said aloud, "I'm here, but I've got to get some gas." She hoped that would cue her friend that she needed to go.

"Chyna, he'll understand, he will, it will just take some time. He'll forgive you, he's just hurt, you know how sensitive he is," Tish tried to assure her friend. "He loves you so much, it's just hard for him to admit that, okay?"

"Yeah," Chyna said, no longer listening. All that had transpired between them couldn't be relayed in a matter of moments on her dying cell phone. Chyna spontaneously had tried to reach out to one of the few, true friends she had, only it had been so long since they'd talked. Unfortunately, Tish just wasn't up to date on the latest Chyna and Dean saga. Chyna stopped her car at the pump, continuing to make herself listen enough to say okay at the right times.

"You're not listening to me, Chyna!" Tish protested.

"I'm sorry, what?"

"It's hard for him, it's hard for him to admit his feelings, Chyna, but you do believe he loves you, don't you?"

Not really, she wanted to say, but "yes" was her reply.

"Good, good, I know all that you want, Chyna, I know, and you'll have it. We're your family. We are here for you."

"Uh-huh," Chyna whispered before her tears and her emotional state filtered through the line. She rushed Tish off the phone and said good-bye, feeling more alone than she ever had in her entire life.

Sitting down heavily, Tish eyed the phone as if magically it would ring again and everything, her best friend's life, her brother's love life, would be in order. She believed that they would reconcile, it just seemed as if it was taking years and years for them to do so. Her attention to her friend and her brother's problems was tucked into the back of her mind as her perky little boy entered the room.

"Mama, you okay?" Thomas asked.

"Yeah, sweet pea, I'm all right," Tish said, thinking of her friend, her brother, and their bumpy road to love. Tish felt so out of touch having moved to Georgia, but even if she'd been living in Virginia, she knew no one could solve their problems but them. Looking back at Thomas she took a deep breath and smiled. "But I was just thinking that like the late, great H.G. Wells, what if we could stop time and you could stay eight forever?" She raised an eyebrow, waiting for his response. As of late Thomas was into time travel, space exploration, and history. His questions were endless at his age and his quest for knowledge unquenchable. As a teacher, she welcomed the deep discussions they got into and Tish was continually amazed by his young insight. On maternity leave, she missed the many opportunities teaching provided her to get into the minds of her pupils.

Thomas shrugged a shoulder. "That'd be cool, eight's great." He smiled at his play on words, and was thoughtful a moment longer before he said, "But that means that the twins," and he pointed to her protruding belly, "would still be baking inside your tummy. They'd be stuck in there for infinity plus infinity," he hooted. "They'd never get out of there if we stopped time, Mama," he finished and rubbed her stomach in a circular motion as he'd often seen his dad do.

Tish was shocked. As horrific as the idea seemed, she managed to let out a hearty laugh in spite of herself. Thoughts of carrying around not one but two growing babies forever was absolutely unthinkable. "How'd you get to be so smart?" she asked as she struggled to lift herself from the low chair. Thomas instantly helped. When she stood, she looked expectantly at him.

"Grandma. She told me to tell you that."

Tish laughed out loud again. She moved toward the door and gave one last look toward the telephone with thoughts of her friend and her brother, saying a silent prayer that one day they'd find the happiness she had at present. Even she, Tish thought sadly, had faced tremendous obstacles on the road to love, but she'd made it, and she believed her brother and her good friend since childhood would find happiness together too. She faced forward and let her son lead her to the kitchen where dinner awaited as the two tiny beings growing inside her stomach demanded she feed them.

Idiot. That's what Dean thought of himself as he pointed his car back home. He didn't know where Gary Williams lived and he should have known Williams would be gone from the senate building at this hour on a Friday night.

He was back where he started, at the house, because he hoped and prayed that Chyna had returned. She hadn't. In the back room where Dean had converted the small space into a bedroom for Chyna while her leg healed, Dean noisily shoved papers, taking out his anger and frustrations on any object in sight. When an old newspaper article with a yellow Post-it note caught his attention he brought it closer and switched on the lamp shade to read it.

Here's the article I mentioned—JINA.

Dean read his sister's slanted script and lifted the note to read the entire article. In the corner there was a picture of Warren Hardig with Lisa Stephens draped on his arm.

Under more piles of paper, notes for Chyna's articles, Dean found subsequent articles that discussed the Hardigs' real estate and retail empire.

On a yellow lined legal pad was Chyna's handwriting that asked *Why is Gary calling me?* He moved on to rove over useless notes about the elderly and then found more notes with her thoughts. Almost ripping the sheet,

Dean turned the page over and saw another newspaper article.

> . . . if Hardig is successful, this entire dying strip of Springfield retail will be his. Chauncey Hardig says the buildings will make Springfield a better place, increase property value. Residents say they don't want such a dominant force in their back-yard. Now, as it stands, only three offices will have to move. The other retail facilities and office build-ings have long since gone when the transit construction first started years ago. Dr. Dean Jame-son's will be one of those buildings to relocate. Hardig says he isn't worried about Jameson; they are friends and whatever benefits Hardig could benefit the Jamesons. There's definitely space for his small optometry practice among the new plans.
>
> The other two retail shops are small stores, a bakery and small bicycle shop. Hardig says he's al-ready started negotiations and is offering well above what the property is worth. Deals should be finalized any day now.

Dean abruptly put down the stack of papers in disgust when he heard the front door open and the light tap of footsteps move down the hall.

He started to run to the door and call Chyna's name until he heard, "Dean? Sweetheart? Are you in here?" A female voice that wasn't Chyna's. Hairs on the back of Dean's neck stood on end. With a new alertness made possible by all that he'd just read, he turned around to regard Lisa Stephens in a whole new light.

Chapter 18

"Hey, there you are. The door, honey," Lisa said, pointing a thumb over her shoulder, "was just open so I let myself in." She made her way over to where Dean stood.

Dean smiled falsely and quickly turned back to the desk. "I was just cleaning up," he said, as he began reorganizing the scattered papers and other contents of the desktop.

He didn't bother to turn back around to greet her as he might have if he still trusted her. He would ask her to leave, as soon as he figured a way to get at least some of the questions he had answered. With Chyna's thoughts, and then Lisa conveniently showing up, the night he'd poured his heart and soul out to her came flooding back. It left a terrible taste in his mouth and sickened his stomach.

He had been so wrong. He was a complete and utter fool. One single night came floating back, the night he got drunk and poured his heart, soul, and feelings about everything, including his practice, to Lisa Stephens.

When he felt Lisa's arms come around him, he topped the tablet containing Chyna's notations with another stack of blank legal pads and pushed it to the back of the desk. Strategically, he placed other things in front of it.

"Oh, Dean, I'm so sorry about all that's been happening. I, I saw the news, this is terrible," Lisa said as she commenced to massage Dean's shoulders. "Gosh, you're so tense, this must be devastating,"

"Yeah," Dean said, his thoughts still occupied trying to hurriedly jigsaw the puzzling pieces of information together until everything fit. After what Chyna had come up with, there really didn't seem to be much figuring left. Except maybe the reasons why?

"That heifer didn't deserve you. I thought you'd be over here sulking." She laughed lightly. "I don't mean to make a joke out of this, I'm sorry, but I think this time you'll realize what I've been trying to tell you all along. I know it seems like I'm always around, but I just care so much about you." Her hands stopped massaging Dean's shoulders to wrap around his waist from behind. Standing on the tips of her toes, she kissed the back of his neck.

You're always coming to my rescue, you're right about that. I guess I need a savior, huh, a pretty one like you? he thought disgustedly. He didn't even desire her. He'd never desired her. Her light-colored contacts made her look as if she belonged on the set of some vampire movie. Her acrylic nails were much too long, and their color, he guessed, she'd picked out to match her hair. Everything about her was fake. Her skirt was too short, her bosom in his face all the time. For once he looked at her, really looked at her, and wondered what in the world he had ever said or done to make her think he wanted something more than friendship from her.

"Oh, Dean," Lisa said, turning to touch his face.

"You seem to show up at the right time, when things just fall apart."

Shrugging away from Lisa slowly, but not so much that he pushed her away, he shifted lazily to the bed where he sat down, hunched his shoulders a minute, then lay back and covered his eyes with his left arm.

"How do you always know when I need someone?" he asked nonchalantly.

"Oh, I've got a sixth sense about such things. I may be a lawyer but a part of me just knows when a friend needs a friend."

"I just don't understand, I trusted her," he said for effect.

"She wasn't worth it. I know you'd never burn your place down on purpose. That night, drunk and depressed, I hope you knew then I'd never betray your confiding in me. That Chyna would. I knew you'd never actually do that."

"Yeah," he said, wondering if she even realized how what she said should make him suspicious. "Man, what a fool, huh?"

"No, no, you're not a fool. Not at all. Don't you ever think such a thing. She was vindictive, she didn't deserve you."

Dean removed his arm, squinting at the assault the lights brought back to his eyes when he opened them. He looked over at Lisa, trying to see more than he had originally. His eyes then moved to her naked earlobe, then the other ear with one of the earrings he'd bought for her last Christmas. They'd been a gift of friendship and nothing more. She'd come bearing gifts over the holiday and instead of giving them to Chyna as he had intended, Dean had given them to her, only as an afterthought.

"You, uh, lost one of your earrings," Dean said, reaching up to touch her earring-less lobe with his index finger and thumb. For effect he rubbed it lovingly when really it took a sheer force of will not to yank it harshly.

"Hmm? Oh, I must've left it in Warren's office." She reached up to touch her ear where his hand lingered, then shrugged nonchalantly. "It's probably by the phone. I always take it off to answer the phone, but I make a habit not to lose them, they're the ones you bought me for Christmas. Remember?"

Dean nodded. "Yeah," he said hoarsely. "I forgot you

work at the Hardig building." He was beginning to feel sick. Did she even know she'd said Warren or did she forget the script to her act and ad lib? Dean wondered. "You and Warren, the both of you being lawyers, you guys must keep running into each other."

"Yes, they, the Hardigs, get a tough rap, but Warren's all right. Lawyers can be labeled ruthless, cutthroat people, you know? He mentioned that you would be joining his team and I may be doing some work as well. It'd be awesome if we could all work together."

Dean sat up straight, as if he'd been catapulted from a springboard. Without looking at her, his body went rigid, impervious to the constant stroke of her hand up and down his back. "Man, oh, by the way, I never got a chance to thank you, for helping my mom." He raised an eyebrow. "Jina, my sister . . ." *What a fool,* Dean chastised himself over and over again. "Jina, my sister," he repeated, and watched Lisa shift uncomfortably, "said you helped our mother out with the finances. I'm sure she appreciates that. You didn't have to."

"Everyone needs an objective eye at a time like that. I realize that each of you were more than capable, but it was important for you guys and your mother especially not to make any rash decisions. All kinds of mistakes can be brought on by stress. I just felt I could help, so I offered to take a look at your father's financial statements and records. Good thing I did, your father's bookkeeping, well, it was a bit of a mess.

"Dean," Lisa said seriously, "I know how important family is to you. I know that . . . Chyna couldn't give you those things. I'm sorry but that just shows you it wasn't meant to be. I know you'd want to be a father one day . . . and that Chyna . . ."

Dean nodded, and stood so fast he felt winded but resisted the urge to sit back down. He had heard enough. "I think you should leave now," he managed to grind out.

"What, sweetheart?" Lisa said, sitting up to look at him. Smiling, she also stood.

Dean turned abruptly to face her, leaving her hand to stroke the air. "Get out!" he said coldly, more forcefully. She was so completely wrapped up in her ploy. Her theatrics could win her an Oscar if she were in the running. But she'd hear him loud and clear in the next few seconds.

"I don't stutter, Lisa." He pulled her hand, yanking it from an attempt to make one more caress. Then by placing an index finger under her chin and pushing it upward, he helped her to close her mouth. When she backed away, her expression was disbelieving. Dean leaned down, looking into her eyes. "I said get out of here . . . as in out the door, walk quickly to your car, scoot your lying butt in the seat, start it up, and drive away. Drive far, far away from me, away from this house, away from my sight, and out of my life, and after you do that, don't ever come back.

"That mouth of yours, lawyer, legal assistant, financial adviser, whatever the hell you're calling yourself these days, just slipped and got you into big trouble. You see, I should've realized your motives for everything you've ever done is to get what you want, to get Chyna out of my life. You always appear, out of thin air. It's like, it's like you're watching my house, and just waiting for Chyna to leave and then, poof, you appear. Nice idea you had trying to change the records, but I've been to the bank and we don't owe anyone a dime."

"How can you say this to me? I didn't change anything, Chyna's a conniving little—"

"Don't finish that," Dean warned.

"Don't finish what's true? Why the hell not?"

"Tell me what you and Warren are planning."

"What?"

"You heard me," Dean snapped. "Tell me what you

and he are planning for us. You do have a plan, don't you? You're not stupid, you're smart, and this, this mess, this is good."

Dean advanced on her when she continued to look as if she hadn't a clue what he was talking about, and before she could turn, he'd grabbed her arms.

"Stop!"

"My life, you're messing with my life, so tell me the whole plan before I hurt you." His hands squeezed her arms a bit harder and the only thing he could think about was that it wasn't only their doing that had ruined his life, but his own mistakes as well.

"You're hurting me, I'm sorry, I'm so sorry, I love you, I just wanted you to choose me," Lisa sputtered.

"You call this love? How did you know about Chyna's pregnancy?"

"Warren told me . . ." Lisa breathed.

"How the hell does he know?" Dean demanded.

"That, I don't know, I really don't, Dean. Dean, please, you're not a violent man, please don't do this . . . Warren has connections, he uses people, he used me . . . he's in love with Chyna."

Dean didn't know when or how it happened, let alone what had happened. It seemed one minute he heard someone racing down the hall, it sounded like the authoritative voice of his brother, and the next minute he was on the floor.

"What the hell is your problem?" Jojo Jameson said as he readjusted the bulk of his weight that now pinned his younger brother to the floor.

"At present?" Dean didn't wait for an answer as he spoke again. "That would be you. Now get off me." Dean looked toward the door but Lisa was gone. He heard the rev of her truck's engine and the squealing of tires as she sped away.

"Why don't we have a little talk first?"

"I don't have time."

"Make some," Jojo ordered.

Jojo pulled Dean roughly into a sitting position and instead of hoisting his brother up like he intended, he left Dean on the floor and took a seat in the chair.

Dean didn't bother to get up. His brother didn't look as if he planned on leaving any time soon, so while Jojo delivered his talk or whatever it was he came to share, Dean took the time to think about where Chyna could have gone and prayed that wherever she was she was all right. Reaching into his shirt pocket, he removed his cell phone. Watching his brother from the corner of his eye, he frantically pushed the numbers to Chyna's cell phone. When her voice mail came on, he hung up and put the phone back in his pocket. He'd try again as soon as he got rid of Jojo.

"Messed up again, huh?" Jojo asked. Removing his jacket, he placed it over the back of the chair opposite Dean.

"You know every damn thing, you tell me."

"You think you're going to get her back with that attitude?"

"No, but there's always force."

"That the way you operate nowadays? Pushing people around. I take it you seen the news?"

"You want to cut to the chase, brother? And yes, I've seen the news."

"You blamed Chyna, that why she leave?"

"What do you think?"

"I think you're a fool."

"Well, good for you! I don't think too highly of myself right now either."

"That's a step in the right direction."

"You're getting on my nerves," Dean replied, mentally counting the places Chyna might have gone. He was up to only two places, but had counted at least five people he could call and inquire of, including the brother-sister team that hated his guts, Charlize and Samson Godfrey. Dean mentally scratched their names off his list. They'd tell him to go to hell before they helped him with anything where Chyna was concerned.

Going to her place would be too easy. That's the first place he planned to look, however.

"Good, that's good too, you wanna hit me?"

"What?" Dean looked up, lost in his own thoughts.

"I said you wanna hit me? It will help get some of your frustrations out."

"Gimme a break, will you?"

"Where would you like it?" Jojo replied.

"I don't have times for games, Joe!"

"I'd let you go find her, but, well, I think you need to calm down just a bit."

"I'm calm, thank you."

"Could've fooled me, I come in here and find you roughin' up Lisa Stephens."

"I didn't hurt her, what I felt like doing was nothing compared to the little she got. And I'd never hurt Chyna!"

"But didn't you? Hurt Chyna? Maybe not physically but emotionally?" Jojo raised an eyebrow. "You see, I stay out of people's business, well, your business anyways. I thought for once you and Chyna had it together, but now I see you can't seem to do nothing right on your own. You need your butt kicked."

"I'm not sixteen anymore, you know."

"True, true, but it's been a long time since we pounded up on each other, might do you some good, you're a little worked up."

"You done?" Dean stood, ready to leave. What Jojo proposed sounded like a good idea, though he pictured Gary

Williams's face, or better yet, Warren Hardig's mug on Jojo's body. He smiled. He liked that idea much better.

Dean was wary, mad enough at himself without Jojo trying to further irritate him. It had worked when they were adolescents but not anymore.

Jojo continued, "Chyna ran clear across to California and I finally got why. Just another fool in love and unfortunately she was on the receiving end of your anger, and your stupid misconceptions. Your one true love and you treat her like dirt."

"I didn't . . ." Dean started, but his brother was right.

"Sure you did, what else do you call it?"

"I thought she betrayed me, all right? I made a mistake!"

"Again! You keep making the same damn mistake, because you're afraid."

"Well, I'm sorry I couldn't hop in and out of bed. You change women like you change your drawers."

Jojo only laughed. "I tell you whose bed I missed, that if I knew you were going to jerk her around, I would have gladly held her tight at night."

"Shut up, Joe. Don't go there."

"Why the hell not? Isn't that what makes you mad, Gary was keeping her warm at night? You snooze, you lose. One time too many and someone's gonna get her, whisk her away. Steal her right from under your nose. She's divorced, you idiot, but instead of sweeping her off her feet you keep acting like a jackass. Anyways"—Jojo fluidly switched gears again—"getting back to my story, I was saying, the first time I knew you were in love with Chyna Lockhart . . . I came home from college . . . just two years away at VSU, Chyna saw me, man, she was capital F-I-N-E!"

When Jojo laughed as if he and Chyna had secret memories of their own making, Dean's back went stiff and he looked at his brother, waiting for him to continue but also as if he'd lost his mind. Dean hoped the story ended soon before he took him up on that offer to fight.

"Man, at sixteen," Jojo continued, "fine, I mean, don't get me wrong, she still look good . . . filled out . . . but there's something about that age. That innocence, me being older, I could appreciate that, you know?

"I remember the look on your face. All that long black hair, those big, pretty brown eyes, and that wide rump of hers. Man, if I weren't serious about Angie, I'd give you a run for your money.

"But I came into the house, you and her talking or arguing, whichever you were doing at that time. She took one look at me, leaped into my arms, gave me a big hug and a kiss, right here," Jojo said, pointing to a spot on his cheek. "Man, she looked at me like I was her long-lost brother, only you know, Dean? I know you know. I was thinking I was anything but her brother."

"I said shut up."

"I even told her one time, things don't work out between you and Dean, she could come see me."

"Are you deaf? I said, shut up!" Dean flexed his hands into tight fists. For several moments, he contracted and released them as if that would make some of his anger dissipate. When that didn't seem to work he stood up to his full height, only an inch shorter than his brother.

"Come on, Dr. J, you wanna fight? I used to wonder where all your anger and frustration went. Now I know, poor Chyna, in love with a complete fool! Those long legs, she'd probably wrap 'em around you twice if you asked her."

Chapter 19

That was it, the last straw to his misery. Dean rushed his brother, seeing red. He knew Jojo's tactics well. Running his mouth, to get a rise out of him, to make him respond. His stupid play had worked this time.

Dean shoved a fist into Jojo's gut, then his jaw. He remembered that day as if it'd just happened hours and not years ago. Jojo had dropped his duffel bag at the door. Chyna had taken one look at him, him looking all intelligent, six feet four, shoulders like a stack of solid bricks from working out in college. A few years of college, and Joseph Jameson Jr. seemed even a bit educated, grounded, and Chyna, with Dean standing there, disregarding the fact that he even existed, had unashamedly leaped into his arms like the two existed on a very personal level.

Dean's hand throbbed from pounding his brother, but Jojo merely grunted. Not only did Jojo barely fight him, his brother took each blow without any depiction of pain or fear on his face, like Dean knew he could. And their battle, rather Dean's constant punching, took the fun out of doing so. The fact that his brother didn't fight back angered Dean even more. The more he punched, the less the anger seemed to leave him like it should've. He was fighting a winless battle. Knowing he could give his brother as good as his brother gave him did little for his ego even.

"Fight me back. You started this whole thing, come on!" Dean yelled at his brother.

Jojo shrugged his shoulders, dropped to his hunches, where he threw out a leg, and kicked Dean's out from under him. Dean fell to the floor, where he lay dizzily on his back.

Dean struggled to get up and he thought Jojo was helping him until he swiftly flipped him over onto his stomach and pressed his knee into his back.

"Get off of me!" Dean said, breathing hard. His knuckles crackled as if they'd been burned and his ears rang from the heat that rushed to his head. His brother's massive weight pressed on top of him, and the concentration of that weight seemed to center inside his chest.

"I'm bigger than you, you forget!" Jojo said.

Dean couldn't see anything but the floor, his face pressed into the odorous pine boards he'd laid a few months ago. When Jojo flipped him over, his brother leaned into him and told him how lousy he was. How unthankful he was and Dean couldn't agree more.

"You're pathetic!" Jojo continued. "You didn't have to work for much of anything, Dean. You made straight As through high school, through college, honor societies, stupid chess club, you nerd!" Jojo looked up and around the room, before looking back down. He hadn't moved an inch while he observed the renovations Dean had done and still managed to keep his brother pinned to the floor. "You can do everything but love with ease. Dean, that takes work. The one thing you gotta work at and you're hopelessly bad at it." Jojo moved back to bring his brother brusquely to his feet. They stood at eye level, Dean moving away, shoving his brother's grip from his shirt.

"Real hard work, and there aren't any damn classes. It's a crash course of trial and error, and you've mostly erred . . ." Jojo lifted a shoulder. "You've made enough mistakes in your life when it comes to that girl. She's doing all the work and you're sitting on your butt waiting for things to fall into place. Don't screw this up too."

After taking a deep breath, Jojo finished his monologue. The shoe was usually on the other foot, Dean thought sadly. It was Jojo that had the relationship problems but as he and Angie's relationship grew steady, it seemed as if everyone forgot his playboy ways. All of a sudden he was a freaking expert.

"Now give me a hug," Jojo said.

Dean looked at him as if he'd lost his mind. "Go to hell, Jojo," Dean said, rubbing his sore hand in a circular motion.

"That's what I thought," Jojo replied as he pulled his stiff brother's solid frame roughly into his arms, hugging him bear tight before he let go. He moved to the door and looked back at Dean for a moment to say, "I'll take the long way home, see if I see Chyna anywhere, you take I-95."

Dean looked up and nodded. Before Jojo could get into his truck, Dean had his own keys in hand and made his way to his own car.

Seconds, it seemed, after Dean exited onto the highway, he had to turn his wipers on high. He reached for his phone when it began to vibrate against his chest. Quickly he set it in the small device that would amplify the caller's voice. Using a series of voice commands, Dean kept both hands on the steering wheel. "Yeah," he said when his brother called his name.

"Found Chyna's car," came Jojo's reply. "A ways up Franconia Road, the Mobile station."

Dean nodded, then realized Jojo said he'd seen her car and not her. "She there?" Dean inquired frantically, maneuvering his car off the next exit to go back the way

he'd come. He was a good ten minutes from where Jojo
said Chyna's car was located.

"No, looks like there's something wrong with the car,
won't start."

"What about . . . where could she . . . anything?" Dean
said. The phone beeped and an error message flashed,
the connection broken due to the storm. Dean pressed
the redial button only to get a busy signal. He stop trying
to reach him altogether as he sped up the car and was able
to get to the gas station in under ten minutes. He quickly
maneuvered his black Lexus behind his brother's truck.

"Yo," Jojo said.

When Dean exited the car, he moved quickly to the
driver's side. "Where the hell could she be?"

"I don't know," Jojo replied.

Dean looked down, noticing for the first time that the
driver-side window wasn't rolled down, but pieces of the
window's glass littered the seat, indicating something
or someone had smashed the window.

"Whoa, just calm down, it's probably nothing," Jojo
said, holding up his hands in defense, waiting for his
brother's outburst.

"Like hell it's probably nothing. Why would her window be broken, Jojo?" Knowing his brother didn't have
any more answers than he did, Dean went inside to ask
the cashier about the owner of the car.

Jojo followed him.

Inside the small minimart, Dean waited until the man
in front of him settled his bill and left.

"The woman who owns the car out there, you seen
her?" Dean frantically asked the man who looked as if he
hadn't understood a word Dean said. "What happened to
her?" Dean demanded again of the short Middle Eastern
man.

"No trouble," the man replied, eyeing Jojo behind
him. "I got gun."

"The woman who owns the car with the broken window?" Dean asked again slowly, his hands up to indicate he meant the man no harm. "Is she all right?"

"Broken window," the cashier repeated, his voice rising an octave with each repeat. "The woman, tall, very nice . . . then another woman, this one crazy! Drive big, big car, came and be real mean to her . . ."

"Another woman?" Dean did a double take when the cold sweat of fear poured down his back.

"Yes, crazy woman, in big, big car."

Jojo moved up to clarify. "A truck, you mean?"

Dean no longer listened to what the man said.

"Yes, truck," the man went on, "that's what I say, big, big car! Hit the woman car, tore her window with crowbar, woman crazy, very, very crazy!"

Dean looked back at the man and then at his brother. "Lisa drives a truck."

Chyna was home—or she was at her house, she never quite saw fit to call it a home. The steps it took to get there, however, caused her a little more empathy for Alice in Wonderland, or even poor Dorothy and her little dog Toto—she too felt like a character that had the unfortunate task of doing battle with all kinds of villains when all she wanted was to hide under the covers of her bed and never come out again. Her villains: a blinding, torrential rain, thunder and lightning that at times left her paralyzed with fear. If that weren't enough, throw in one crazy woman with a crowbar for added effect.

She'd been at the gas station, getting her tank filled up like normal people do; she paid inside, got back into her car, and inserted the key that should have started the ignition. Only her transmission merely grunted in response. Chyna hated that car. She could handle that, she thought silently; after all, it seemed fitting for the finale to her day.

She had exited the car, ready to make her way inside to inquire about the availability of an on-site mechanic, when the sound of a loud blaring horn stopped her dead in her tracks. The truck barreled to a stop in front of her, its horn deafening her and its lights shining in her face. For a moment, Chyna thought she had gone deaf and blind at the same time.

The truck continued to run, the door opened, and a blurry figure leaped from the driver's side and ran toward her. Once her eyes readjusted from the blinding lights she came face-to-face with Lisa Stephens.

"I'll kill you, I swear I will! He's mine and I love him," Lisa had screamed over the thundering rain.

Chyna shook her head in disbelief as she backed up from the deranged woman. She grunted in pain when she backed into the cold metal, sharp-edged mirror of her car. Quickly Chyna moved away, bringing a hand up to rub her bruised backside. She looked down and focused her eyes on the heavy object dangling from Lisa's hand.

When Lisa waved the crowbar frantically, Chyna stiffened and reared back again, this time in shock when Lisa swung the metal bar so hard it smashed through her driver-side window. "That's my car! What's the matter with you!" Chyna yelled, barely able to hear herself over the traffic and the roaring of the rain and then a sudden clap of thunder. *It wasn't the best car* was her first thought, but it was paid for.

Chyna wiped the damp tendrils from her forehead, watching as Lisa Stephens moved closer to her, her bosom heaving, her black hair with burgundy highlights flat and having lost its bounce. Her makeup ran, leaving her eyes to look like those of a raccoon, and her entire face was now nothing more than a loose shell that sagged and wrinkled. She moved forward, leaning again near Chyna, and whispered, "I'll get you, take this as a warning!"

"Hey, what's up here? What's the problem?" A man wearing a light blue shirt and the word *Mobile* across his chest ran from the small building, closer to where Chyna stood. Before Chyna could get her thoughts together about what happened and relay them to the gas station attendant, she watched in a daze as Lisa moved quickly back to her truck and hopped into the driver's seat. Chyna stared after her in disbelief as Lisa screeched away, blowing the horn, darting into the oncoming traffic without looking, and sped off.

The gas station attendant asked Chyna if she was okay again and if she wanted him to call the police.

"No, no. Just need to call a cab, please, and my car . . ." Chyna didn't see where she placed her hand until the tiny shards of glass bit into her palm. She quickly withdrew it. "Oh, ouch," she muttered and withdrew her hand to examine it.

"You're bleeding," the man said, frantically gesturing toward her hand. It trickled blood down her arm.

Chyna had to assure the frazzled man that she was all right. He abruptly shoved a dingy rag at her and she proceeded to wrap her hand in it. She'd think about oil, someone else's sweat, and gasoline residue seeping into her bloodstream at a later time. Smiling at the man, she thankfully pressed the rag to the middle of her palm where the cut bled.

"I need to call a cab," she stated. The man led her into the building, thrust the phone into her hand and a raggedy yellow page that'd been torn from the book for such occasions. She then dialed the number someone else had circled.

And here she was, having fought the villains, having secured her car for service and repair at the station's adjacent garage. She stood now, in her own home, for the first time in almost three months. A sense of apprehension and loneliness immediately descended over her and cloaked her as if someone had just dropped the heaviest, most oppressive cape on her shoulders.

She continued to move down the hall from her front door and to the back of the house where disaster had once been, noticing every change that had transformed her place into a livable area again. To her amazement, there was nothing that indicated the roof had caved in at all. Nothing appeared to suggest that not long ago pieces of the ceiling and chunks of her walls floated like rafts on the water that almost drowned her.

"Everything mighty tidy in here?"

Startled, Chyna turned around and found Bubba standing at the door. She nodded, resisting the urge to rush to his arms and bury her face in his chest like she could do when she was a child. Instead she said, "You didn't have to do all this, I . . . I . . ." It was so much more than just simple repairs, but new carpeting, she saw, looking down. The paint she had planned to use was no longer in canisters awaiting application, but on the wall. Even her ceiling fan with its lighting fixtures had been put up. She didn't have to purchase much more than a few chairs and a table. "I, I don't know what to say," she said, looking up at the older gentleman, then at her ceiling in awe, not a drip or rip anywhere. It was perfect.

"Least I could do for you, little girl."

Chyna smiled, wishing she were a little girl. "You don't owe me anything, I . . ."

"Sure I do. Me and my Georgia, we owe you much, a hell of a lot. This is the least I can do, just as I said."

Chyna nodded and realized that for the second time that day she was being rude and ungrateful. "I'm sorry, Bubba, I just, I don't want to be mean to you. I just . . ." She sighed. "Thank you for everything."

"What happened to your hand? Don't stain this new camel-brown carpet by bleeding all over the place, now. You should take your shoes off. This fussy stuff cost a bit, but it'll sink your toes," Bubba continued sheepishly, displaying the pride and joy he took in sparing no expense to make her place more than just livable again.

"Let me see that." Bubba gestured toward her hand and reached for it when she hesitated.

"I'm all right, really. I . . . just a cut."

"Nothing around here to cut yoself on, I made sure of that."

"No, no, nothing around here," Chyna assured him. She winced a little when Bubba removed the bandage from her hand. The blood on the cut had begun to dry, causing the rag to stick to her gash.

"This place looks beautiful, Bubba. I mean, you didn't spare any expense. Unfortunately," she whispered, "I think I'm going to sell it."

"Wait till you see the upstairs. Jameson did most of the decorating work up there. He wasn't any good with the power tools," Bubba snipped. He continued the neat reapplication of the bandage. Wrapping the fabric tautly around her hand, he tied a secure knot before he looked at her strangely. "What you talking about selling this place? That's nonsense!"

"Dean helped work on my house?" Chyna asked.

"Sure he did, helping out when he wasn't tending to you. Put a pretty penny on the upstairs. I just took care of this room here and the roof. Upstairs was the work, he bought you all that frilly stuff you women like. Wait till you see it."

She wouldn't see it. Bubba's disclosure should have made her feel differently, fall harder in love with Dean, if that were possible. He did everything . . . everything, right! With his actions, Chyna amended. His outward exhibition was like no one else, but he obviously didn't trust her, and where were they if they didn't have that?

"I gotta start over somewhere," she said, recalling the subject she and Bubba discussed at present. "Too many memories here," she said by way of explanation when it was so much more than that. "Here is just not the place for me. I gotta leave. I just keep getting myself into a mess. I keep trying and it doesn't work."

"What's gotcha talking like that?"

Chyna shrugged.

"That newscast?" Bubba harrumphed. "What a crock o' bull. Never heard anything so silly in my entire life! You know, little girl, if I had a daughter, I'd want her to be just like you. . . . Georgia and I couldn't have any children but we'd **of**ten say that if we had a little girl, we'd want her to be like Chyna. Precious. Parents just messed over you but look at you, you turned out just right."

"Oh?" Chyna said, never realizing he felt that way.

"You're sweet, you're kind. We all mess up, sometimes. That Williams boy ain't help your matters none. I'm old, but I could take my belt to him if you'd like."

For the first time Chyna laughed, imagining Bubba whopping a grown man, no matter how much he deserved it.

"I'm serious. Big bully, that Jameson is, too . . . but, well . . . things will work out. Now, don't shake your head at me. Don't nobody go to that kind of expense if he don't love her. I'd break my back five more times building Georgia twenty houses if I could have her back.

"I'm an old man but I know what I'm talking about. This will blow over and you'll be happy, just a little bit longer, I know it."

Chyna nodded not because she believed what he said to be true but because to argue with him would only prolong his attempts to make her think otherwise. "I'm sorry Georgia . . . died," she said.

"Me too." Bubba smiled. "But she was comfortable when she left, and that was only because of you. You have a special gift for taking care of other people, and you made her life comfortable before she passed. I couldn't boil water for the tea she liked. You did that and helped her with her bath, and she lost all that weight, though I didn't like her so thin, but I loved her and I thank you much. Bet you didn't think I was paying attention, did you? I used to come home and she smelled all nice, you really into those smellin' soaps and thangs. She liked that. So, I can't repay you for that. This house, the little fixing up I did, was a drop in the pan, nothing compared to what you'd given my Georgia in her final days. Someone's going to take care of you real good, just you wait. I just know it."

Chyna nodded and tried not to cry. Letting him have his memories and leaving her own problems for just a bit, she wished she could have the years. Even if her husband died or if she died, she just wanted that love that when you got old, you held on to and remembered.

"You start crying, girl, I'm running. I leave the room when a woman starts getting all teary eyed on me."

Chyna laughed. "What are you going to do now? It's been years since she died. I thought you'd have retired."

"I'm in semiretirement." Bubba smiled. "I may go down to Florida, visit my brother, help start some no-good young Sparks carpenters. Will you write me a letter?"

"If you send me a postcard," Chyna replied and they laughed together.

Bubba turned to leave after giving Chyna a brief pat on the shoulder.

She walked him to the door and when she opened it for him, Dean stood staring back at her.

Chapter 20

"I'll, uh, I'll see you, Bubba, and thank you," Chyna said as Bubba moved through the door.

"You be good. Dean," Bubba said, nodding in acknowledgment to Dean.

Chyna eyed Dean warily. With his icy, silent stare she felt the physical chill of the rainwater soak into her bones. She looked away and covered her mouth as she sneezed. She was soaked to the core. When she was done with a brief fit of sneezing, she rubbed her arms and wished for a nice hot bath to warm her up.

Instead she moved to the kitchen, where she pretended Dean wasn't there at all while she commenced to make a pot of tea.

"I'm sorry," she finally heard him say. He'd followed her to the kitchen but stopped at the entrance.

"Yeah, you really are," she said, not bothering to look up from her task, watching water boil.

Moving to the table, Chyna pulled out a chair and sat down heavily. With Dean's arrival, her thoughts became awry with the constant replay of a short three-minute segment on the six o'clock news. That single event had sent her world flying off its axis.

"I'm sorry, Chyna. I'm very sorry."

"You mentioned that, can you get to the gist of your apologizing?"

"I shouldn't have jumped to conclusions." Dean thrust his hands into his pockets, not knowing what to do or say.

"You didn't trust me, Dean. That hurts."

"You didn't trust me either. You went to see your ex-husband—"

"To get some answers," Chyna defended.

"Couldn't you have told me that?" At least she was talking, Dean thought to himself. He'd take her outbursts, her quick comebacks any day over the silent treatment. For the most part, he thought, as he scrutinized her closely, she looked all right and unharmed but he made a mental note to get to the issue of her car in a minute.

"I didn't have anything to tell at that point," Chyna said, "but I was going to tell you tonight that I'd been to see Gary. But instead of waiting for my explanation, instead of trusting me, you assumed that I harbored enough anger and that that anger ran so deep I was willing to ruin your life?"

"No, I was just upset, and you were the closest thing for me to release that anger upon."

"As always! We are part of a vicious cycle, we keep going through the same old thing over and over again, and I'm tired of it."

"I am too and I want to make it right."

"How?" Chyna pleaded. She didn't see any kind of reconciliation now or in the future.

"Whether we can work this out or not, Chyna, hinges on one question."

Chyna rolled her eyes. "And what would that be?" she asked skeptically.

"Do you love me?" Dean asked quietly.

She looked away, baffled. Whatever she had thought the question would be, that wasn't it. Was it really that simple? Her eyebrows knitted together as she thought, scrutinizing other possible questions that surely had as much weight as the one he proposed, if not more. She couldn't answer, not yet, and she was thankful when Dean went on.

"I have been telling you that I love you, and you haven't told me whether you love me, and that makes me crazy, I guess. Makes me angry . . . I want to tell you something else," he whispered before kneeling in front of her. "We can get past all of this, we can, and whether we continue right here really does hinge on if you love me, Chyna, because I do. I love you with all my heart. And maybe I'm just scared of every possible thing you could ever think of."

Chyna was doubtful. "Like what, Dean?" she asked, wondering what in the world Dean Jameson could possibly be scared of: snakes, natural disasters? That all came to her mind, but they were discussing love. What was so difficult about loving her, or why did he make it seem difficult by fighting it as hard as he did?

"For one," Dean said, breaking into her thoughts, answering her silently posed question, "that I will get sick and you'll have to take care of me like Mom had to do for Dad. I don't want that to be your burden."

Chyna, surprised, shook her head at such thoughts, ready to protest when Dean went on.

"Two, that you'll get sick, that you'll die and leave me. I couldn't bear that. I'll forever regret not telling you that I loved you sooner. Giving myself totally to you exposes me to the possibility of your leaving and my not telling you at all. My letting you go, my pushing you away did us both a favor.

"Three, and this one causes me the most horror, Chyna. I can't measure up to the men you've known. Gary Williams, he's a jerk, I'll give you that, but he's . . . he's commanding, he has money, status, power. I'm just your ordinary regular optometrist. What could you possibly have with me that you couldn't have with him? We're so different. I don't measure up, Chyna. Not in the least. To see you coming out of that building, Chyna, I was mad. So mad I couldn't think. So mad that I thought I'd lost you. I hate him, I wanted to kill him. He's had six years of your time, of seeing your beautiful face, of rolling over and waking up next to you, or making love with you. And . . . I . . . can't . . . stand . . . it!"

Dean stood to pace the floor and when he stopped to look at her, to lean against the stove, he crossed his arms and silently with a look of expectation, indicated he'd passed the ball to her.

She was thoughtful, that last one, number three, foremost in her mind. She'd get to it in a minute. If she had the nerve she'd tell him about Gary's skill in the bedroom, that no one ignited her body and stimulated her mind like Dean Jameson. But Chyna shook her head. Bringing that up might launch a kind of ego match she didn't care to deal with. Not only that but she'd have to admit the times she'd had sex with Gary, that before, during, and certainly afterward she'd wished she was in Virginia, how she longed for Dean's arms to hold her. She wasn't proud of that but it was true. She was only human and reminded herself of that fact when the feelings of guilt said she was to blame for her marriage's end result. She'd made a mistake in marrying Gary Williams in the first place. She'd married him for all the wrong reasons, but for now she kept those facts to herself and focused on the issue at hand. She took a deep breath as she began to address all that Dean's fears constituted, now realizing what he meant. She felt some of the same things he did, only pushing him away wasn't her answer to those insecurities, as seemed to be his way of dealing with them.

"Well, for one," she said, ordering her thoughts in much the same manner Dean had. She began not wanting to admit her feelings one way or the other. "If you get sick I'd take care of you. I'm an experienced caregiver."

"Yes, and that is why you shouldn't have to," Dean quickly interjected.

"But I would want to!" Chyna insisted.

"Wouldn't you call in others to help you? Mom waited forever to ask for help and no one thought to see if she needed it. Sometimes everyone is so busy dealing with their own grief they can't see over that long enough to ask what they can do to help. Instead they focus on what they can't do, and do absolutely nothing. I don't want you to go through that!"

Chyna nodded. The fact that he'd thought about it that way was so amazing to her. She'd seen many families that broke apart, instead of banning together like they should have, when a vital unit of their family took ill. The Jamesons hadn't been one of those families. They may have been slow to help Ms. Alfreah, but they were selfless, every one of them. "Okay, this is all hypothetical, Dean? You're not sick, are you?" Dean shook his head and Chyna felt an unexpected and fierce gladness come over her. "When someone you lo . . . care about gets sick, people pull together, and if I was your wife that's what I would do.

"I'm a professional but I would ask your family for help. I would tell them where I needed help. That's what a marriage . . . that's what loving someone is.

"But even if I didn't ask for help, I'd take care of you because I loved you and I'd want to take care of all of your needs. For better or worse, it doesn't say in sickness jump ship. It says in sickness and in health and for better or for worse."

"So you love me?" Dean asked, searching her eyes for any sign of something.

Chyna abruptly stood to move before the stove again. She turned off the burner and didn't dare begin to pour the hot liquid into the mug for fear she was shaking so badly she'd spill it.

"I said this was all hypothetical, Dean."

"So you don't love me?"

Just one more time, say it! a tiny voice inside her chanted. Could she risk her heart just one more time?

"For two," she said, ignoring Dean's attempt to get her to admit whether or not she loved him. She didn't remember if she'd made her first point yet, but she had to move on. "For two: people die, it's what you do with the time you're on this earth. You seem to be wasting yours bickering back and forth and if that's what you want to do, that's fine, do it by yourself."

She ignored part three altogether and asked instead, "What are we . . . what are you . . . going to do about Gary?"

Dean reached out to turn her around to face him. Her eyes stared intently at the dark, golden sandy skin of his open shirt. When he tilted her head up, she closed her eyes to keep the soul-showing windows from telling him her every dream, her love, and her true feelings for him that would never seem to go away.

"What about point three?" Dean asked.

Chyna opened her eyes again. "Point three?" she breathed, suddenly angered by his version of point three. She pushed him from in front of her and walked around him. "That's just your own twisted ego. Sounds more like a matter you should take up with Gary and whomever else you think I've got the hots for. Your jealousy is a personal problem! It's all up here." She tapped her temple. "I don't know what more you want me to do or say."

"Do you love me?" Dean measured each word carefully for what he hoped was the last time.

"Would you stop asking me that?" Chyna yelled. "Of course I love you, with all of my heart, but it hurts, Dean. I won't take another of your potshots, another rejection slip because you can't or won't. You won't," she spat, "let me love you. I don't have time, I'm getting old! It hurts me too. . . ." She rubbed her chest when it seemed something inside eased. Her feelings were out in the open, all the cards, all of her heart lay on the proverbial table.

"I love you, okay? Me . . . I love you. I've been here since I was eight years old. . . ." The tears ran down Chyna's face and she talked faster. "I've been here, in this house, this stupid empty house, and I used to go down the street to yours. Your family were the kindest people I'd ever met, you know them?" Chyna turned around. "Because sometimes you act like them, and sometimes you act like a jerk!"

"I won't hurt you again, I promise. I'll take care of it, I'll make it right, just let me try, please?" He took her hand in his own, holding it there for a moment, then wrapping her in his arms.

"You're already in here, Dean, but if you hurt me again . . ." This didn't quite go as she had planned. For some reason she thought herself exhibiting more resistance, but she'd grown weary.

"I won't! I . . ." He nipped her lips and when she stared at him astonishingly, he closed his mouth over them again. His tongue sought entrance and he took her breath away when she let him in. "It's you . . . I love."

She did love him and there wasn't any resistance left, because she hadn't stopped loving him. Ever. When she felt her knees buckle, she wrapped her arms around him for support, and he lifted her into his arms.

"I got a little crazy, Chyna." Dean set her atop the sofa just outside the kitchen.

"A little?" Chyna responded.

"Okay, a lot," Dean amended.

"Be sure, Dean. This time be very, very sure. You threw our trust out, even if for a few crazy moments, you threw it away, and that hurts so bad. I'd never, ever hurt you,

I'd never hurt your family, because I wanted, I hoped to be a part of that."

"You are," Dean assured her.

"Am I?" Chyna looked at him skeptically, wondering if he could truly understand the extent of all that encompassed what he, his family meant to her.

"You are, you are. You're a part of me, you're a part of my family. I think they'd gladly rather get rid of me than lose you, Chyna," Dean said, trying to assure her, before he assaulted her with more kisses.

Chyna smiled, no longer listening. Desire reigned over everything. She didn't hear his constant chants when he laid her on the sofa. The only thing she could do was feel and see, when he laid the center of his weight on top of her.

"Chyna," Dean pleaded, trying to get control of his runaway desire. He felt himself grow heavy just thinking about loving her, just wanting to love her and hoping she wanted him to. "I want, I need to love you, now, right this minute, I can't wait, not another day," Dean whispered.

"Please," Chyna added when he touched her breast.

She froze when he grabbed her injured hand and held it in his. "What the hell happened to your hand?"

Then as if someone had dumped cold water on her he said, "And what happened to your car?"

Chyna took a moment to reorient herself. She blinked rapidly and looked up at Dean above her. He sat on his haunches and looked at her expectantly. She started to tell him that she was more concerned about his expressing his newfound *I promise not to mess up again* love for her and that he was doing a really good job of it, but she doubted that maneuvering the conversation off her hand and the details surrounding the damage to her car was possible.

"Dean, listen."

"Lisa," he said, more of a statement than a question.

"How did you know something happened to my car?" Chyna asked.

"I went looking for you, Chyna. Your car was at the gas station, the window smashed, and that no-talking attendant said a woman in a truck smashed your window. Now, you want to tell me the rest?"

"No, Dean."

"Well, what then? Chyna, what happened? Where's your first-aid kit? Keep talking, I'm listening," Dean said, lifting himself off Chyna. He frantically opened and banged drawers shut. When what he wanted wasn't there, he moved through Chyna's living room, down the hall, and to the bathroom. When he came back with a white box in his hand, he knelt in front of her, grabbed her hand, and threw away the present bandage in disgust. "Tell me!" he said, looking at her expectantly.

"She knocked out my window with a crowbar, Dean. . . . But I rested my hand on the windowsill, and the shards. It was an accident. I did it to myself really."

"Does that make it better, Chyna? You wouldn't have hurt your hand had it not been for her, a damn crowbar, for God's sake." He was silent as he blew on her hand to cool the mild burning of the solution he used to cleanse her cuts. He placed the gauzy bandage across her hand and pressed it to make it stay in place, then secured the padding with surgical tape.

"I could have her arrested for this."

"Dean, no!" Chyna said, grabbing the arm that moved for his pocket cell phone.

"She was upset," Chyna said in Lisa's defense.

"She's lost her damn mind," Dean exclaimed. "She's not just after me, Chyna, she works for Warren Hardig."

"I know, your sister told me." Chyna stopped to turn, rethinking her recent defense to spare Lisa Stephens from formal assault charges. "Well, your sister said that a photo of Lisa and Warren were taken recently in the business section of the paper."

Dean nodded. "I told her, Chyna. About how I felt about my place when I was drunk . . ."

"You what?" Chyna said.

Dean nodded and a host of other questions came to her mind. "I'm sorry, Chyna, that I could ever believe you did what I thought. I feel like a fool. I'll never forgive myself. This mess is somewhat of my own making."

"You were hurting, Dean. But it's not of your own making. Hardig doesn't like you," she told him.

"They never liked my family. That goes back years."

Chyna nodded, feeling only slightly relieved. At least Hardig's focus wasn't totally on her, as she had started to believe.

Dean shook his head. "I know Warren Hardig doesn't like me, Chyna. I know his father and mine have years of dislike for each other, but you've yet to tell me why you don't like him."

Chyna shrugged her shoulders. *Dislike* was such a non-threatening word. What hatred, what utter disgust she had for Warren Hardig required a word more descriptive than simple *dislike*. She looked up and saw that Dean waited for an answer. "I mean he and Gary are friends, that's reason enough to despise him. Gary's a jerk, the people he hangs out with are jerks." If she just didn't think about it, if she didn't tell anyone else, she could pretend it never happened.

"Chyna, look at me, okay? Please tell me, I don't believe a word Lisa says. I don't know what to believe but she said that Warren is in love with you."

"What?" Chyna said, horrified.

"Chyna, look at me," Dean said again, turning her face back to him. "There have to be no more secrets, all right? I don't care what's in the past. We've both made mistakes, but we have to get everything out so we can solve this, so we can get on with our lives. Right?"

Chyna nodded her head. He was right, but she didn't want to think about months of someone she'd never hinted at liking calling her when her husband was away as if she had given him a reason to do so. She didn't want to think about working up the nerve to tell Gary that his supposed friend had crawled into their bed only to have Gary laugh at her as if she would lie about something so devastating.

It only took one time for Gary to laugh at her, and she'd never mentioned the incident again. What good would it have done? He'd told her that the Hardigs had deep pockets that could afford him more money than he could raise legitimately for his campaign. That single talk, lasting only a few minutes, had told her what she could do with her talk of Warren Hardig's advances. She was surprised Gary hadn't asked her to sleep with Warren just to get more money and ultimately advance his political candidacy.

Chyna looked away, knowing that as much as she would like to forget that night, she had to tell Dean the truth. If Warren was proclaiming his undying love and affection, then something was wrong. She had underestimated the depth of his feelings and now they were back to haunt her.

"One night," Chyna began, then stood, "Gary was having a business meeting in the house and Warren was there. He and Warren, after everyone left, both got drunk. Gary had passed out on the couch downstairs and Warren . . . Dean . . . he came upstairs and crawled into bed with me."

"You're not serious?" Dean said incredulously.

"I wouldn't lie about something like that, Dean."

"Chyna, I'm sorry. I . . . Why didn't you tell me?"

"It happened years ago. It's part of an entire time I'd rather forget!"

"Did you?" Dean stuttered.

"Did we have sex?" Chyna said incredulously. "No! Dean, I wasn't so sleepy that I couldn't recognize my own husband. I threw him out of the bed. He tried to come after me, but the alcohol made his coordination a little off."

At times she questioned if he was really drunk at all. "I was able to get away. I left the room." Chyna shook her head. "I left the house, with a pair of pants and a shirt, and I spent that night at a motel."

Chyna shook off a chill, remembering her house, how it never felt the same. How she didn't want to return to her home. How Gary, her own husband, didn't seem to care that his friend exhibited such poor judgment.

"What'd Gary say?" Dean asked.

"Nothing," Chyna replied, laughing. "What could he say? His friendships, his connections meant more to him than I ever did. So you see . . ." Angrily she turned to face him. Her anger wasn't directed at him, but at her life then. "My years of waking up next to him, his seeing my beautiful face"—Chyna quoted Dean's words—"must not have been that beautiful to him if he could treat me so bad. And you think I want to go back to that? You think I'd subject myself to such brutal humiliations?"

"Chyna." Dean gulped. "I'm sorry, I'm so sorry."

"I made a mistake and married a man for all the wrong reasons. I think back now and I don't think that I loved him even. That's what I get, that's my punishment for marrying him when I wasn't sure."

"No! No one deserves that kind of treatment." If Dean could order Gary Williams's execution, he would.

"Against my better judgment, I went to see him today and I'll regret that for as long as I live. I thought he'd changed, I thought he'd be different. I thought he might try to offer some apology to me. But he hasn't changed, not one bit. And I was happy living with you down the street. I wanted to show him that I was happy . . . and I got back and everything just fell apart."

"It's not apart, we're together, we've reconciled, we're fine."

Chyna laughed.

"I mean it," Dean said and crushed her to him. "We'll figure this all out, we'll figure it out and fix it. I'm sorry I made you rehash that. I won't let anyone hurt you, I won't let Gary or Warren hurt you."

Chyna nodded against his chest. "I'm sorry I went to see him."

Dean shook his head, a thousand regrets in his eyes. It didn't matter anymore, nothing else mattered but getting through this. He kissed her and he was so thankful when she kissed him back.

"I love you, Dean."

"I love you, too."

They'd work everything else out, but right now she just let Dean work the only magic she'd ever wanted. Amazed by how fast her desire came back, she reached for the hem of his shirt and pulled its damp fabric from his chest, up and over his arms, and then over his head. Rubbing his warm naked skin every place her hands could find to touch, Chyna removed her shirt, and Dean's hands reached for the button on her pants.

He tugged them downward, leaving her in her bra and underwear. He backed her to the sofa, Chyna sat down and Dean quickly removed his shoes, and his own pants. He didn't want to wait another second and removed his underwear too before rejoining her back on the sofa.

"I guess we should do this in a bed."

"No." Chyna shook her head. "I only have so much forgiveness left and I won't forgive you for another interruption."

Dean nodded, without uttering another word. He

searched quickly in the back pocket of his discarded pants for a condom and rolled it onto his jutted length.

Chyna made quick work of her underwear. Kicking it aside, she held Dean to her and he moved to join them together in slow and torturous thrusts.

Looking at her, Dean took her face between his hands, reacquainting himself with every one of her features. He kissed her eyes, her nose, and finally her lips. "I missed you so much." For a moment he just stared at her, remembering the fear and the jealousy that took a stranglehold of him from thoughts that she'd gone back to her other life: a life without him. "I love you and only you," he whispered in her ear as he withdrew and entered her again.

"Do you trust me, Dean? I mean really trust me, that I'm here with you, that Gary, that status, that power isn't important. That those things I never wanted. All I wanted was to be loved and to have a family that loved me," Chyna said.

"That's all I want. But if we don't have that, we have nothing," she added, taking his face in her hands.

"We have everything, I have everything I ever need, right here, with you. I trust you, Chyna, with everything." Dean shifted, and his hand reached down, pushing her breasts higher to meet his mouth. His lips found her nipple through the cottony fabric of her bra, his tongue flicked over their hard, rosy peaks before he reached to undo the front clasps and remove the garment entirely. He bent his head again, opening his mouth over one to suckle it. He moved his head to lathe the other with his tongue again and again.

Chyna was lost in a lovely haze that Dean Jameson created. She felt his body, the very length of him pushing, pulsing into her, and still it didn't seem like enough. She wanted all that he had to offer, to give. Before she could request that he go deeper, move faster, he told her what he needed with one single word.

"Lift," Dean whispered and Chyna raised her legs higher on his back. She crossed her legs one on top of the other to hold him tight. He plunged deeper into her heat and she gasped.

Her body was on fire and she reached to wrap her arms around him, to stroke his back, to knead the taut muscles of his shoulders as he stroked himself inside her.

Dean knew everything there was to know about her tendencies when making love and he wanted to bring each and every sound she made from her lips. He knew she didn't say much at all, but he knew that when she panted she was close to the edge. He marveled in remembering how tightly she closed around him, how he always went very slow until she moaned aloud, and only then was that his signal to work it faster, more powerfully. He did it now, frenzied with want, holding her close, flicking his tongue over her earlobe, her neck, until the blood rushed through his body and his heart pounded. His love for her was so intense that it scared him for the first time. He had given Chyna Lockhart a piece of himself, a piece he couldn't get back.

She whimpered and he looked at her. "I'm sorry," he said, easing the force of his thrusts. "Too rough?" he asked.

"No, oh God, no," she breathed, shaking her head to assure him it was anything but that. "I'm just . . ." She shook her head, and he nodded. She knew he knew. Tears filled her eyes, and she loved being loved by him. Her flesh was burning, his flesh warming her from the inside out, and her stomach coiling so tight until it burst and she cried out Dean's name over and over. "Oh," Chyna said, her breath coming in fast gulps. She bit her lip and Dean kissed it.

Her legs continued to hold him tight until moments later he let go. She felt him, the tightening and easing of his manhood.

Dean continued exiting and entering until the downward spiral was complete. God, he loved her, desired her, wanted her as his forever.

"Chyna," he whispered in her ear.

"Dean," Chyna said, wiping with her hand the fine sheen of sweat that beaded across his forehead. "I love you, oh, I love you so much. You had to know. I know you know."

"I do," Dean said as he pulled one last contraction from her body. He bent down and kissed her lower lip. For moments, their tongues mated like their bodies had just done.

When he was able, he moved back only slightly to lie against the sofa, bringing Chyna directly on top of him, kissing her lips, and holding her tightly to him.

"I'll just never tire of hearing you say it. I love you too. We can get married now that all that's out of the way."

"Are you . . . are we?"

"If you'll have me?" Dean asked.

"Yes, yes."

"Chyna?" Dean said, looking down at her. He had one last question.

"Hmm?"

"Did my brother ever tell you to come see him if things didn't work out between us?"

Chyna lifted her head and looked at him. "Your brother would never say anything of the sort. Why on earth would you ask that? Everybody knew I loved only you. Except you," she reminded him.

Dean shook his head, smiling. "Just checking." He kissed her on the top of her head, thinking he didn't want to have to go to jail for murder.

Chapter 21

"You know what, they will probably be married by the time you get your act together," Lisa said. "While I'm telling you all that's been happening since you been in God knows where. I hate dealing with your father. I'm sick and tired of dealing with him every time you decide to go on vacation."

"Is that what my father told you?"

"Yes, that's what he told me!"

Warren shook his head in denial.

"Well, where the heck have you been?" Lisa threw up her hands in exasperation. "And what the heck is wrong with your face?"

Warren looked up in confusion.

"Your face, you're breaking out or something."

Warren swiveled in his chair. Opening the side drawer to his desk, he removed a small mirror. Holding it closer to his face, he scrutinized the tiny bumps. "The medication."

"What?"

"Nothing," he said. "I'm having an allergic reaction to something I ate."

"Well, find out whatever it is, so you can stop eating it! You look psycho."

"Don't call me that."

"I wasn't calling you that, I said you looked—" Lisa

ducked when the mirror Warren had been holding smashed behind her head.

"I said don't call me that!"

She stood slowly. Horrified, she watched him as she backed away. The glass cracking under her feet almost made her lose her balance, but she remained upright until she reached the door and disappeared through it.

"I'm not psycho," he said to the empty room. He pulled open another drawer where he had a folder containing more than a hundred pictures of Chyna. Only he couldn't seem to get a shot of her alone. She was always with someone. In California it was him, and now this guy, his father's nemesis's youngest son. Why wouldn't she ever love him?

Warren gripped the picture tightly in his hand, searched through another drawer until he found a pair of scissors. Ensuring that her perfect face remained unscathed, he carefully cut out the man beside her.

It seemed when Chyna awoke, it was in a foreign place. She sat up in the bed, a bed she'd never seen before. White and lace enveloped her like a cloud and, somewhat frightened, somewhat delighted, she cleared the sleepy grogginess from her voice to yell for Dean.

Dean turned on the coffeemaker he'd recently added the grinds to and, hearing Chyna's voice, moved quickly up the stairs and entered the bedroom. "What's the matter?" he said when he came before the bed.

"This bed, this, this . . ." She finally got out of the bed to look around the new room. The curtains hid the new window, and she peeked through it, recognizing what looked like her needing-a-serious-mowing backyard. She turned back around to Dean and looked to the side, seeing the oak side tables, and when it seemed to overwhelm her she sat in the new sitting area. It was like nothing she'd ever seen.

Dean was before her, kneeling. "You don't like it, we'll change it. I have no sense of color, but I tried to look at books and stuff—" He stopped talking when she put two of her fingers across his lips.

"You did this?"

Dean nodded. "After Bubba built it back, you needed a bed, and I just—"

"It's the most beautiful thing I've ever seen. I can't believe you did this. This room, it was nothing but a shell, a raggedy rug, a scratched-up dresser, the bed . . ." She couldn't remember if the bed was worth anything, but its brass replacement definitely wasn't what she had before. She looked up, noticing the fresh paint, the blue like the sky. The entire place seemed so much different than what she knew was there before the disaster had happened. She had plans for making it better, for tackling the renovation, but nothing could compare to this.

"I want to give you everything, Chyna," Dean said, breaking into her thoughts. "Make this place something you like, you might even love, if you don't get a headache from my mismatching color schemes." He smiled and Chyna laughed. "Just because there was this unhappy time here doesn't mean you can't try to change a few things, some coats of paint. You can remove the old memories and create newer, happier memories. But if you want to move, we'll find a new house and we'll start over."

He was so right, Chyna thought.

Chyna blinked her eyes to remove the tears. He would make her so happy. "Are we gonna make it?" she asked when he picked her up in his arms and carried her back to the bed.

"We will. I promise you," Dean said.

Chyna wanted to believe him and a part of her did,

but danger lurked in their future. She didn't know the first thing about the kind of tactics those who wished Dean's demise would use to get to him. She didn't know what Warren was capable of or how deep his so-called feelings for her ran.

"Hey you?"

Chyna lifted her head to look up at Dean. She studied his brooding features, his dark concerned eyes.

"Where were you?" he asked.

Chyna hated to ruin the moment, but the thoughts of the Hardigs entered her mind when she thought of her and Dean's ability to move on with their lives. "Just thinking that we gotta talk about what we can do to—"

"Not now we don't."

"Dean, please." Chyna couldn't help laughing out loud when Dean tickled her ribs with hot kisses.

He reversed their positions. Looking down at her, he grew serious. "I promise to listen to you, but later. I want you to know that everything is going to be all right. Your ex-husband, Warren Hardig, Lisa Stephens—they won't touch a hair on your pretty head ever again. That's my word, Chyna. You trust me?"

"Yes."

"You love me?"

"Yes."

"Then show me right now," Dean requested and for most of that morning she did.

Chyna Lockhart was in love and right then, nothing else seemed to matter. She'd been thoroughly made love to for the better part of the morning and to her delight one more surprise lay beyond the new doors that allowed her to exit her luxurious master suite.

The fragrant scent of burning candles wafted through the confines of her new bathroom. She wouldn't believe it if she weren't about to experience the ultimate bathing experience. Her bathroom was almost as big as her bedroom. Bubba had knocked out walls to enlarge the space and Dean, she sighed as she swung one leg and then the next over the tub, had purchased and paid for the installation of her brand new pedestal bathtub.

When the soothing water raised over her calves she slowly descended into the frothy bubbles and the relaxing heat massaged her muscles. Her tired and taut limbs were just now getting a bit of a reprieve from her and Dean's exercises. Chyna smiled with remembrance. When it came to the department of making love, that area of their lives never needed assistance. They had voracious appetites for each other, and now that Chyna knew all secrets were out—her past almost behind her—she and Dean could get to living their lives, together. With the flick of the plastic curtain, Chyna drifted to an island of tepid blue water and warm brown sand.

Thinking about her refurbished master suite, the room downstairs and all its newness, she didn't think she could stand any more surprises. But this one, she gladly accepted. She planned to show Dean again and again just how thankful she was. To top that off, he was making a trip to the store to get food to fill her belly.

"Yep." Chyna lifted her arms to lather them with her favorite lavender scented bar, then reached to turn off the running water and all was quiet. "Dean Jameson will be my husband," she whispered to the air, believing that this time nothing would keep them apart and that she loved him with all of her heart. "Love you, love you, love you," she sang and snorted aloud at the silly rendition of her made-up song.

"Do you really?" Warren said as he pulled back the curtain to the tub.

In horror, Chyna crossed her arms over her chest as the stifling height of Warren Hardig loomed over her.

"What the hell are you doing here?" she said, thinking that he was much crazier than she ever could have imagined. "I suggest you leave right this minute. Dean will be back any moment!"

"Really? I just saw him skipping down the aisle of the local grocery store. You tell him about us?"

"There is no us. Does he know you crawled into the bed of your supposed friend's wife? Then yes, I told him, blamed it on your state of drunkenness, but I'm beginning to wonder if that's what it was. If you're not just some wacko with a little too much time on his hands."

"It's not nice to call people names, Chyna. I'd have thought better of you."

When Chyna heard the door close downstairs, she snatched the curtain from the metal rod around the tub, using it to quickly wrap herself. "Dean!" she yelled, attempting to leap from the tub. Before she could get to the door, Warren grabbed at the makeshift cover. She managed to get almost to the door when his hands pulled her leg and groped her wherever he could touch. Chyna screamed more to get Dean's attention downstairs than from any pain he may have caused her, and when he flipped her on her back she managed to shove her knee into Warren's groin. She slid away, crawling as fast as she could, yelling the entire time and wondering why Dean hadn't heard her.

"Go downstairs."

"Dean." Chyna looked up to see Dean standing in the doorway. She knew he'd kill Warren, judging by the look in his eyes. It was a look so deadly it made her scared.

"Do it now, Chyna," he repeated. He practically picked her up off the floor with one hand and shoved her toward the stairs without ever taking his eyes off Warren.

"Hey, man!" Warren said as he stood up, brushing off his suit as if he'd just been planting roses in a flower garden.

"You got a death wish?" Dean asked him coldly.

"No way, Chyna invited me over—" Before he could finish his statement, Dean had bent and kicked Warren's legs out from under him.

Dean stood to his full height. As Warren got back up, Dean used his fist to knock him down again. When another retort came from Warren's mouth, Dean rested his weight on the center of Warren's chest, pinning him to the floor. "You underestimate me, Mr. Hardig. You look at her again, I'll kill you, you invade her privacy again, I'll kill you slowly. You get it through your head that Chyna Lockhart is my woman, not yours, not Williams's. You stop coming in here trying to ruffle my feathers playing your little punk games. Find another pastime, one that doesn't have anything to do with the Lockharts or the Jamesons."

Dean couldn't see much anything except his own rage, his own anger that placed his thumb across Warren's windpipe and pressed down. The loss of oxygen left the man gasping, practically wiggling with his last breath. Dean did, however, feel Chyna's hands on his back, and her pleading penetrated his ears.

"Dean," she said. She'd rushed on a pair of pants and a shirt. Once downstairs, she paced for two seconds and called the police on the third. It was not for Warren but for Dean. She knew Dean could hurt Warren for what he'd done, but she wouldn't let him go to jail for murder no matter how much she agreed Warren deserved to die. She wouldn't lose Dean over anyone, but especially not Warren Hardig. "Dean, honey, please, please, he's not worth it, stop this,"

Dean heard her, and was up. Keeping his hold on Warren, he loosened his grip slightly as he dragged Warren down the steps and out the door. The sirens seemed to come immediately, growing louder and louder as they got closer. Finally a state car pulled into Chyna's driveway and without waiting for the officer to ask any questions, Dean had the door open with one hand. Keeping a hold on Warren with the other, he shoved him into the car and shut the door.

When Dean could see straight and was calm enough to talk, he took over from Chyna, telling the officers the more heated version of what happened. "You get him out of here, you tell me what I need to do for a restraining order."

"Yes, Mr. Jameson," the man said, taking down all the orders. "You might have to come to the station to sign the charge, Ms. Lockhart."

"Fine, fine, whatever you need," Chyna said, her focus on Dean and his state of mind, not to mention his torn shirt. He contracted his hands into tight balls of fists and then released them again and again in quick succession. She didn't register what the officer said, but whatever it was it must have had the word *good-bye* on the end, because he got into his car and sped away.

Chapter 22

Inside, it seemed as if time had stopped. Neither of them said or did anything for a few moments. Dean robotically emptied the bags of food he'd bought, putting things away in the fridge, and moved back again for the things that went into the cupboards. She watched him move stoically.

"Dean." Chyna felt compelled to break the silence when she noticed that he put the milk in the cupboard and a box of cereal into the fridge. "Dean," Chyna repeated, this time more forcefully.

Dean looked up. Taking a moment to gather his thoughts, he brought Chyna roughly into his arms. "Are you all right?" he said and kissed her cheek. Chyna nodded.

"Are you sure?"

Chyna nodded again. "Dean, sit down."

Without protest, Dean took a seat at the small kitchen table.

"I'm fine, okay? I'm all right."

"And if I hadn't come? Who knows what the hell would've happened? He's got problems, Chyna. Serious, like mental, you know. He thinks he can go wherever he pleases, do whatever he wants. He's got to be crazy."

"I know, I know, but I'm all right. I am," she reassured him when he looked at her.

"You hungry?" she asked and moved to find the milk

he put in the cabinet. After that she retrieved a sauté pan and eggs.

"I think I could scramble these without getting shells in them," she said, trying to lighten the mood, knowing that would be awfully hard, considering all that they had to contend with.

"No, I'll make them." Dean smiled and stood to wash his hands. After drying them on a paper towel, he didn't reach for the eggs; instead he turned to Chyna and said, "I want you to leave town."

"What?" Chyna looked up to see the concern evident on Dean's face. She softened, knowing his good intention, but wasn't comforted by it.

"I only want you to go away for a week or so." A week was the minimum but he wouldn't tell her that. Not now anyway. Taking a deep breath, he said, "Warren is after you, Lisa wants your head on a platter."

"And you?"

"She wants me, but she'd never hurt me. Warren, I can handle him."

"And I can handle Lisa."

"Can you handle Warren, Chyna? This isn't a game, this is serious. You got a woman after you, and an obsessed man who almost . . ." Dean didn't want to think about what almost happened. "I know them," he said. "If they think you're still here, in town, they'll continue to try to get to you any way they can. They'll use you to get to me. He may have no intention of harming you, but sometimes things never work out like they should and someone gets hurt. Lisa's obviously a lot more involved than we thought.

"If this is a joke"—not that Dean believed it was—"then you come back after a few days. The person closest to me, and not just in proximity but in this whole mess, is you. You are a pawn."

"So remove the pawn from the board, it's still there,

you know, your opponent just can't see it is all, doesn't solve anything," Chyna said, flopping onto the sofa.

"But it does." Dean took a seat on the sofa at the end by Chyna's feet. "When you can't see something, when it's removed to an undisclosed location, that eliminates the potential and likelihood that it will be harmed."

Taking one of Chyna's feet into his hands, he massaged her heel in a circular motion. "Tish will be happy to see you and I'll fly up this weekend."

Still no response. Dean continued. "I'm only asking for a few days to see what that presents. If nothing happens, then you come back." When Chyna placed her other foot in Dean's lap, he smiled.

Scrunching up the pillow underneath her head, she looked at him through lowered lashes and pushed the hair from her face. "What do you think is going to happen? What if something happens to you? What are you planning? You're planning something, I can tell it!"

"Whatever happens, I don't want you near it . . . for it to happen to the both of us, just me is better . . ."

"Don't say that." Chyna sat up straight in alarm. "Don't even think like that, and if that's the way you feel, I'm not leaving, I'm staying right here . . . You can't just say that and expect me to say, oh, gee, yes, that's a brilliant idea, Dean!"

Dean turned his body to the side so that he was able to face Chyna. Bringing an arm around her, he lifted her closer and whispered as if he had a secret to tell her, "I love you, please just trust me."

"I do, you know I do . . ." Chyna said, rising up to straddle Dean's legs.

"Then know that I'm only thinking of you, that I only always think of you."

Slumping, Chyna placed her head on Dean's chest. She was thoughtful a moment, hating all the while that Dean was so right even if the whole thing was stupid.

When Dean's cell phone rang, he moved to retrieve it from the small coffee table and pressed the button. "Yeah." He smiled. "She's right here."

Chyna was suspicious, but still she took the phone from Dean's hand, placing it against her ear. "Hello," Chyna said and that single greeting launched her into a long discussion with Dean's youngest sister about her upcoming visit.

Chapter 23

Dean had called his sister while in the grocery store and had been thinking about an out-of-town trip even before the last battle with Warren.

Chyna had been duped and was none too happy about it. But there she sat at Ronald Reagan International Airport, among a bustling crowd of people all going someplace, all supposed to be someplace already. Chyna was ready to back out of everything she'd originally said, everything she'd agreed to.

She felt nervous, jittery, carrying a bag, only one, she had insisted, which to her meant not packing enough to warrant a long stay, which also meant Dean's constant protest the entire time.

The whole scheme seemed fishier by the moment. A flight just ready to take her to Atlanta had just one seat left later that same day. Not tomorrow, or next week, but right then. While Chyna had packed, Dean had conveniently made all the arrangements for her departure. And the conversation with Tish. What would Chyna possibly say without making it seem as if she didn't want to see her dearest friend, who also didn't know much of anything about all that was going on in Virginia? How could she, Chyna wondered, go play pretend in Macon, Georgia, while Dean got into whatever he was planning for Warren Hardig? He was planning something, of that she was certain.

With love and just an ounce of hate, Chyna looked at Dean, who sat quietly reading a paper next to her. "Are you sure you want me to go?" she asked sadly.

Without looking at her, Dean stared across the room blankly as he closed the paper he read. "No," he said slowly.

Chyna almost jumped for joy until Dean looked at her fully and said, "I'm sure you must go, however, and I'm sure I want your safety."

Crossing her arms over her chest, Chyna looked away and harrumphed. When her flight was called she sat completely still and watched as Dean stood folding the paper and placing it on the chair next to him where he'd found it.

Taking her hand, he led her to wait away from the gathering line where a crowd of people filed in to begin the slow and tedious process of getting their tickets fed through the machine.

Bringing her closer into his arms, Dean didn't seem to care about the onlookers staring at their public display of affection. "Don't forget to water Ms. Alfreah's plants," Chyna said as he brought his arms snugly around her waist.

Dean nodded. "I'm coming to see you, this weekend, I promise."

"Until then, will you call me?"

"Every night before you go to sleep."

When the line dwindled, Dean looked toward it and when Chyna's eyes also wandered toward the line, he brought her face back around to meet his and kissed Chyna lovingly, pouring the depth of his feelings into the meshing of their lips. It seemed so intense, and it was so fiery, it rocked her to her toes and lifted her spirit, leaving no doubt in her mind that he had anything other than love and caring for her well-being, and her safety.

"I'm only staying a few days."

"A few days? Five."

"Three."

"Four. We'll play it by ear. And something else."

Chyna sighed in exasperation. "You've reached your request limit."

"I love you like I have never loved anyone."

Chyna gasped, surprised by his honesty, those sentiments. She didn't know what she could say and knew that anything she did offer to his statement would sound insignificant and small compared to that.

"I loved you first," she said, smiling that she'd upped him one with the truth.

Turning to leave, Chyna and Dean held hands until she passed the gate and reluctantly let go only at the very last moment.

Dean waved one last time until he could no longer see Chyna. He knew she would be safe and truly believed she could only be safe far removed from the entire situation, while he, Jojo, and a longtime trusted friend of the feds prepared to do battle with a bunch of crooked business tycoons and one corrupt governmental officiator.

Dean turned on his heel after seeing the huge white plane tramp down the runway and soar into the cloudy skies. For some reason he still only felt slightly optimistic. He couldn't place the reason and chalked it up to nerves and not knowing what dealing with Warren Hardig would involve or what kinds of secrets and lies lay wrapped up in his father's finances, in his building's charred rubble, and if Warren really had designs on Chyna or was just using her to get at him. So many questions, questions he didn't necessarily want answers to, but questions that kept him from moving on with his life, kept Chyna, his future bride, in danger.

Dean knew that the woman he loved and cared about more than anything was safe and sound but what he didn't realize was that he wasn't as safe, not when a man in dark clothing emerged and followed him out of the airport.

Tish Jameson-Alton made her way to the door with just a twinge of apprehension in her gut. When the door opened and her friend walked in with a huge smile on her face, some of that tension left immediately. "Hi," she said and returned her friend's smile with one of her own.

"Hey," Chyna replied. "You have a sweet husband. He chatted the whole way here with endless stories about you and Thomas. I'm so glad you're so happy."

"He's had that effect on me, yes. He gives me everything I want and if he doesn't, my little boy does," Tish said, smiling as her husband, Chase, walked in. He bent to kiss her cheek, before turning to Chyna. "I'll put your bag in the guest room. It's upstairs and to the right." Chase nodded and disappeared. In a matter of moments, he'd returned and said, "Would you like something to drink, Chyna?"

"Well, got anything with lots of caffeine? But . . . you gotta promise not to tell Dean. I'm on Dean's caffeine-free regimen, but just one little splurge?" Chyna laughed at the raised eyebrow and puzzled face Chase made as he turned to look at his wife.

"I think that can be arranged. We won't tell, will we; honey?" Tish said.

"If you asked me to keep it from Jojo, I would've said no way," Chase said seriously.

Chyna looked back and forth between the two of them, not understanding what Chase had meant.

Tish hugged her friend and stood back. "Chase is scared of Jojo," she said.

Both of the women laughed, and Chase's face remained serious as if there was nothing at all funny about the issue before he disappeared into the kitchen.

"And thank you so much, and, you guys, I could've gotten a cab from the airport, you know. . . ."

"I didn't mind," Chase said from the hall.

"Nonsense," Tish amended. "Come into the den, we'll talk." She turned from her friend and led her to the end of the hallway.

"This is a beautiful home," Chyna commented as she followed distantly behind Tish, taking time to look at the pictures on the wall, the structural ornaments, and other things that piqued her interest, realizing for the first time how design-conscious she'd become since renovating both her and the Jamesons' home.

"Thank you," Tish said. Upon entering the den she flipped one of the many switches on the wall panel. One of the many lights that blinked on bathed the room in a soft glow.

Chyna took a seat feeling completely relaxed and happy but in the back of her mind yielded to a sense of impending danger she'd have to manage to keep from Tish and Ms. Alfreah—which, now that she had arrived, seeing Tish face-to-face, she no longer believed she could do. The resistance to caffeine she'd managed to turn down on the plane had snapped as soon as she landed safely. But thoughts of Dean returned and maintaining a calm front for his pregnant sister would only work with the help of a jittery, calming cup of Joe.

Determined to maintain the farce, she concentrated on the decor Chase and Tish had chosen for their home. She looked around the place, noticing some of the intricate patterns. Patterns she and Dean could implement their own spin-offs of, giving them a uniqueness they'd had the ability to create on their own and that already existed around the Jamesons' home.

Taking a deep breath, Chyna sat down on the couch opposite Tish. After her eyes wandered one final time around the glorious room, she placed a hand under her chin. When her eyes landed on Tish's, she recognized the look of sadness and Chyna's joy dashed immediately. "Hey, what's the matter?" Chyna asked alarmingly, and sat up straighter in her chair and placed her hands together in her lap.

"Are you happy, Chyna?" Tish asked. Subconsciously, Tish placed a hand over her stomach. "I just feel so bad about, you know . . . I'm so glad you're here, but I want you to be all right with this. I worried about it . . . that when Dean said you were coming, or suggested that you come, I wondered if he knew how you would handle that, how you would feel about . . . but men are so clueless sometimes. I didn't want you to say you were all right, just to pacify him, and me, and to avoid the both of us being worried about you. Are you okay with . . . with this?"

Chyna waved a hand dismissively. "I wouldn't have come if I wasn't going to be okay. More importantly, I would never come and bring such negative energy to your home and most importantly to those unborn babies. I think . . . I think I am . . . fine." *But Dean's in trouble and he's taking on this man that hates his guts because of me and he might get hurt!* Chyna took a deep breath, closed her eyes and her ears to the thoughts that wanted out of her head, but managed to keep them inside. She couldn't bring Tish any worry or distress. It was unhealthy for her and her babies.

She nodded back at Tish as if to bring her mind back to what they were discussing. "I am," she said again, "I'm so spectacularly fine. I probably couldn't, well, I know I wouldn't have said that a couple of months ago, but I'm so happy for you . . . much too happy to focus on my own loss; that would be utterly selfish," she acknowledged again. Despite the short talk that she and Dean had about her feelings, the jealousy would be considered human, not at all selfish. She was a selfless person. "And I won't do that. You said that I should tell him, tell Dean.

When I did, it started everything all over again. But I did feel as if something had lifted from my chest, my heart. It didn't happen right away but it did happen . . . eventually, and even after we talked, there was still some tension but I'm sorry I kept it from him at all. I'm sorry I placed you in such a terrible position. He knows, you know."

Tish shook her head in denial. "Yes, he was upset, not very happy that I knew, but I'm his baby sister." She smiled. "The fight seemed to zap out of Dean when we talked. He only wanted to know you, Chyna, understand why you left. That hurt him."

Chyna nodded, feeling sorry she'd done what she had.

"But that's over now." Tish waved her hand, not wanting to make her friend feel guilty. "Speaking of Chase, though, you really have him to thank for my insisting you tell Dean the truth. See, we talked, or I asked Chase if I had lost the babies would he have wanted to know? Hypothetically, I mean . . . if I'd lost them before we got married. He said that it would kill him not to know, because loving someone, no matter how painful whatever's going on, it's the not sharing that's selfish. I think he's right as far as I can analyze this without having dealt with it personally. That's the part that hurts—not that going through it alone wasn't difficult too. But Dean, he's always been so sensitive when it comes to that stuff."

"I know, and we're all right, we are," Chyna confirmed and repeated in her mind, even when his sending her away left her feeling somewhat slighted, though she knew it was meant only to protect her. "Someday, I hope that we'll have our own children. He means everything to me." *And I don't want him to get himself hurt!* the tiny tell-it-all voice shouted in Chyna's head.

Tish slowly exhaled a loud sigh of relief, then smiling

more genuinely, she said, "I'm so glad," and took a deep calming breath. "I'm so happy for you guys."

"And my ring, I didn't show you. . . ." Chyna pulled out her buried hand and waved it before Tish's eyes.

"Well, keep still, would ya? Let me get a look without getting cross-eyed."

Chyna was immediately up on her feet. "Oh, I'm sorry," she said, moving to stand and close the few feet between them. "Sit down."

"This is our great-grandmother's ring. Oh, it looks so new, but it still has the antique finish."

"Yes, he told me he had it reset and cleaned. I used to see it in your mom's jewelry box. I used to wish he'd put it on me," Chyna said.

"You got your dream," Tish said in wonderment.

"I did," Chyna replied, looking up toward the ceiling, her eyes glazed with happiness and blurred by tears. "I got it. Do you think it's silly, my dream, I mean?" she said, looking at her best friend.

"I think it's silly, your wanting my big dumb brother," Tish replied jovially. When they laughed, Tish sobered and said, "But seriously, I . . . Without dreams, Chyna, we have nothing to attain, nothing to desire, and then we have nothing to pursue. What have we, what are we, if not beings floating blindly along, existing in a space, with no drive, or determination, or aspirations? So, no, I don't find it silly. You're strong, you're so strong, and you've held on to fight for what you wanted, with every possible adversity. It's easy to give up, it's easy to let go, but it takes someone real to hold on and fight."

"Thank you so much, T.T.!" Chyna said, calling her friend by her childhood nickname. She then blinked rapidly to remove her tears and laughed at Tish's startled expression. "So! What are you going to call these beautiful babies?"

Just as Tish was about to tell Chyna about the plans for the twins' names, her mother walked in.

"Hello," Alfreah said, moving slowly into the room.

"Oh, Mrs. J. How are you?" Chyna stood and walked to the woman that had taken her in as if Chyna were one of her own.

The two women embraced each other, holding hands until they moved to sit down together on the sofa.

"I'm doing quite well now that my third daughter and my silly son are acting like they have some sense," Alfreah said matter-of-factly, wasting no time in cutting to the subject on the tip of everyone's tongue.

"Be nice now, Mama," Chyna heard Tish warn, then looked back at Alfreah, waiting with bated breath.

Alfreah merely smiled, looked over at her daughter, and said, "Did I call your number?" Seconds passed, silence swelled, and Chyna bit her tongue to keep from laughing when finally all the women in the room laughed heartily.

Chapter 24

"Good night, you guys," Chyna said to Tish, who tiredly moved slowly up the stairs, her husband leading her, or rather shooing her from the kitchen and up the stairs to bed. "He's so protective of her, it's so wonderful." Chyna turned once Tish and Chase had left and regarded Alfreah.

"Yes, he's a good match for her."

"How are you, Ms. Alfreah, since . . . uh . . ." Chyna struggled for the words.

"Since Joe died?" Alfreah finished, and continued when Chyna nodded her head. "I'm all right. . . ." Taking a deep breath, Alfreah shook her head. "I'm all right," she said again. "How's everything in Virginia?"

Chyna bit her lip, wondering just how much she should relay and if Dean had planned to tell his mother anything. "Things are good, the house is looking very beautiful, and you should see the work Dean's done. We've referred to the idea journal you left full of ideas. We've implemented a lot of them. You had a wonderful vision for the place. I hope you like it," she said enthusiastically. But from the way Alfreah looked away, Chyna could tell she was disinterested to hear more about the changes to the house.

Alfreah nodded and looked at her hands. She bothered the wedding ring on her left hand, and twisted it around her finger before saying, "I'm sure it looks nice." She stood abruptly. "I'm going to go to bed now."

Chyna touched the older woman's shoulder. "It will get easier, it just takes time."

"I know, sweetie pie," Alfreah said, patting Chyna's shoulder and turning to leave.

Chyna knew then that it wasn't the time to let her know about the finances, the Hardigs. Dean would handle it, and when she got back to Virginia, she'd help him clear up the rest. Here right now, however, she remained, looking at the kitchen's dirty dishes, and for lack of something to do she wiped down the counters, cleaned off the table, loaded the dishwasher, and headed up to bed.

Chyna hated to admit that all the activity didn't keep her mind off Dean, especially at night. Tish and Alfreah had visitor after visitor from the school and the local church, and Thomas had friends over and they blasted music and pretended they were up-and-coming rappers.

To her surprise Chyna had enjoyed readying the baby room for the arrival of the twins. Per Tish's request, she painted just a few little flowers and butterflies around light switches, and in a faint border pattern around the wall, little girly things since they already knew the twins' sexes. It was the first time she's painted anything since her first miscarriage.

Chyna also spent time playing with Thomas, who had a dose of endless energy. But when it was time for bed, Chyna tossed and turned, waking up only with thoughts of Dean.

He'd called her back hours later after something had happened, something she still hadn't gotten to the bottom of, but something she knew Dean was keeping from her. He said there'd been problems with his car, but hadn't elaborated beyond that. Chyna hated how much harder it was not seeing him face-to-face to accuse him of lying. He'd only deny it, and what good could it do to accuse him otherwise?

"Ahh." Chyna pounded the sheets in frustration. She'd planned to return home after just a few days, but a week had passed and she'd already called to see if she could find a flight to Virginia, or anything even remotely connecting her to Virginia from Atlanta Hartsfield International, but the days she'd checked, they were all booked up. If something didn't give, she'd just as well take the red-eye, which was an idea she was heavily considering.

Turning on her back, Chyna looked at the clock to see it was almost one o'clock in the morning. She didn't realize that she'd dozed off until voices from the downstairs woke her abruptly.

She wondered who'd be stopping by at that hour but then not enough of her interest was piqued to actually get up and investigate when the voices quieted.

With her back to the door, Chyna closed her eyes and proceeded to count sheep. Familiar scents and someone opening the door to her room rendered her wide-awake again, however, and she sat up abruptly.

"Dean?" she said when his body filled the doorway.

"You were expecting the tooth fairy?"

"Oh, Dean," Chyna said, jumping up from the bed to rush into Dean's arms.

Dean released the sport bag he carried, dropping it to the floor, and pulled Chyna into his arms.

He kissed her soundly and backed her up to the bed where they both fell upon it.

"Why couldn't you come up yesterday?" Chyna asked, moving more fully onto the bed and pulling Dean with her. She removed his shirt and flung it across the room.

Fixing the covers, she pushed them to the end of the bed until Dean removed his shoes and pants and climbed in with her, pulling the covers over the both of them.

"I told you . . . I got tied up."

Chyna nodded. "Any news?"

Dean merely shook his head.

She was ecstatic that he was there, but something was on his mind, that she was sure of. "I know there's been at least one development, Dean, so spill it! Is Warren out of jail?"

"Man, I missed you, and this mouth." He kissed her lips and smiled satisfactorily when she kissed him back. "I missed that the most. You want to help me here?" Dean said, running his hands up and down the sheer gown, trying to find a place that would give him access to her flesh.

Leaning back from kissing him, Chyna stilled his way-ward hands. "You have to answer my question first, and besides, we're a guest here, we can't."

"Oh, please, they're way down the hall," Dean said in-credulously.

"Dean?"

"Did you miss me?" he said, kissing her lips again.

"Yes," Chyna said, turning back on her side away from Dean.

Taking a deep breath, Dean knew he'd have to tell her what was going on but he didn't want her to worry and he didn't want her back in Virginia. Taking a moment to study her face, he said, "Someone wrecked my car." Then silence for a moment as he waited patiently for the outburst.

"What!" Chyna turned around to face him again and sat up in the bed.

"The car, someone smashed it up, Lisa probably . . . Gonna cost an arm and two damn legs to fix it. They have it at the shop, but it's being investigated for prints, whatever else they could find." Shaking his head, Dean went on. "My beautiful car, I loved that car," he said dreamily. "Oh well, maybe I can get me a truck. What do you think? Chevrolet or . . . get me an SUV, four-by-four, a man's truck, I should ask Chase about his Navigator—"

"You! Would you stop it, please? You are telling me . . . asking me about my preferences for a damn truck, are you all right?" Chyna asked, running her hands over Dean's chest, then lightly touching his brow. "Don't you see why I should be in Virginia? And stop going on about some stupid truck! You want to rewind to the part about someone smashing up your car? What happened?"

"Shh, I wasn't in it, I was seeing J and Anthony in D.C. I parked the car and took the metro. And you're getting all in a huff. You know I don't want Tish or Mama to be worried, so keep your voice down. I'm handling it."

"Dean," Chyna whispered this time, "tell me this: when you booked your flight home, did you get two tickets?" she asked this even though she already knew the answer.

"No, I didn't, I got only one because you're still staying here, for just a few more days."

"The hell I am, Dean."

"Can you come here, with me, back to bed? I came a long ways and you're all in a huff. Didn't you miss me?"

"Of course I did, but I will miss you even more if something happens to you . . . do you understand?"

Dean nodded and Chyna settled down into the bed, just out of Dean's reach.

"Can we not talk, not right now?" he asked.

"Well, we can just sleep, because we're not going to do it!"

"Like they aren't doing it."

"Dean, shut up. That's your sister, for goodness' sake!"

"You're right, I feel nauseated."

Chyna laughed but sobered quickly when Dean's hand traveled past the elastic of her underwear.

"Dean, I'm warning you."

"Really?" Dean said, bending his head where he closed his lips over her nipple through the material of her shirt.

"Ah," Chyna gasped when she felt Dean's hot mouth tug at her breast.

"Shh, you're a guest!" Dean admonished her, as he combed his fingers through the tuft of hair at the juncture of Chyna's thighs. He smiled when she opened up to him and turned to face him.

"Dean?"

"Hmm?"

"You're a naughty boy!"

"Love you too," he said, kissing her lips. "I like this spot, here," he added, inserting his finger into the small orifice.

"Oh God, this . . . discussion . . . Dean . . . it isn't over, okay?"

"Okay, shh!" Dean said and watched her eyes light on him. He was instantly aware of her, her heat closing around his finger. He smiled at her when he inserted a second finger and swirled his thumb around her secret button in a circular motion.

Chyna grabbed his shoulders, burying her face in the crook of his neck when Dean exhibited that he knew exactly where and how to touch her. The very spots that drove her to the brink of insanity. "Oh, Dean, there, um . . ." she whispered and her teeth lightly nipped at his shoulder.

"Yep, you missed me." He laughed, and pulled her close, showing her just how much he had missed her.

The two days Dean came to visit went by unbelievably fast. The family caught up discussing the twins, Thomas's Little League game and Chyna and Dean's plans for nuptials. Already they'd eaten dinner and it was time for Dean to get ready to go back to Virginia. Little did he know that exactly five hours after he was there, Chyna's flight would depart for Virginia's Dulles-Washington Airport. She'd timed it perfectly, sneaking to find out his departure time from the ticket in his bag and then using Chase's downstairs computer to book her own flight.

"I got a little bit, you want to . . ." Dean said as he moved onto the bed to look over Chyna's shoulder. He was shocked to find a list of what looked like paint supplies as well as a flyer for the local paint store. "What are you doing?" he asked, raising a skeptical eyebrow.

"Tish asked me to paint some butterflies in the baby's room."

"And you agreed?"

Chyna smiled and nodded. She put down the piece of paper and the sales circular from a local arts and crafts store after highlighting in neon pink one last sale item she would get later that day. She turned to face Dean.

When his face continued to remain alarmed with raised eyebrows, she graced him with a long leisurely kiss. "I love you, Dean, and I thank you."

"For what?"

"For giving back to me something that I thought I'd hate forever, that I'd associated with tragedy when it brought me so much joy. When I get back home, I'll paint Ms. Alfreah's backsplash."

She'd known for a while that she would paint it. She wanted to do her part to complement the beautiful work Dean had already done to the house. She wanted to be sure of her skills so as not to mess it up.

"Since you're feeling so thankful, we've got a bit of time before I go." He smiled, lifting a corner of his mouth conspiratorially.

"Uh-uh," Chyna said, moving out of the reach of his greedy hands. "I wanted to tell you that I noticed how we had seemed to reconnect. Dean, look at me." When Dean looked back at her she continued. "I'm not the only one you pushed away. You pushed away your family by staying in Virginia by yourself, dealing with the loss while everyone moved away. I bet you didn't think I noticed, but I did. We worked on us and that was important, but now you need to work on you and your mom. Have you talked to her? I mean really talked to her? I know you think you're . . . you're cleaning up this mess with your father's finances, and you're dealing with what's going on with Warren, even though you won't tell me what that entails, but talk to your mom, okay? Don't just handle things and clean it all up, but include her. I know you don't want to bother her with this, but just give her a small dosage at a time.

"Also, Dean, I told her about the renovations that have been done to the house. I was surprised when she didn't seem all that impressed or excited. I don't know exactly what that means, but it can't be good." When Dean took on a serious worried look, Chyna reassured him. "I'm not sure, I just think if you're talking about things, you should see where she is about that, how she feels. Make sure she's all right with the changes. It's one thing to request some minor renovations, but quite another to return home and find things so vastly different. I don't know, just a hunch. She shared so much time in that house, with your dad, that things, little changes can seem so three-sixty, they can seem almost too different, foreign.

"I'll go, um, go help Tish clean up. I'll see ya." She kissed him and when she moved to leave the bed, she stood for a moment while Dean held on to her hand, preventing her from leaving. When she turned, he brought her hand to his lips, kissing each one of her fingers. "Looks like I'm the one who needs to thank you."

She nodded. "We've got the rest of our lives to thank each other." She nodded again, leaving the room and Dean, alone with his thoughts.

Chapter 25

Chyna was right; Dean knew that as he moved down the steps and into the den. It was much easier for him, if he really took the time to analyze it; it was easier just to smooth things over concerning his father's issues and present to his mother a nice neat package. It seemed that's what she did for them. That's what mothers did. Just cleaned it up for you, and he was glad to have the knowledge, the know-how to pay her back for all the years of her sacrifices, her care, her patching up the numerous boo-boos he and his siblings seemed to create as adolescents. But he did have questions. Questions that might shed light on some things and better help him to understand why it seemed the Hardigs had it out for just him or the Jamesons as a whole, and was there some history before he came along that was a precursor to what he and Chyna were going through at present?

In the den, he found his mother sitting alone in a far corner, her still frame outlined by the low lamplight. A book situated on her lap was closed and so were her eyes, Dean noticed as he moved closer. Her dainty reading glasses hung from the beaded chain around her neck to rest on her bosom.

Taking a seat on the floor like he used to do when he was a child, Dean looked up, tucking his knees under his chin and resting his arms across them. "Mama," he said, gently touching her knee.

Moving with a start, Alfreah looked out across the room and then down at her son.

She smiled. "Hi," she said groggily.

"How are you doing?" Dean asked, not quite sure how to broach the subject, then wishing his mother was in a cut-to-the-chase mode as she often was.

"I'm doing all right."

"Are you?" Dean wondered aloud.

"Well, I'm sorry I ran away from a mess," Alfreah said, quickly changing the subject.

"What mess?" Dean said, thinking his mother not only cut to the chase, she'd picked up telepathy. He looked up abruptly, however, ready to deny that anything was wrong, but even as quickly as she had switched subjects, he could tell she had indeed known something was going on at home in Virginia. "I didn't think that you knew . . . anything." Alfreah nodded. "I can handle it, Mama," Dean finished.

"You shouldn't've had to . . . I knew your father had bills, but he never told me about them. I guess I just turned a blind eye to them."

"That's just it, Mama. Everything is paid off. There aren't any outstanding debts. There's a larger problem, however, but none of it's on Dad's end."

"What?" Alfreah leaned forward and the book she'd been holding in her lap slid down. Before it reached the floor, Dean caught it and placed it on the side table next to where his mother sat.

"It's the Hardigs and Lisa Stephens," Dean said, unsure at this point what he should hold back and what he should reveal. "They've conspired to do us, our name, in."

"That property?"

Dean nodded and watched his mother close her eyes as if recalling something terrible.

She smiled for a moment and then her look saddened

and Dean waited patiently for her to relay a story he knew was coming.

"I had told your father that building was . . . I just couldn't see any use in it. We as black folks owning a three-story, nice brick building in a popular plaza strip seemed so unheard of in the sixties and seventies. But he roughed his hands building the place that would go to his youngest son. A man gave him that place, a Caucasian man that had too much money. He and your father, they were friends. And old Chauncey Hardig . . ." Alfreah stood and Dean was on his feet to help her. After standing a moment, Alfreah looked up at her son. "Hardig was a man who made his money, created his destiny or took it, wheeling and dealing, cheating people to build his empire. . . . Your father, the man I loved, was a kind man, and sometimes people just gave him things . . . like Elliot Poynter did with that new brick building. See, Chauncey Hardig always wanted what a Jameson had, that property . . ." She left off other parts about Hardig's want of her. "He had no regard for what wasn't his. I think that he's instilled that same drive and take-all attitude in his own son, honey." She felt saddened that Chauncey Hardig would hold something so long, but something inside her, the part that didn't want to go back to Virginia, knew that he would.

Shaking her head, Alfreah turned back to her son, focusing on the matters at hand. "The office? Do you think he burned it down?"

"I don't know about Warren, but Chauncey Hardig? Just to be mean? Just to kick me when I'm down? Dad had just died," Dean said, trying to fit all the pieces together. "Warren keeps sniffing around Chyna, that's why she's here."

Alfreah nodded, thinking, *Chauncey keeps sniffing around me now that your father's dead. That's why I'm here.* But she kept those thoughts to herself. "I know that you enjoyed your practice, honey, but I also know that in the last few years you lost your passion for it, your desire waned, and it's up to you but perhaps when things are cleared up, you should sell the property. Not"—she waved a hand—"not because it was what Chauncey wants but because it's no longer in you.

"I know in your heart you're over optometry. It's just hard when everyone tells you you're over it, and not wanting to admit it for yourself." Alfreah nodded knowingly. "You could do some consulting."

Dean nodded. He'd thought a million times about what he could do with his life, what he should do next. Consulting, yes, but teaching? Thoughts of teaching seemed to stir something in him.

"Teaching," his mother said as if reading his thoughts.

Dean nodded and looked up, feeling not one shred of surprise that his mother knew him so well, but more concerned about all that he had to absorb with what his mother had relayed about Chauncey Hardig. "You and Chauncey Hardig . . ." He left it open for her to fill.

"Before I met and married your father," Alfreah said adamantly.

Dean nodded, knowing even if there had been something then, his mother had loved his father no matter what the past had held. "Gotta move on with our lives."

"You'll fix it, sweetheart. If I thought you weren't capable of doing so I would have stayed and I appreciate you and your brother. You'll handle it. But optometry, let it go, baby."

Dean nodded and smiled.

"I'm glad to see Chyna so happy," she said, changing the subject again.

"I'd do anything for her."

"I know, honey. I've been thinking about the house."

"She said that you didn't seem enthused about the changes she mentioned."

Alfreah nodded. "Your father and I used to joke that when you all left, we'd move into a small apartment so none of our kids would have room to move back." She smiled sadly. "I think I'd still like the small apartment. Springfield is a bit too congested for me."

"You wanna sell the house?"

Alfreah shook her head. "I was thinking I'd give the deed to my new daughter-in-law. Someone who used to wish she lived there, as a little girl . . ."

Dean's eyes went narrow for a minute, then he raised his eyebrows, unsure of how he felt about living there. With Chyna he knew he could live anywhere, but to give it up—could his mother really do that or was the pain of the memories she had outweighing her long-term feelings about the house she and his father once shared? "Are you sure, Mama?"

Alfreah nodded and Dean shrugged again, not sure what to make of his mother's decision. Dean chanced a look at his watch, knowing he had to catch a flight soon and needed to repack and say his good-byes before he left for the airport.

"We'll talk about it another time," Alfreah said as they both looked toward the door where Chyna stood.

Standing, Dean turned to face her and waved her inside the room. Taking her hand, he pulled her back onto the seat beside him. "Is everything all right?" Chyna asked, looking back and forth between mother and son.

"Yes, yes. I'm going to see what the future Will Smith is up to. Excuse me." Before Alfreah left, she kissed Dean on the cheek and to Chyna's surprise kissed her as well. "The ring looks beautiful on you," Alfreah said and left the room.

Chyna looked toward the door, tears in her eyes, and then tried to blink them away before she looked back at Dean.

"Hey, quit that," Dean said, lifting her face to meet his.

"Shut up," Chyna replied, using her fingers to rub her eyes.

Dean leaned back against the sofa, bringing his arms around Chyna. His mind had wandered back to the conversation with his mother about Warren Hardig, then about his mother's gift of the house to the both of them. Whatever the case, whatever his mother would decide, he realized that letting go of the house would be a huge deal. He could see living there with Chyna, raising a family, but exactly where they did it didn't matter. He would ensure that his mother was okay with his doing so before he mentioned anything to Chyna. Wherever they called home wasn't as important as the fact that they were together.

When Dean arrived home late that night deep in thought, he didn't realize the need to be more alert until it was much too late. Something was wrong.

He stood at the entrance, the door ajar the number-one sign that something was amiss. As Dean reached for his cell phone to call the police, he stopped punching in the number when he heard a noise and something made of glass crash to the floor.

He prepared to go inside and confront whoever it was that decided they could just up and wreck his parents' home when he heard voices, two of them, and thought better of having to get the jump on two people instead of one. What Dean didn't count on was someone with a heavy something that propelled him through the door.

Dean gritted his teeth at what felt like a two-by-four biting into his back. As quick as he could, he rolled from the blow, moving farther into the house, and stood again on his feet.

When the man came at him again, Dean struck out with his fist and punched with as much force as he could, landing a few good blows to the man's gut.

Someone pulled him from behind and dragged him away, letting him know there were three people and not two as he thought. The one behind him pinned his arms behind his back and, using his weight, Dean pushed the man back and they landed on the living room table where the legs snapped under their combined weight and sent it crashing to the floor.

Dean struggled against the man who held him and from the corner of his eye he saw the other man pull a metal object from his pocket. The metal was sharp and its mirrorlike surface reflected the moonlight cast from the window.

Dean was up in a matter of seconds, his knuckles throbbing and his lower gut hurting from the blows. He managed one man from behind, his burly size and breadth thicker than Dean could imagine any human being. He had him in a choke hold, though, and using his thumb and index finger, he applied a pinching pressure to a prominent point within the man's thick neck. After a few seconds, the bulk of his weight was overcome by the pressure Dean's fingers applied and the man went listlessly in an unconscious heap down to the floor.

The man holding the knife stilled as if he'd been rendered speechless and unmovable. "What the hell'd you do to him?"

"He got a little sleepy," Dean replied and then before he could set himself for reaction, the other man threw the force of his body against Dean, sending them both backward. The knife was still in the other man's hand, and to Dean's dismay, he felt the sharp stab of the blade slice through the flesh just below his chest. The pain was sharp and piercing, but his doctor's sense kicked in and he knew he'd be all right, but only if he got to the hospital.

Dean staggered to the man as he backed away, his own fingers reaching to hold the knife in place as he resisted the urge to pull it out, which might cause him to bleed to death. But keeping it in was more painful than he could have imagined. The first of the pain was immobilizing, and Dean dropped abruptly to his knees. The portion of his chest was on fire and he was in agony. He kept his hand on the knife and managed to slide it out slowly, painfully. His shirt was soaked with blood. It ran in red rivulets and pooled in the palm of his hand.

Dean felt himself fall the rest of the way to the floor. A piece of the damaged furniture met him in the face, nicking his lip, and frayed edges of a table leg scratched his cheek as he turned his head. He tasted his own blood before things went blurry. He managed to turn his face the opposite way where the man grunted as he dragged his friend outside, and the clanking of cans pierced his ears, then the opening and shutting of doors and the revving of an engine and yelling. Dean tried to remain alert, awake, and the smell of gasoline met his nostrils before it seemed someone turned out the lights around him, and everything went completely black.

Chapter 26

With a new flight alert system, Chyna received a call that her flight had been delayed. Much to her dismay she was stuck at the Alton house four more hours than she had expected. She looked up from sipping her tea. The agitation over Dean's having gone back to Virginia seemed to intensify more than when she'd first left him a week ago in Virginia.

"Have some of your coworkers thrown you a shower? I'd love to throw you one," she said, trying to get her mind off Dean and chat with Tish. They sat in the living room sipping cups of hot tea.

"There's been some talk of it. I think it's a surprise."

"I suppose you could have two, one from them and a smaller one given by your family."

"I suppose." Tish nodded, noticing that her friend seemed to look toward the door repeatedly.

Chyna rubbed her stomach and a new kind of pain seemed to eat at her gut. It had started when she first arrived in Macon, when she'd left Dean, and now that Dean was gone she felt it creep back little by little. Each time it came Chyna knew it was her own signal that danger approached.

She set the tea down hurriedly, spilling its contents on the table and droplets on the rug. She looked down and then at Tish. "I'm sorry."

"Let me get something to wipe that—" with the

phone's piercing shrill Chyna nearly jumped from her skin. "Who's that?" she said as if her friend could read the phone lines and know who was on the other end without answering it to find out.

"Chyna? I don't know, someone else must have picked up. What's the matter?"

Something was wrong, terribly, terribly wrong.

"You're so nervous!" Tish said.

Dismissing her friend's correct assumption, Chyna asked quickly, "Can I use your computer?" and then looked at the small laptop computer in a corner. A sense of urgency so strong it nearly stifled her had come and gone with the ringing of the phone. It shifted only slightly but still she felt a need to be anywhere but there: home in Virginia to be exact.

"Sure," Tish said, standing. "You can use the one right here. Just—"

"Thank you."

"Chyna, what's the matter? You're shaking."

"Nothing," Chyna said and counted to ten, then to twenty and thirty when that didn't seem to work to calm her suddenly jittery nerves.

She then used that nervous energy on the keys to open the programs she needed. In a matter of minutes, she was listening to the computer as it painfully dialed the number to connect with the Internet.

"You think something's wrong at home?"

"Nah," Chyna said exaggeratingly. She waved a hand nonchalantly and smiled, though she wouldn't dare look at her friend.

"Are you lying?" Tish said, placing her hands on her hips.

"Of course I am," Chyna said.

"Lying?"

"Um-hmm." Chyna scratched her head, folding her hands between her legs while the small, thick blue line of the site took forever to move to the other end. "You need direct service link, T.T.," Chyna said and then laughed nervously. "Listen to me, the computer techie . . . I don't even think that's what DSL stands for, it just sounded good to me." She laughed again.

"Yeah, Chase mentioned getting a Digital Subscriber Line—Chyna!"

"Huh?"

"What's the matter?"

"Dean," she whispered.

"Something's the matter with Dean?"

"No."

"Chyna!" Tish said again and this time took Chyna's hands in her own. She looked down at them, noticing how they trembled in her own hands. "Talk to me. Are you having some kind of premonition or something? I've never known you to do that."

"I've never had them, not really, I just knew when something was wrong, a sixth sense."

"Okay, what does it feel like?"

"I have to go home, like now, Tish, like I can't stay here! Dean . . . fire . . ." Chyna said, looking back toward the computer. "There's gotta be a way out of this place." Chyna managed one of her hands away from Tish's grip, enough to allow her right hand to work the mouse to open another site. "Tomorrow? Tomorrow night? Oh, geez," Chyna wailed. "I could drive. I could rent a car. What's the name of that place?" Chyna managed her other hand away and was able to use both of them this time, the tiny tap of the keys echoing in both Tish's and Chyna's ears. "Oh, look," she said, scrutinizing the computer monitor. "There's another airline I've never heard of, it's Blue something—"

"Chyna, please, take a moment to sit down, like over here, I mean," Tish said.

Chyna moved to the chair at Tish's coaxing. Once near the sofa she sat down abruptly.

"Now, just start from the beginning, tell me what's going through that fast-paced mind of yours. When's the first time you've had something that came true?"

"Just once, I had a feeling, that time."

"What time?" Tish pleaded.

"I was doing my chores, Tish. I was coming, but I didn't get there fast enough. I tried, but I couldn't."

"When?" Chyna took her friend's hands again, shaking them to get her to focus and tell her all that ran through her mind.

"The fire," Chyna wailed. "I was too late, and you got hurt too, I'm sorry."

"That wasn't your fault." Tish shook her head frantically.

"But if I tune into things, if I could just sit still for a moment, I'd hear it before it's too late, if I'd just listen, and I never should have left Virginia. This is Dean's fault, his stupid ideas . . ."

"I thought you wanted to come here?" Tish asked.

"I . . . I did, but . . ." She couldn't explain further without more questions so she stopped talking completely.

"Chyna, listen, I am sure Dean is fine."

"What if he's not?"

"Then Jojo will call."

"Not if they don't want me . . . us to be concerned, they won't."

"What is going on that is to be so concerned about?" Chyna didn't answer. "Well, then, let's call them," Tish went on.

"Good, good, yes, you call them, let me talk to Dean. Don't tell him I'm coming home though," Chyna said as she stood up again, took two steps back to the desk where the computer was situated, and sat down, commencing clicking over the keys again.

Tish moved to the phone where she dialed both of

her brothers' telephone numbers and then Jojo. Tish didn't want to alarm either of them so she left a casual message.

"Tonight!" Chyna squealed, taking a deep shaky breath. "I found a flight tonight, the red-eye, that's all there is," she said, frowning. "Well, I'm taking it." She spoke to the computer, and hit the enter button after typing her personal information into the computer prompts.

"Did you get Dean?" Chyna asked without relaxing her fingers on the keys, without looking up. She knew the answer and she knew in her heart it would only confirm the terrible thoughts her mind conjured up.

"No, I left a message and Jojo's line is busy," Tish replied.

Chyna nodded, feeling only slightly better as if some of the danger had passed, but not enough that would get her to cancel her flight and remain in Macon.

When the phone rang, Chyna jumped again. She looked at Tish, who picked it up and spoke to someone. Chyna knew it was Jojo after Tish asked about Dean's whereabouts. She wasn't prepared when Tish looked at her, still holding the phone, and said, "Yeah, she's right here, what—" Tish turned and handed the phone to Chyna.

Chyna took the phone. "Hello," she said shakily after placing it against her ear.

"Hey," Dean whispered into the phone.

Dean tried to shift himself higher on the bed. Looking up at his brother, he rolled his eyes exasperatingly and recognized the look that silently said, *You're pathetic,* as his brother stood over him holding the phone to his ear. Turning his head, Dean tried to readjust so that his ear could rest more comfortably on the phone, but it was useless, the pain in his side left him immobile, almost paralyzed.

"Dean? What's the matter?"

"Why? Nothing," Dean replied hoarsely.

"Don't lie, I got a flight out tonight, I'm coming home."

"Don't do that, Chyna," Dean said more forcefully, feeling the pain of everything, even organs and limbs that didn't originally hurt, center in his side where he'd been stabbed.

"I have to, you're hurt, I can hear it. How bad is it?"

When a rustling sound came over the phone, Chyna called Dean's name over and over, while Dean's protest grew distant before another, stronger voice came through the line. "Jojo?" Chyna said. "How bad is it, Jojo?" she began without waiting to confirm he was listening.

"Oh, he's all right, really. Someone did a little job on me, but he's cool," Jojo said into the phone.

"I'll be there soon. Is the doctor around?" Chyna asked.

"What's the matter, you don't trust me, girl?"

"No, no, I don't!" Chyna said matter-of-factly. More calmly she said, "When it comes to this, I don't. I know you're trying to make me feel better."

"That's what family's for."

"Well, damn it, it's not working!" Chyna screamed, belatedly looking at Tish with a silent apology. "When I get there I'll talk to the doctor myself. I'm taking the next flight into Dulles. Don't worry about picking me up. I'll catch a cab. Either way I'll be there by the early morning. Tell Dean that I . . . I'll be there soon, and that, oh God," Chyna said. The revelation that all of this, the entire mess, was all her fault came crashing down on her like nothing else she'd ever felt in her entire life, not her miserable marriage, not her divorce. "I . . . I love him." Chyna said good-bye to Jojo before hanging up the phone. She moved past Tish to place it in its cradle and when she looked up again she found that not just Tish, but to her dismay, Ms. Alfreah also occupied the room, both of them staring at her, expectantly waiting for the story she'd have to tell them, about all that was going on back home in Virginia.

Chapter 27

"You're certainly good for not one single damn thing!" Dean said as Jojo replaced the phone in its cradle.

"I'm in better shape than you, little bro," Jojo replied. "Got some facts on these people?"

"Yeah, they carry knives!" was all Dean offered. "And they're big," he added.

"And why the hell didn't you tell me what was up? My brother, handle every damn thing by himself? It's a family affair now," Jojo said and looked at Dean as he nodded.

"I'll go down to the station, check out the house, and get back in time to meet Chyna," Jojo offered, looking at his brother.

Dean could only nod in return. He didn't want Chyna anywhere near the hospital or within one foot of the state line, but considering it hurt like hell when he simply exhaled and inhaled, he was in no position to do anything and he hated it. He nodded to Jojo, who quickly left the room.

Chyna nearly banged her own head against the automatic doors of the Inova Alexandria Hospital, but she stopped just in time, allowing the doors to open before she moved again through them. Her legs felt as if they stomped against the floor like wood and as they ate the ground before her, they still didn't seem to move her body fast enough and get her to her destination.

She was on the verge of tears when she finally saw Jojo's head swim high above others. He smiled reassuringly and she tried to retract her tears immediately. She wouldn't feel like crying if her plane ride had been a bit more pleasant. The airline no one had heard of was a kid-friendly company. The only adults were parents of toddlers, the rest a bunch of loudmouthed, I-just-got-my tonsils crying babies that just woke up from naps, it seemed, as they got on the plane. Oh, Chyna winced, how could she forget the other adults, herself, and an ancient lady that plopped beside Chyna, dumped two pills down her throat, and was immediately, mouth twisted, head practically on Chyna's shoulder, fast asleep. If Chyna had been a mean person, she'd woken the old hag back up and asked her to regurgitate one of the pills so Chyna could join the land of the snoring sleep, but no such luck would befall her. Chyna was wide-awake, worried sick with nothing but strong coffee to keep her company as her endless thoughts ran rampant from the time she sat down till the time the plane landed with enough jerking to put all the coffee she'd drunk on the floor. But she hadn't gotten sick, not yet. The contents of her stomach remained intact.

This entire mess was a farce Dean had deemed necessary to keep her safe, but no more. He would stop sheltering her at this very moment. *When I get my hands on him,* she thought to herself and calmed only slightly, *I'll tell him how much I love him . . . and then I'll beat him up.*

Trying to dismiss her thoughts, Chyna moved before Jojo when he finished talking with a nurse. Unfortunately, she'd only been able to catch the tail end of their conversation and nothing offered had been any kind of help. Chyna focused on Dean's brother and couldn't help viewing him as just another nuisance to deter her from getting to her destination. "Where?" she said without greeting. Considering the circumstances, she also knew that Jojo of all people wouldn't care if she'd greeted him or not. If he didn't show her as she requested, she'd mull him down too, though considering the size of him, that might prove difficult, but she could try.

She finally noticed him, really took a moment to scrutinize his stiff back, the guarded stand made more impressive with his army fatigues and his eyes stormy as if he were ready to do the combat he'd been trained for at a moment's notice.

The thoughts traveling through Chyna's mind hadn't been good. Each time she thought of Dean lying somewhere, she'd torture herself with blame all over again. Seeing Jojo, his serious eyes, his guarded look, Chyna began to wonder if he might have blamed her for her role in this entire mess. After all, Dean wouldn't be here at all if it hadn't been for the deranged criminal and fool she'd married seven years ago. Chyna wouldn't, she couldn't fault Jojo or Dean if either did blame her. The entire plane ride, she'd thought of several reasons why her future husband's entire family should hate her, should blame her, why his entire family should loathe the very ground she walked upon when everything, everything was totally her fault. Telling Tish and Ms. Alfreah hadn't been easy when she was trying not to upset them. They were trying to move on and she didn't need to bring the baggage of Warren Hardig into their lives.

Ms. Alfreah had seemed the most distant, and that was what Dean didn't want. It hadn't been six months since her husband died. She needed her own time, and Chyna felt as if her mess wasn't helping matters any.

"You going to calm down and wipe those crocodiles?" Jojo said, standing stiffly.

"I'm sorry," she said, hastily running a hand over her face, not realizing she'd let her tears fall until she smeared the wetness.

"Ms. Lockhart, I was just telling Mr. Jameson here that Dean is stable." Chyna looked down at the man standing next to Jojo. He was short, the lab coat making him seem even shorter, tan skinned, and he spoke with an accent that lifted the ends of each ending syllable of the words he said. Chyna looked back and forth between Jojo and the man, wanting the man to continue speaking, to get to the gist of the extent of Dean's injuries. When he said her name, Chyna belatedly felt just a twinge of relief, relaxing and realizing that Jojo had made introductions and had said that she was Dean's fiancée.

"Your fiancé, uh, Mr. Jameson, has sustained what looks like a knife wound to the upper torso. We've done a CT scan of the torso to ensure that there was no internal damage to any vital organs. Thankfully the object didn't pass through the pleural cavity. It looks like they, whoever did this," the doctor stammered, "narrowly missed the membrane of the abdomen, which if the knife had penetrated this tissue, he would've needed to have surgery . . . and that's a very good thing, as we try to avoid this in every case, and are thankful for cases like these. He's very lucky.

"Dean is very groggy. We've repaired some tissue and muscle damage. There wasn't a lot of fatty tissue around his chest area. We've given him some blood," the man said, gesturing with his head in Jojo's direction. "The only concern right now is the pain and the blood loss. He is very weak.

"He seems rather excitable, but I urge you to keep him calm. . . . The police were here earlier. Mr. Jameson, I assumed you talked to them—"

Chyna watched as the doctor stopped talking abruptly

when Jojo slowly shook his head, indicating for the doctor not to continue any further.

"What?" Chyna looked from the doctor, then up to Jojo. "What is it?" she demanded.

"I'll let, uh, I'm on call . . . if there's any trouble, I have some other patients to see but will check back in just a bit," the doctor said and hurriedly turned to leave.

Chyna turned as Jojo guided her away from the nurses' station and down the hall. "Is this the way to Dean's room?"

"He's going to be fine. Take a walk with me," Jojo said as he nodded in the direction of a long hallway. He crossed his arms over his chest and shuffled lazily away from the nurses' desk as if he hadn't a care in the world.

His demeanor, his nonchalance was only stirring Chyna's temper and she wondered at times if he was really that unflappable or if he did it to aggravate her. One more evading comment and she'd planned to let him have more than a piece of her mind.

Despite wanting to turn to the nurses' station and ask where Dean Jameson's room was, she immediately moved in step with Jojo. Still she questioned, "Is this the way to his room?" knowing she wouldn't believe the words that came from anyone's mouth, other than Dean's. The shelter-Chyna act was no longer working. She'd known these people too long.

"How are you?" Jojo said.

"Fine," she clipped out quickly as if that would help him hurry along. But if Chyna had learned anything it was that Jojo Jameson never did anything fast. He let you stew if he thought you believed he was reacting too slowly. He could move fast, talk fast, and comprehend things fast when he wanted. He wasn't a special agent of the government for nothing, but in situations like this and most others, he seemed to deliberately take an abundant amount of time when he knew others were in a hurry to get to the bottom of something and to find answers. But Jojo Jameson seemed to execute time at a pace he deemed fit.

She wanted to tell him that he shouldn't be concerned with how she was when it was her fault his brother was laid up with injuries that almost caused him to bleed to death. As if reading her mind, Jojo said, "This isn't your fault," and Chyna looked away.

"Dean would kill me if he knew that you took the redeye to get here, so tell me the truth about how you are doing and we'll go a little further."

Chyna could only stare at him in disbelief. Straightening her back, and standing as tall as she could, she took a deep, exasperating breath. "I'm worried, okay, so what do you propose I do? You're taking all day to get me to him knowing he's my only concern, and you stand here with idle chitchat. I don't have time for this, I really don't, Joseph, so quit your jabbering and tell me what room he's in." Belatedly after taking a deep breath, she added, "Now!"

"Good, didn't that feel better?" Jojo questioned. He didn't wait for a reply and turned slightly to place a hand on the door directly to his right. Chyna was surprised when he pushed it open and motioned her inside ahead of him.

Dropping her bag at the door, Chyna rushed to the bed where Dean's large form was soundless and still. The lights were turned down and the beep of a machine made whatever injuries he might have had seem all the more real. If the room had been silent, except for Dean's light snoring, she could've borne what she saw a little better, but the machine's faint beeping noise, the suctioning of air pressure rising and falling, the contraptions, and all the monitoring they did made her nightmares all the more realistic.

Moving closer to his bed, she looked down. Gently she

placed her hand over his forehead and rubbed his brow. His body jerked and his eyes fluttered open. "Hi," she whispered, trying to keep her emotions in the deepest part of her heart even as it broke into a million pieces.

One of his eyes was swollen and bruised. Chyna looked down to where the thick pad constituting a bandage lifted the sheets slightly away from the frame of his chest. His eyes were hazy and confused and Chyna knew he'd been given something for the pain. His lip looked cut, bloodred, and inflamed and then her mind seemed to go on and on conjuring a thousand other injuries the naked eye couldn't see.

"How's it going?" Dean said groggily.

Chyna smiled. "I'm all right. I . . . I . . ." she faltered.

"Good," Dean replied and closed his eyes momentarily.

"I'm so sorry this happened to you, I'm sorry," she said, reaching for his hand and realizing belatedly that it too was wrapped fiercely in gauze and pinned with a shiny metallic clip.

Chyna's eyes traveled back up to his face. Not knowing what else to do with her hands, she quickly withdrew them from him and folded them together. When that wasn't enough to do with them, she wrung them together and finally crossed her arms over her chest and placed a hand under each armpit. She didn't know what to say or do, so she paced. Once away from the bed and back to it again, she said, "Getting here was a nightmare," taking a deep breath before continuing. "There was no one to talk to, babies crying, I sat by this lady, she fell asleep, then I drank a lot of coffee and had to pee, which I should have known better considering how tight those bathrooms are. . . ." Near hysteria, Chyna took a deep breath and relaxed again. Looking down at Dean, she said, "Are you sure you're all right? Are you sure? Because . . ." Chyna looked around for something to pound. "Because . . . I'm going to hurt someone." She accentuated the end of each statement by pounding her fist into the palm of her hand repeatedly. Running a hand over her head, she pushed away too-long bangs when they began to irritatingly tickle her forehead. "I'm going to hurt Warren and the rest of his sorry gang of governmental, crooked professionals. Oh, Dean. I'm sorry."

"Come here," Dean managed to whisper when Chyna's mouth finally closed. "Here," he repeated, and then he awkwardly patted his chest with his bandaged hand, and with his other he rubbed the small space next to his thigh.

"I don't want to hurt you," Chyna replied even as she stood immobile, frozen to a spot far removed from the bed. Her face was tight with fright, viewing Dean as if he carried some type of communicable disease she had given him. When he patted the space again, she moved closer to his bedside.

Inches within his reach, he managed with his good hand to pry her folded hands away from her frame, and working enough of his hold up her arm, he pulled her closer. She resisted with little success and was forced to lean down over him. She splayed her hands on the upper part of his chest to keep herself from falling completely on top of him.

"I'm all right, stop worrying," he said, using the thumb of his good hand to rub away the frown line between her brows. Finally she graced him with a sad smile. "Give me some sugar."

"I'm so sorry you're hurt."

"Yeah, you mentioned that and I said give me some sugar."

Chyna acquiesced. Bending her head down, she fleetingly brushed her lips against his. She smiled again when she opened her eyes to regard Dean.

"You must be joking, that wasn't sugar."

When Chyna leaned in again, Dean pressed the back of her head gently. Sliding his tongue past her teeth, he sighed. "Better," he whispered, his eyes a shade darker with desire.

"You're terrible, even in your state—"

"I'm not dead, you know."

"Don't joke! Dean, this is serious."

Jojo moved into the room after a few moments. "Ya'll all right?"

Chyna nodded though Dean was the first to speak. "I'd be better if you'd have woken me. For someone who gives orders you sure don't follow them very well."

"That's why I give them," Jojo replied seriously. "Look, I'm going to head out." He looked at Chyna, then back at Dean.

"Yeah, do that," Dean replied.

"Do what?" Chyna looked back and forth from one brother to the other. "Don't you both dare try to keep things from me now, let me know what's going on, what are you planning? Do they have proof Warren is behind this?"

Without further word Jojo disappeared from the room, throwing a courteous "I'll be in touch" over his shoulder as he left.

Chyna's furiousness grew by the minute. "What's been happening? What's going on? Did you get a look at who did this to you?" she rattled off.

"Shh."

"Don't tell me to *shh!* Do you know what I went through? Do you understand what you mean to me? Now look at you, you're laid up here." She gestured toward his bulky frame that covered most of the twin-size hospital bed. "It's all my fault, and you're still protecting me, you're still trying to. I can do something, I'm not helpless, you know!

"You're all I have left!" she pleaded more softly.

"And I'm still here. . . . Climb up here with me."

"No."

"Please."

Moments passed while Chyna stood before Dean's bedside, hands on her hips. She dragged a shaky hand across her forehead and wished for something to pin back the bothersome bangs. Concerned, she watched as Dean raised his head off the pillow and when continuing to hold it up proved difficult, he blew out his breath harshly and plopped it against the pillow.

Chyna wanted nothing more than to pound some sense into that thick head of his, to shake him for scaring her. Instead she moved nearer, releasing the railing to lie beside him. Turning on her side, using most of the bed and trying not to lay too much of her weight on him, she felt his arm come around her in an almost deathlike grip and to her surprise he managed to pull her more snugly against him. With his other hand, awkwardly, he lifted the sheet and brought it around them. Chyna kicked her shoes off.

"Keep those legs still, will you? There's a drawers thief in this joint, stole my underwear."

Chyna smiled just a little and rolled her eyes. "You're incorrigible!"

"They didn't hurt certain parts of me, you know . . . I think things are still working just fine. We can try it later."

"Don't be facetious, and would you stop?" she said, reaching a hand behind her. She stilled Dean's hand as it wandered low, past the dip of her backside, to rest proprietarily on her rump. "Please? Please stop joking around," she pleaded even though a sense of humor from him, anything of the sort, was better than what could have been, she reminded herself and was grateful.

"My gown's got really easy access. Did a man invent the miniskirt? Rather drafty but do you find my gown sexy?" he finished.

Chyna couldn't stop herself that time. She did her best to suppress it but a laugh bubbled from her mouth regardless and she felt Dean let go of a relaxing sigh from his body.

"Am I hurting you, do you hurt anywhere?" She looked up at him.

"My lips."

Chyna propped herself up on her elbow to look at Dean's mouth. "They're a little chafed and dry. Did they punch you . . . with their fists?" she said, rubbing her index finger over his lower, bruised lip. Her thumb then grazed over the cut at the corner of his mouth. She turned to retrieve a small tube of ointment she'd seen lying on the tray table. After reading the many suggested uses, she applied a small amount to the tips of her fingers and then smoothed it over Dean's lips even when he tried to turn his head away from her.

"Busted my lip all by myself, doubling over from the pain those punks put in my side, and geez, Chyna, I meant for you to kiss me again. That stuff is disgusting, it tastes awful," Dean said, turning his head from the hideous smell of the ointment.

"You're not supposed to eat it," Chyna reminded him after she recapped the tube and set it aside. "They stabbed you?" she asked. She lightly touched Dean's side, feeling what felt like corrugated card stock, hoping the side of the bandage actually touching his wound was softer. She placed the blanket back over him.

"Little pocketknives, Boy Scout rejects, bunch of punks," Dean muttered. "How was your flight?" he added, trying to change the subject.

"All right," she replied this time, realizing her earlier spiel of that flight ordeal had gone unheard.

"You've had some caffeine, I smell it," he said as a statement of fact rather than speculation. "Café latte? Espresso roast? Or I know, a double shot?"

Chyna nodded her head against his chest. "Actually, it was Maxwell House . . . on the flight. Almost six cups. They were little paper cups," she offered poorly in her defense, wondering why she'd been so forthcoming in the first place with her caffeine intake. She quickly dismissed her sudden bout of honesty and chalked it up to stress and worry. "Listen," Chyna began, dismissing her sudden honesty. With her index finger she drew light circles on Dean's chest while she tried to get her thoughts together. "I want, I need . . . you . . . to, to work with me on this. Togetherness, isn't that what we're about? We're trying to start working together." She didn't wait for a response from him, either his acquiescence or his protest, which she was certain the latter would probably be the most likely. "We can make better sense of everything together, with our facts, than we can with just you and your brother trying to protect me. I've got some information too. I can ask Gary what he knows about Warren, see if he'd be willing to tell the authorities. Then there's the proof . . . I could go to Warren . . ." Chyna exhaled and inhaled deeply, ready for Dean to have a fit. She hadn't quite mapped out the matters to get to Warren Hardig, but slowly her initial idea was coming together more solidly in her mind. "Like a sting operation."

Chapter 28

She knew Dean would never go for it. She'd have to revisit that idea later. "I need to know what Jojo is doing and I need to tell you everything I know and vice versa!" She tapped his chest, wishing he'd say something, even an outburst, but when she looked up, his eyes were closed, and with the steady rise and fall of his chest, she realized he hadn't been listening to one word she said. He was asleep.

Chyna laid her head back down on Dean's chest. "I'll fix this," she whispered. "I love you. I love you so much, Dean," she continued as she kissed his chest, "but I can work this out, I can. I know I can." She said so as much for him as she did to talk up and solidify the plan that was coming to her mind, and to motivate herself to be brave enough to follow through with it.

She lifted her face, angling her head to kiss Dean just under his chin. She inhaled deeply through her nose, his natural scent interspersed with the medicine smell of the ointment, before snuggling back under the flimsy sheet. Then she wrapped her arm low around his lower waist, careful not to injure or jostle his wound. She knew she would spend just a couple more hours with him before she needed to leave to find Jojo and implore him to use her to help bring down Warren Hardig.

* * *

When Dean awoke, he blinked his eyes and rolled them heavenward, disgusted by the fact that his sleep hadn't been interrupted by Chyna's light snoring, or her finding a new position next to him, but instead by the irritating sound of his own machine with its incessant beeping noise. It was apparently daylight as the light from the sun shone through the dingy white and tattered curtains of his room. Though what day it was, what hour, and just how long Dean had been in and out of sleep remained a complete mystery. He wasn't concerned about the hour as much as the fact that Chyna was no longer beside him.

To his dismay, he tried to bring his body upright as best he could but relaxed immediately when the door swung open. His uneasiness increased, however, when the subject of his question wasn't the one to walk through it. He watched as Chyna's friend Charlize, also unfortunately known as Nurse Ratched, as far as he was concerned, moved quickly through the door with a tray.

"You seen Chyna?" he asked, once she set down the tray on his table and proceeded to remove the coverings to display what looked like breakfast.

"Well, I'm sorry it's only Tuesday to you too!" Charlize replied. "Here's your breakfast, and I saw Chyna . . ." Charlize thought for a moment, "for a brief moment early this morning."

"Where is she now? What time is it?" Dean questioned and when Charlize wiggled the tray in front of him, he pushed it back from his immediate view. Just the sight of the eggs, let alone the other unidentifiable stuff, made his stomach quiver with disgust.

"I don't know, Dean, to your first question, and to your second, it's about ten A.M.," Charlize said testily, looking at her watch.

"Are you the only nurse in this joint or something?"

"Nope." Charlize shook her head. "But I handle the

ornery patients." She read the data on the many monitors, and noted them on the flip chart she held against her hip. She put the chart back in the slot at the foot of Dean's bed before saying, "I'll be back to take your vitals, so get your attitude in check. I'm sure Chyna will be here to fuss over you any minute, so stop worrying."

Dean would never stop worrying about Chyna, that much he knew. He wished he could have stayed awake to hear all that she was talking about the night before, but the medication had made him sleepy and he dozed off. He watched as Charlize backtracked a minute, waving her finger at him as if he'd been a naughty boy.

"There's a trick to this whole hospital thing," he heard Charlize begin, and he rolled his eyes. "You cooperate," she continued, "you get your vitals stabilized, you show improvement—that starts with a good attitude and being nice to the nursing staff doesn't hurt either—and you check out . . . which I'm sure is number one on your list of priorities. Try some of those steps I just gave you and we'll see what I can do. It starts, by the way, with eating your breakfast," Charlize finished, pushing the tray once more in front of Dean, close enough to where he could reach it. As she backed up, she pushed the button that caused the television to loudly blast some news talk show. Charlize waved at Dean one last time before exiting the room.

Dean was alone only a matter of seconds and his pulse immediately calmed when Chyna finally walked through the door.

He smiled internally, but lit into her. "Where the hell have you been?"

"Well, good morning to you too," Chyna said, carrying a brown bag with the famous golden arches on it. "I brought you breakfast." She held the bag up and waved it like the swing of a pendulum. When she leaned down to kiss his lips, he held her there a moment longer. "You look better, I'm happy to say," and she thanked God he did. His color was returning, his usual smooth, healthy pecan-shell color instead of ashy brown, and his eyes just a little more alert and of course accusing as he continued to eye her. Chyna looked away, smiling. Anything, even attitude, was better than when she'd first seen him yesterday.

"You didn't go to the house, did you?" Dean asked worriedly, knowing it would break her heart to see the place in the complete shambles Jojo had told him it was. He knew there was some damage from the scuffle, but complete and utter destruction was what Jojo had said and his brother never sugarcoated anything. The place they were rebuilding, reconstructing, and had worked so hard together to renovate, seeing its destruction would upset her, try as she might not to let it show. Dean knew she took it to heart.

"Yes, I, uh, I was there," Chyna whispered. Barely able to get through the door, she had seen the lovely antique secretary in pieces. It blocked the door and she had to push hard just to get inside. She and Dean had salvaged that piece from the attic, sanded it, and painted it a nice dark maple. Now it was chipped, its legs broken, and the repair of it would be virtually impossible, its sentimental value irreplaceable. It must have crashed during Dean's and whoever's scuffle.

Chyna nodded and closed her eyes. She'd been there all right. Couldn't help herself from picking up just a few things and piecing them back together or setting fallen pictures where they once had been. The destruction had stifled her elation in renovating. It was the house she had loved, but it had history and belonged not even to her but to her family, the family she was a part of in her heart; and looking down at her ring, she knew she was soon going to be a part of it on paper.

Seeing the destruction, all of it, had worked up her

temper all over again, which really didn't take much considering she hadn't truly calmed. What Warren had done was ruthless, and hateful. She thought back to her plan, which was almost complete, and things were about to be set into motion. She'd been at the house long enough to shower and change, packed up the nice dress she planned to use for her ploy, then stopped for food for Dean, all under a couple of hours.

"We'll fix it, Chyna," Dean said solemnly, watching the emotions flit across her face. "They're just things, material possessions."

Chyna looked over at Dean as if she'd just been transported back to the present. She nodded. They were things, but they'd meant so much more than objects. There were familial stories hidden in every single piece. She could've agreed with him had there been a fire, Mother Nature's brutal natural disaster, but the destruction came from another's own hands. Chyna smiled sadly and not knowing what else to do, she nodded again. "I know we will," she said aloud, thinking to herself that she'd indeed fix it. There wasn't a doubt in her mind.

"What are you thinking?" Dean asked, the new aromatic smell of hot greasy food getting the better of him. He was starving and though he rarely ate fast food, he could go for something greasy right about then, considering his rubbery alternative.

"Oh, nothing," she said quickly, "just a plan . . . and that I brought you a sausage sandwich. I even got some jelly." Reaching into the bag, she pulled out the fat white packets with a head of grapes on them, wiggling them in front of Dean's eyes. "For your biscuit, I thought you'd like that."

Tucking her lip between her teeth, Chyna looked up, recapping the cover to the meal compliments of the hospital cafeteria. She removed it entirely, placing it on a nearby chair, and proceeded to cover a small space on the table with several napkins. After spreading out the sandwich, she took each half of the biscuit, tore open the small packets with her teeth, and squeezed a generous portion of jelly onto it.

"So, Chyna, what's the plan about?" Dean said seriously, while he eyed her skeptically. A picture of interlocking wheels turning one into the other might as well have been stamped on her forehead.

Chyna turned the biscuit over, taking the other side of it to spread the remainder of the jelly. "Well . . ." So much for her efforts with the jelly and the biscuit, she thought to herself. "Well, um," Chyna said again while she pressed the halves back together. She broke off a piece, fed it to Dean, hoping to take his mind off her big blabbermouth entirely, though she knew even under mild sedatives, he'd still have a ton of questions for her.

Startling them both, the phone in Chyna's tote bag rang loudly. Chyna smiled falsely, wiping the corner of Dean's mouth, then her own sticky hands on the paper towels, and reached for the phone.

Dean watched as she looked away from him while she spoke and he also noticed the fact that she didn't say much of anything, that she simply nodded, uttered a bunch of *yeses* and *I understands,* then cheerfully ended the call with a "thanks for calling." She pressed a few buttons and placed the phone back in her purse.

When she turned back to him, Dean eyed her expectantly.

"That was a friend of mine," Chyna said to his silent question.

"What friend?" Dean asked angrily. He knew she was up to something and knew to his further agitation, he was in no position to stop her. "Talk to me, Chyna! Who the hell was that? What is the plan, Chyna?"

When she didn't respond, Dean chewed the leftover

food in his mouth, swallowed quickly, and said very calmly, "Damn it, you better tell me, Chyna, this isn't a game. Jojo and I will handle this, I won't have any harm to you on my head."

Chyna looked at him as if he'd gone completely crazy, and her anger at his words and the entire situation rose to meet Dean's. "Oh? But I can have yours on mine, is that what you're saying?"

Chyna shook her head as if she could retract the words she spoke. She dismissed what Dean said. She needed to concentrate and she would have to get into a totally different mode to deal with Warren Hardig, to make him believe that she no longer loved Dean and that she wanted to be with him instead. That was her plan.

After running a hand down her face, she moved her purse to the end of the bed, and went back to the head to whisper to Dean, "Will you remember something for me, Dean?"

"What?" Dean snapped.

"That I love you, only you, okay? With all my heart, Dean," she finished and kissed him quickly before he could grab her, prolonging her stay and melting her resolve to stick to her plan. She moved toward the door, slung her tote over her shoulder, and placed her hand on the doorknob. "Please eat your breakfast, and be all right so you can come home to me, so we can move on with our lives, so we can get married. I've gotta go, I've got something to do."

"Chyna, no!" Dean pleaded. "Listen to me, listen to me. We believe that Lisa will help us, that she called the police after they beat me up. They were going to burn down the house. Lisa . . . we think . . . is the one. We've got an FBI agent to help, a friend of Jojo's, to get Lisa to trap Warren." Dean reached farther up the railing where his hand gripped the cold metal bar. It tightened and he used it to pull himself upright even as the pain bit into his side. It felt as if his stitches burst open with every inch he tried to sit up. "Warren is into so many different things, illegal things . . . The police are already on to him. We're just going to get Lisa to be the decoy to do the sting on him. My mother, my mom and Chauncey Hardig, he loved her and those same feelings for all the Jameson men he thrust upon his son. Damn it, he's dangerous, he is, please don't go, please."

"I have to," Chyna said, as she stood at the door ready to leave. Her mind was already made up. "I have to fix it."

Regretfully, Dean could do nothing except nod in acquiescence, and sadly he watched Chyna go. "Please be careful," he whispered belatedly. The pain of breathing deeply trying to explain in just a few minutes the vendetta the Hardigs had against the Jamesons left nothing improved.

Dean was silent, trying to concentrate on calming himself while the pain was alleviated only slightly. He was thoughtful as the words *Come home to me, come home to me* repeated over and over, rolling around in his head like loose marbles. There was no doubt that he was going to come home all right, but what if she wasn't? He knew she was planning something, the kind of thing that just might get her killed or as close to the grave as one could get.

Chyna was that stubborn, that upset, that worked up about Dean's own carelessness, about his inflated ego that let him think he should try to take on three oversized bullies who meant to end his life.

Taking another bite of his sandwich, Dean chewed thoughtfully for a moment, trying to figure all the possibilities of what Chyna knew, what she would do, and how far she would go. His temper, second by second, seemed to fester like a sore, bleeding with every minute that passed, until it boiled over and Dean threw everything from his tray onto the floor.

Removing the covers, he managed to reach for the phone. He gritted his teeth at the pain, at the exertion, but after jerking the cheap phone to his bed, he took a deep breath and proceeded to dial Jojo's number.

"Get over here, now!" he said the first moment the line cleared, not knowing whether it was Jojo or not. Dean hung up just as quickly. When he picked up the receiver the second time, listening for a dial tone, he dialed his friend, also on the case, Special Agent Terrance Trent Dunbar.

Chapter 29

Terrance Trent Dunbar, better know as Trent to most of his friends, sat in a dark room with a lining of television monitors on each wall. Surveillance was his specialty.

"Damn it, why isn't she here?" Jojo said.

"So she's not coming, she backed out? If she was coming she'd be here by now."

"Look, Trent, I appreciate your coming to help me."

Trent waved a hand. "You know I'm cool. I'll wait as long as it takes for her to get her butt in here."

Jojo nodded to his longtime friend from way back and kept pacing the small room. As he checked his watch for the umpteenth time, his anger grew.

"How's Dean, man?"

"He'll be all right, but this is the last straw, nobody puts a knife in my brother and lives to see the next hour, let alone the next day." His friend nodded and Jojo looked at the door again. "Where the hell is she?"

The door swung open. "Where the hell have you been?" Jojo said heatedly, but when he finally took a moment to look at the face above the cheap getup the woman wore, he realized to his dismay, she wasn't at all whom he had been expecting.

Chyna Lockhart realized that to play dirty, you had to become another person entirely, especially so because it wasn't in her nature. Getting into a certain underhanded, conniving mind-set, and executing seedy dealings with the rest of those who threw caution to the wind when it came to obeying laws, was difficult for someone, anyone not accustomed to that sort of lifestyle. But for the moment, Chyna shook her head, trying to convince herself that it was what she needed to do and exactly whom she needed to become to fix things and make it right.

For the last year and a half, Chyna Lockhart had forgotten who Chyna Williams was. She'd forgotten everything she'd learned, everything she knew about Gary's friends, fellow senators, White House officials, and aides to the highest executive branch of office. Because she wanted to forget her life, and have nothing to do with that time, she'd put that knowledge in the most repressed part of her memory, but she never really forgot. It was back there, down deep in the recesses of her mind: who was having an affair with who, who was stealing money, what senators' wives were in the best position to help her, considering their own illustrious affairs. She had favors to call in that were a mile long. It took only a couple of hours to discover what Jojo was up to.

She stood at the entrance of the office in an outfit meant for seduction. A provocative getup meant to make a certain man forget to keep his secrets and utter the secrets that would ultimately bring him to his final demise: to justice. With a simple, black dress, Chyna had combed her hair, pinned it high on her head, brought down a few wisps, and added a cheap necklace she'd hastily purchased at the store along with the dress, the stiletto heels on her feet, and the sheer black panty hose covering her legs. She stood at the door expectantly, waiting for the men to say something.

"What the hell are you doing here?" Jojo was the first to speak up. He moved to the door, pulled her in, and closed the door behind her.

"What do you think?"

"Everything all right?" asked a short and stocky woman wearing tattered jeans and an oversized shirt. She addressed the men and then looked back at Chyna. "She's all taped up, we should do a mike check. . . . How's that wire feel, Ms. Stephens?"

"You're kidding me," Trent said and stood from his chair.

Jojo did a double take before he exploded, "This isn't Ms. Stephens, this is Chyna Lockhart."

The woman shook her head and Chyna could only stare at her, her mind too focused on what she was about to do to feel sorry for the woman and Chyna's hand in duping her.

"She told me her name was Stephens. . . ."

"What are you, a temp or something?"

"Hey, Jojo," Trent said. He stood and placed a hand on Jojo as if he might go after her and do bodily harm once he had her in his grip.

"Come on, Trent, damn it, she should know what Lisa Stephens looks like."

"Wait a minute, just how many other people would come in and say they're one person just to get wired? Not like that happens every day, and, well, geez, I'm sorry I didn't know."

"Yeah, I'm sorry you didn't know too. This is a mess!"

"Well, is Lisa Stephens here?" Chyna asked, though she pretty much knew the answer already.

"No," Jojo snapped.

"Then I'm all you got," Chyna broke in. She didn't know if Lisa had showed or not. She didn't know where Lisa was, but somehow her cowardice didn't surprise her.

"She is already wired up. We can do a mike check and—" the female officer said.

"That will be all, thank you, Carla," Trent said, and

without another word, the female officer left the room, her head bowed as if she'd been reprimanded.

"I'm not doing this. You want Dean to kill me or something?" Jojo said.

"You're bigger than him," Chyna reminded him pathetically.

"Did you do something to Lisa?" Jojo asked, raising a skeptical eyebrow. "Is she bound and gagged in a closet somewhere just so you could take over?"

"No, but that sounds like a good idea if she decides to show up. But, I can do this, he won't hurt me," she said.

"No, Chyna, go back to the hospital, clean that stuff off your face, and get the hell out of here."

"I'm not leaving. You help me or I'll do something on my own. You have nothing right here, nothing, and no one can help you better than I can, I'm all you got!"

"No!"

"Yes!" Chyna said one last time, and as a testament to the seriousness of her mission, she held her left hand by her right hand, studying the ring that symbolized everything she wanted for the future and everything she held dear. She removed it and tucked it in the small beaded handbag dangling against her hip. She then looked at Jojo and launched into the argument she'd been preparing since she received a phone call from the man she'd had follow Jojo from his Alexandria apartment to Special Agent Terrance Trent Dunbar's workplace.

It seemed almost too easy; that meant the hard part was getting his confession. She stood, trying to remember everything they'd talked her through, a twenty-minute session on how to act while wearing a wire, and she couldn't remember many of the instructions she'd been given. They seemed numerous. "The mike is just there," Terrance had said. It was there all right. She tried to adjust her shoulders as if that would take away the tiny tickle the wire made as it inched around her waist, the gray tape holding it securely to her chest. It stuck out just enough for her to know she was wearing it and not enough for Warren to see anything other than her bosom pushed up by the tight-fitting bodice of the dress.

"Act natural. We have surveillance in his apartment too, so there's no need to be really close to him to get all that he's saying; he'll become suspicious. Act natural." That was Jojo's friend, Agent Dunbar, a special under-cover agent for the FBI. "Ask open-ended questions," Trent said. "Don't worry about the wording so much as getting him to talk. That's his downfall, we'll get him on that alone."

So she was there at his Georgetown apartment, a two-bedroom, sterile, cold place with limited furnishings. She sat on a nice sofa she might have admired at any other time but she couldn't right then. Trent and Jojo had thought much more ahead than she had. They got dinner from a take-out restaurant and a bottle of ex-pensive wine.

Not sure where to put everything, Chyna moved to the small dining room. She set up the place with what little serving ware he had in the bare cabinets. Then she lit two long tapered candles, took a seat, rehearsed ques-tions, and waited for Warren to arrive.

"I brought some dinner, I wanted to talk with you," she said, silently chastising herself for not hearing him enter.

"How did you get in here?" Warren asked, as he loos-ened his tie and placed his briefcase by the door.

"The landlord couldn't resist my outfit. I bought this for you, do you like it?"

Warren nodded and she thanked God for the ability to change subjects quickly. "I . . ." She looked around,

feeling out of place, naked almost. She never wore anything so hideous, provocative, and revealing. Dean
would hate her looking so trashy. She was a casual
clothes person. Even for her job, she didn't have to buy
anything other than a uniform, nothing businesslike. "I
had hoped . . . we could talk over a nice dinner. . . ." She
turned to raise her hand to indicate the spread laid out
on the small table.

"I'm not really hungry."

"All right," she said, quickly trying not to seem put off
or discouraged by his attitude.

Not knowing what to think, Chyna watched him move
away from her farther into the kitchen. From the refrigerator he removed a beer, popped the cap, and turned
it upward, consuming half of it with a long chug. He
wiped his mouth and turned again to regard her.

"I don't stay here often," Warren said, looking at her
and looking away as if he was nervous. "I bought this place
to get away from my father. I do a lot of my business here,
but I'm in the process of moving."

She tried to concentrate on him to find an opening to
get down to the business she was there to conduct. She
tried to look as if she hung on his every word and tried
to make her eyes reflect a love she didn't feel.

"What are you doing here?"

Quickly she refocused on what he was saying, remembering that she was there for a purpose: to get at the
truth, for her and Dean's life together. "I left Dean." She
looked away.

"You did?" Warren asked incredulously. "I haven't
heard how bad they hurt him."

"They?"

"Yes," Warren said.

Chyna would get that part later. "Well, a knife wound
to his upper torso. He lost a lot of blood."

"Did you really leave him?"

Chyna turned when Warren pulled her roughly into his arms. First she looked down to count the buttons of his shirt and then up into his eyes. Eyes so cold a door might as well have opened and brought a blast of cold air to her skin. "I did, I even gave him back his ring." She held up the ringless finger before his eyes.

"Oh, I wish . . . I wish I could have seen that . . . I wish . . . I knew . . . I knew you'd do it, I believed, I hoped that you would."

She nodded. "You did everything to make me see."

"Yes, yes," Warren shouted. "Dean, the Jamesons, they're nothing. I told my father I'd be better than him. I told him I'd succeed where he failed." Warren let go of her and chugged another swig of the beer on the counter.

"Where, how did he fail?"

"Alfreah, he loves her, my father always wanted what a Jameson man had, but I succeeded."

Chyna nodded and pretended that that revelation had no affect on her. "Wow," she said in awe.

"Kind of like I love you," Warren said as he moved closer to Chyna again and placed an arm around her.

Chyna did her best not to shrug away in disgust. "Your love, though, it's not an obsession, it's real?" she questioned.

"Isn't it probably both?" He laughed. "I hated that Gary had you and when you divorced, I wanted to comfort you. Then it seemed Jameson had you and I did all the tricks in the book to ruffle his feathers to make him think you and I had something going. I just wanted him out of the picture. I want him dead."

"No!" Chyna shouted. More calmly she said, "He's out, you don't have to worry about him anymore, we can be together now." She touched his cheek, repulsed by the straggly facial hair that grazed her fingers and the palm of her hand.

"I still can't believe it." Warren moved to pace the

small kitchen confines. "Do you really mean it? Do you love me?"

Chyna could only nod. "I just want to go slow. I feel bad for leading Dean on, for pretending to deny my feelings for you. That wasn't right."

"I know why you did it."

"You do?"

"He's stable, he has family; it's just my dad and me. I'm sorry I have nothing more to offer you in that way but we'll build our own family, we will be very well off. We'll move away from my father, he's nothing but a washed-up old man, obsessed with another man's wife." Warren laughed again. "Sounds like me, I guess, but I'm better than my father. I'm going to have the woman I've always wanted, we'll be happy."

"Being better than your father, so you were able to bring a Jameson down when he couldn't years ago."

"I guess you could say that . . ."

"The fire, that was ingenious," Chyna went on. "I mean, his father had just died, nothing like kicking a man when he's down."

"Was it? You thought so?"

Chyna nodded enthusiastically.

"I wish I could say I had planned it, but Lisa took care of it for me."

"Well, having him beat up then, leaving him for dead. Why didn't you just finish him?"

"I tried, but Lisa got in the way, she called the police. I ordered them to burn down the house, made it seem like she did that as well."

"That's brilliant."

"You're brilliant. I love you, Chyna. I have something to show you. Come this way." Warren moved, grabbing Chyna by the hand. He led her to the back of the apartment. There he moved boxes, and a door opened and a cold draft enveloped her.

"I've been planning this, the Hardigs' second empire. Dad doesn't know anything about how much I've thought and set this deal into motion."

Chyna watched as Warren moved to plug in a cord leading from the glass box. When a series of lights inside came on, it was like no other planned development she'd ever seen. Even on television.

"This," Warren said as he came back to stand beside her, "the Hardigs' twin buildings, the heart of Springfield, the mall is around the corner over here, but these will be more upscale shops, a piece of New York in Virginia. Right off I-95, people can zip off of this exit ramp, which will be installed after they completely demolish and cart away the rubbish to Jameson's building. It was in the way where it was. I offered him new space, a piece of this"—he gestured toward the model—"he didn't want it. I offered him executive positions on my team, but really only so I could be closer to you, so I could have you. I know you'd never cheat if you were to get married, but I couldn't lose you and plus Jameson brings a lot of pull in the community, at least that's what my father says. If I could persuade him to see the benefit of this development, other prominent people would think it was a good deal and support the project.

"Here!" Warren continued. "The lower garage, people can have their cars parked, and then spend time shopping. Over there"—he pointed to a small park that separated the retail community from what looked to Chyna like apartment complexes—"the planned apartments, pool, tennis courts, spa, also contained within a tower of very high priced living efficiencies."

As Warren clicked a serious of buttons, a waterfall sprouted from a makeshift fountain in front of one of the buildings, and Chyna was shocked to see her name in small neon lights, a minute sign.

"You'll love this, this is Chyna's Shop! An artist bou

tique. You can sell your art pieces here, or you can display the imports from others in your circle. These glass doors . . . you can have a showing, people from outside can look in and wish they'd had your creativity, your mind to produce such fabulous works. . . . I bet you didn't know that about me, that I knew your passion.

"Gary used to invite me over, and I'd sneak up to the upstairs loft where you had your studio. I used to look at your work and admire it. I admit I coveted a few pieces. Oh, all my fantasies are coming together. I'll make you so happy, where Gary and Dean couldn't. I know about the trouble you've had conceiving, but I'll get the best doctors in the world."

"Stop! Stop it." Chyna felt ill, her heart pounding as if she was about to have a heart attack, and her act to coax the truth from Warren went out the window. She backed away and fell against the hard oak doors of a bureau she'd seen on her way in. The doors flapped open and Chyna turned around.

Warren rushed in front of her to close the doors as if there was something he didn't want her to see. "I'm sorry, I've upset you, I'm sorry."

"It's just, it's just too fast, and how did you know about all that?"

"Gary told me, he told me he was glad you hadn't been able to have children, that you'd lost—"

"No, don't . . . don't finish that."

"I'm sorry, I'm sorry I've upset you."

Chyna couldn't think anymore. She watched him, but she moved on to something quickly before she let go of whatever was in her stomach, which couldn't have been much considering she hadn't eaten in almost twenty-four hours. She concentrated, or made herself concentrate, on the way he stood in front of the bureau, hands behind his back. "What's in there, what are you hiding?"

"Nothing," Warren said. "It's just . . . you'll think I'm crazy, you'll think badly of me."

Too late for that, Chyna thought silently to herself, then noticed the way he hung his head, almost like a child. "I won't," she tried to reassure him. "I wouldn't."

He turned and opened the doors to the bureau, sliding each one back until it fit perfectly in a groove. The furniture was the kind meant to house a television, but there was nothing in the empty space.

Warren moved from in front of her, and reached near the door for a small lamp that brought to light a shrine that was apparently dedicated to Chyna Lockhart's life.

"You're sick," she whispered, covering her mouth. She hadn't meant for the words to leave her mouth but the truth and the extent of his obsession with her had shaken her.

Chapter 30

Nearby, with their headphones on, with their eyes glued to the monitors mounted along the van's walls, Jojo and Trent sat watching the screen. "What's she doing, man?"

"Let's go," Jojo said and moved to the van's back door.

"Wait."

"No, no, let's not wait, move it, right now."

Jojo was out of the van and up the stairs of the George-town apartments, his friend on his heels, his gun drawn. "Would you let me do this?" Trent asked heatedly.

"You forget I used to do this too," Jojo said.

"And you forget I'm in charge of this operation," Trent whispered back and moved in front of his friend to the door.

"I know this is a bit much, but I told you I've loved you since I met you at that gala and fund-raiser benefit during the first few years of Gary's career. You were a vision, beautiful, and I guess that night started my fixation on you."

"You need help," she whispered again, but didn't know if he'd heard her. In some ways she wanted him to hear her and in others she knew she had to keep playing along to get more answers out of him, though she didn't know what more she could pretend to be to get him to talk and she hadn't been keeping track of what Jojo and Trent had drilled into her brain. She forgot everything.

Chyna could only nod. She took a step closer, bent down to look at all the pictures of herself. Pictures of her and Gary, pictures even the paparazzi shouldn't have had unless they'd been invited to her home, and personal pictures that she'd never pose for. Then there were pictures of her and Dean at the store, entering the Jameson house. Pictures of her in front of the senate office building, the same picture she'd seen on the news. The one that put serious doubts in Dean's mind whether she had leftover feelings for her husband, or was out to ruin his life. Warren Hardig had submitted that. He and Lisa had worked together.

Startled, Chyna in a blur watched as Warren moved back in front of her and shut the doors with a final snap.

"I'm afraid you know all my secrets," he said as he turned to face her.

She couldn't think. He was maniacal, insane, and further disturbed than she or even Dean had thought.

She moved quickly out of the room to a place where there was more light, where she could not only see, but also think.

"I just . . . there is just so much, it would have seemed easier if you'd told me how you felt from the beginning."

"I thought you loved Dean."

Chyna nodded. *I do, I will always love Dean, not you, you sick bastard,* she thought to herself but bit her tongue.

"I'd have anyone removed for you. They're hindrances to my path to you. I had to do it, and don't you see, it worked. Right down to that picture of you coming from Gary's office. I had my investigator take that of you. I sent it to the media, and Lisa did the rest."

"You're sick, Warren, you need help." She knew that Jojo and Trent were hearing her every word, and ending this farce as she did would signal to them that it was over, that she couldn't continue any longer. She felt literally ill. She didn't know how they planned to enter but she prayed it was soon.

"I thought I could like you at least, but there is no help for you, none!" she hissed.

"Don't say that!" Warren cried. "Why would you say such things to me?"

"Because it's true. You need help." She shook her head as if to pity him. "You need help!"

When the doorbell rang, Chyna jumped but quickly turned as if to let Warren answer the door. When he didn't leave the room, she turned back to face him. "Aren't you going to answer that?"

"No one visits me here, they have the wrong door," Warren said. "I'm not sick, I love you. You just said you loved me, you just told me you were leaving Dean for me."

"Never, I'd never leave him," Chyna spat. She moved to the door when the banging increased, wondering why they didn't just come in and arrest him.

"You set me up?" Warren asked alarmingly.

"Yes! You're going to burn in hell!" Chyna said, feeling overconfident. She didn't mean to rub it in his face like she did, but she felt safe, as if everything was out in the open, knowing help was on the other side of the door, that she was home free.

Warren grabbed her arm and before she could tell him more about how she felt, she halted the spill of everything that was on her mind as Warren reached behind his back, lifting his shirt, and when his hand came back around he held a small semiautomatic weapon.

Looking at the gun, Chyna moved her eyes upward quickly. She witnessed the shift in his eyes, almost as if he'd physically reached for an alter ego, the bad side, nothing like the one that had spoken nice words to her, had caressed and cajoled her earlier. She had turned him, sent him over the edge, she realized, with her harsh words, but she couldn't help herself, he was trying to ruin her life, Dean was in the hospital. She felt as if finally the toll of everything was descending on her. Her life, her happiness, was almost ruined by this deranged, disgustingly sick man before her. She managed to twist out of his embrace, moving quickly toward the door.

"I wouldn't have harmed you." He trained the gun on her and she froze.

Then the door nearly burst off its hinges and in a blur of two tall dark figures, guns drawn, Trent and Jojo rushed in, shielding her. It was Jojo who kept her back, while Trent rushed inside, hollering orders to Warren to drop his weapon.

Chyna heard the click, more of Trent's orders to stop, to drop his weapon, then, "Don't do this, man!" before a single shot rang out. Chyna jumped from the loud bang. She closed her eyes, then opened them again as she rushed to the door behind Jojo. She saw Warren on the floor, a pool of blood spilling profusely from his head. Chyna looked away, felt sick immediately from the sight of blood, which never seemed to bother her before. Then the reason why Warren would be shot in the head dawned upon her. She grabbed her stomach when she began to feel like she'd throw up right then and right there on the floor. She then grabbed her head to stop the world from spinning around her. Jojo seemed to turn his body to regard her. His lips moved, a blurring, deep voice made sound, his eyes, the same shade as those of the man she loved, viewed her with concern, but she couldn't understand what he asked and then his arms were reaching out to catch her before she hit the floor.

Dean was home but he wasn't alone. After pleading with the doctor to let him go, he had to sign a series of release papers stating that he was leaving against medical advice and was let go of his own free will. He'd been warned about the ramifications if he didn't take it easy and allow his body the rest it needed in order to heal.

If he disturbed his stitches at all, they could burst and start the bleeding all over again. If he moved too fast or exerted too much energy, he could faint and cause himself even more damage. So he followed orders as best he could. Moving a bit slower than his normal stomp-the-ground, angry pace called for, he shifted cautiously back and forth before the living room's bay window. It was the only window that gave him a view of the front lawn and the driveway.

He was waiting for Chyna and so was everyone else: his sister Tish, their mother, Alfreah, and even Jina was in the room. They seemed to sit at different positioning points on the furniture, watching him as if they thought he would faint any moment, ready in case he needed carting back to the hospital.

"Dean, why don't you go lie down, please? You know we'll wake you as soon as she gets here." Tish was up on her feet.

It was like they took turns, poking, prodding him to rest, and his agitation grew by the moment. But if there was one person he couldn't get mad at, it was his baby sister, pregnant with twins no less. He placed an arm around her shoulders, thinking back to a time when things were so much simpler. They were the youngest, she and he, thus the last ones to leave the house while their older siblings went off to college. They seemed to be the closest, thick as thieves. He smiled at her, then looked lower to her protruding belly. He thought about the twins she carried, about Chase, his brother-in-law, a nervous wreck who never seemed to leave his pregnant wife's side.

He bent to kiss her on the cheek. "I'm all right, and I wish you hadn't come up here in your state."

"I know you do," Tish said, smiling as she rubbed her stomach. "I'm here now. The doctor said we're all doing fine. It's you we're worried about . . ." Tish abruptly closed her mouth to follow Dean's eyes panning slowly to the window when Jojo's car drove up. As if they hadn't been talking at all, her brother left her side and moved to the door.

Frozen to the spot, Dean stood immobile as Chyna exited the car and walked slowly to the door. His mouth dropped open as he viewed her legs, an indication she was wearing something awfully short underneath the oversized coat that belonged to Jojo. When she exited Jojo's truck, the pieces he'd been missing as to where she was and what she went to do floated into place.

Jojo was at the door first. He opened it, saw Dean, then ushered her inside ahead of him.

Her feet hurt; that had been her first thought, and then she saw Dean and her heart constricted. It took a sheer force of will not to embrace him, to be comforted by him, but she couldn't, not yet. When she entered the house, she felt as if all eyes were upon her, scrutinizing, assessing, detesting, but they weren't really, it was just her imagination. Still, she felt ashamed.

Jojo's arms came on her shoulders to remove the coat and she wished he'd left it on. Chyna didn't want the Jamesons to see her dressed like a cheap trick. He turned and hung it on the coat tree by the door.

Sick to her stomach almost for what she'd tried to do and the terrible way it had ended, Chyna looked at everyone in the room. Everyone, except Dean. It was clear they didn't know what to say. Ms. Alfreah spoke first. She moved closer to Chyna, who felt as if she should run away, but there was no escape. Then she wished she'd gone just a few more yards to her own house. She hadn't known everyone would be there and she wished she were alone for just a little bit longer, but that wouldn't have worked. She owed the people before her so much. They were family. They would understand.

"How are you, honey? Are you all right?" Alfreah said.

"Yes, ma'am," she managed to utter, feeling like a small child. When she felt Dean touch her hand she pulled away from him and apologized with her eyes, then her mouth. "I'm sorry, excuse me, I gotta take a bath." She bent to remove the heels from her feet. With the pointy shoes clutched to her chest, she rushed from the room up the stairs and to the bathroom, where she shut out the rest of the world with the closing of the door.

Chapter 31

"You let her do this. Have you lost your damn mind?" Dean said, watching Chyna's back. He quickly whirled on his brother.

"She came in there and asked to do it. If I hadn't let her, she would have done something stupid on her own," Jojo defended. "This wouldn't even have happened if you had been open about what was going on."

"Don't turn this on me, I was handling it."

"Handling it so much you got laid up in the hospital? That's handling it all right."

"You're a stupid idiot."

"Stop it," Tish yelled. "Stop it right now."

"You never think far enough ahead, do you, Joe?" Dean continued, ignoring his sister's protest, disregarding the presence of his family. "You ever think beyond today, beyond right this moment? What happened to Lisa? See, Chyna wasn't prepared for a sting operation, she's never done anything of the sort. She never lied about anything, but you let her talk you into it. You ever think maybe she couldn't handle the aftereffects of what went wrong once all was said and done? Of just how crazy that bastard was? Something went wrong, didn't it?" Dean knew if something terrible hadn't happened, Chyna wouldn't have shrugged from his touch. She wouldn't have run as if he were the enemy and her eyes certainly wouldn't have evaded his. It was all there, in her eyes, the fact that she took on something greater than what she was prepared to handle.

"So what happened?" Dean repeated again. "If they got him on tape confessing to screwing up my life, the fire, leaving me to my damned death, and whatever else he did . . . if that's all that happened, why the hell is she so upset?"

"Warren killed himself," Jojo said finally.

Upstairs, the water cascaded over her body. Hot like fire, it still wasn't hot enough to wash away Warren's touch, his caresses, the hands of a man that was now dead. The magnitude of all this was so much greater than she thought. He was far crazier than she could have imagined. He had some serious problems, problems she thought were just his jealousy, his greed, and his need to manipulate people like pieces on a board game, moving them, repositioning them to his greatest advantage. It was more than that, it was psychological, serious dementia and Chyna couldn't help feeling as if her last ploy drove him to his final demise.

Wrapping herself in a towel, she bent to pick up the remains of her outfit. Removing the plastic trash bag from the decorative trash can, she dumped everything into it: the black dress, the panty hose, her underwear, her bra, the cheap necklace, the shoes, and the pieces of duct tape that held the wire to her body.

"Useless," she muttered. It hadn't done any good, except to push a man standing at the edge of a cliff over it.

She froze a moment when a light tap rapped on the door.

"Yes," she said, knowing it was Dean.

"Chyna, please let me in. Are you all right?"

"Yes, I'm all right," she replied. "I'll be out in a minute."

On the other side, Dean nodded sadly and moved to one of the bedrooms. He sat on the bed and waited until she appeared at the door.

He couldn't help the sad smile that lit his face. She looked terrible and beautiful at the same time. He felt something tug deep inside his heart when she tentatively smiled back.

"How are you?" he said when her smile fled as quickly as it came. She looked as if she was going to run again.

"Good," she lied and moved farther into the room. She moved quickly to the dresser where she grabbed a bottle of deodorant and rubbed it hastily in the pit of each arm. Next she searched the overnight bag that was still there since she'd been recovering from the accident. She found clean underwear, a pair of seersucker pants, and a cotton tank. With her back to Dean she managed the pants and underwear up, revealing scant skin in the process. The shirt went over her head and she let the towel fall as she pulled her shirt into place.

"Did you get released from the hospital or did you just leave?" she asked, finally turning to face him.

"I signed some papers for my release," he said.

"So you left before you were supposed to," Chyna said, taking a seat beside him.

Tentatively, as if she'd disappear, Dean turned to face her and pulled her into his arms. Moments ticked by and he felt her relax before her body shuddered with sobs. "Chyna? Baby, look at me. It's over now," Dean said. He pushed her back to get a good look at her. "You're the bravest person I know. You did it, you didn't have to, but you did."

"I did it all right. I drove him to kill himself."

"No!" Dean said. "He did that all by himself."

"If I hadn't—"

"Hadn't what? Got to the truth, tried to end his game playing? He would have done it at some other time probably. With all of his dealings, it would have caught up with him, it would have come to haunt him one day."

Chyna knew all that was true, but it was as if he had died on her shift or something. The sting operation had been a catalyst for his death. "I pushed him, didn't I? He said that he loved me. I just used that against him, I just . . ."

"He might have loved you, but his love was sick. It was a twisted obsessive kind of love."

She nodded. "It was sick all right," she admitted but suddenly felt as if the day's toll still hadn't sunk in. She changed the subject. "I'm sorry about shunning you downstairs. I didn't want to hurt you."

Dean shook his head, ready to protest that her actions didn't hurt, but they had hurt even though he understood the reasons behind the way she acted as she did. "I just didn't understand. I was just worried is all. It's all over, Chyna," Dean comforted. "The Hardigs won't bother us anymore."

"How do you know?"

He admitted he didn't, but he hoped.

Chyna nodded, not knowing whether she believed him or not, only praying that he was right. Maybe he knew something she didn't. "I told him I loved him, but I didn't, ever, I never stopped loving you."

Grabbing her ring finger, Chyna shrieked in horror.

"What's the matter?" Dean said, alarmed, but Chyna was up rushing toward the door, down the hall, and into the bathroom.

She searched frantically through the items she'd hastily discarded until she located the cheap sequined bag. Emptying the contents, she shook the bag until the diamond ring fell out and rolled to the floor. On her hands and knees, Chyna located it in the fluffy bristles of the bath mat and placed it on her finger before returning to Dean.

She lay down on the bed beside him as if nothing had happened.

"Is everything all right?" he asked.

Chyna nodded. "I tried to make it right," she blurted one last time.

"You did," Dean said, placing a strong arm around her narrow waist. "You did."

He held her until she drifted to sleep.

"What in the world are they doing up there?"

Tish Jameson-Alton stood with hands on her hips, looking upward from the base of the stairs as if she could see through the walls.

"Probably reacquainting themselves," Jina said as she passed her sister with a tray loaded with food.

"Probably doing what we did to get those two," Chase said, pointing to her belly. "Now stop worrying, whatever they're doing is a great tension reliever, if you know what I mean."

He passed Tish as well, carrying a tray cluttered with drinks. "Come feed my kids," he admonished her playfully.

Tish smiled and followed her husband into the dining room.

"Mama, don't you want to eat?" Tish asked her mother when everyone present had taken a seat but her.

Alfreah Jameson turned to look at her children and her two sons-in-law. She shook her head. "I'm going to run an errand."

"What?" Tish said. She pushed her plate back just a hair and looked at her sister.

Jina wiped her mouth. "Mama, it's almost nine o'clock.

What do you need at this hour? Whatever it is, we'll go get it for you."

"No, I have to go do this. I'll be back," Alfreah said and left through the front door.

Chapter 32

She couldn't tell her family where she was going. In the crisp November air, it took only fifteen minutes for her to get to Alexandria. Alfreah Jameson entered the Hardig building enveloped by the warm interiors, the double-glass doors, their frosted panes with the word HARDIG in lettering so big and wide it seemed to cover most of the door.

"Hello, ma'am. The office is closed now," a man wearing a uniform said. He stood behind a massive desk.

"Is Mr. Hardig in?"

"Well, yes . . . but—"

"Then he'll want to see me," she interrupted the man, who immediately moved to the opposite side of the desk where he picked up a phone and pressed a few buttons. "Yes, sir, a . . . ?"

"Alfreah Jameson," she supplied as she waited patiently to be granted access to the elevators.

"He says to go on up." The man pointed to a series of elevators along the far wall.

As she pushed the button for his floor, she thought of her husband, how if he were living he would hate that she was there now. But she had to end any further disruption to her family once and for all.

The door slid open and Alfreah met another guard casually sitting on a chair where a secretary might have been by day. He nodded sleepily to Alfreah and pointed.

Uncertain of what she would find, she moved to the door and grabbed the knob. Behind the desk was Chauncey Hardig, Esq.

"I knew you'd come visit me," Chauncey said when he swiveled once in his seat before standing. He wasn't a tall man, unlike her husband, Joe. He was just a few inches taller than her five-foot-three-inch frame.

Looking away, Alfreah took a moment to study the pictures lining the walls, the dark interior. A conference table sat along one corner lined with windows that gave view to the other buildings in the surrounding area.

"I must say that you look beautiful as ever. Your hair, it's beautiful completely gray. I wish I could say the same for my own."

Alfreah looked back at him. It was always about him and what he wished for. What had ever attracted her to him?

"Would you care for something to drink? A little chardonnay? I'm having a dinner platter left over from a late business meeting. You're welcome to the platter, or I'll have another sent up if you'd like something else."

Alfreah shook her head. Quickly it came back to her what she had seen in this man when she was twenty years old. Drive and determination, the potential for him to be something great. He had the power to persuade her or any woman. That seemed so long ago now, in another lifetime really, and certainly before she met and married Joe Jameson. She saw it there in the furnishings of the office, the platter of cold cocktail shrimp, and dipping sauces he'd opened placed on his mahogany conference table. The juice bar, metal and chrome. He had everything at his disposal. He was indeed wealthy.

"Free?"

"Don't call me that," she said, trying to remember her

purpose for being there, her desire to pay her respects, to question him in his own role behind his son's fatality.

"I'm sorry about your son."

"Are you?" Chauncey asked, raising a skeptical eyebrow.

"Aren't you? My God, Warren, he was ill. He killed himself, for God's sake."

"No one knows that more than I do. I've spent nearly millions of dollars on his mental evaluations."

"Is that all it was to you, money wasted for time in the doctor's office that obviously didn't work?" She'd forgotten through the years how heartless he was and sadly it all came crashing back. She thought maybe with age, with maturity he would change.

"You forget he wasn't my son, he was my stepson, and I spent years grooming him into something he obviously wasn't cut out to be. He had problems ever since his mother died. I could have kept my money in my pocket!"

"Grooming him? Was he a pet to you?" Alfreah replied incredulously. "Seems like you should have spent time loving him instead."

"That was my way. I did the best I could with what I had."

"Don't quote the words of Thurgood Marshall, you're no measure for such a man, Chauncey. I hope this is all worth it, this, this stuff." She shuddered as a chill ran down her spine. Waving her hands about the space, she continued. "Your caviar, your shrimp cocktail, is this what life is to you? Things to obtain?"

"When love eludes you, you focus your energies on something else."

"Things? They can't love you back, Chauncey."

"And neither did you. Nothing lost, nothing gained."

"So you don't even care that he died, you're here as if the day goes on. As if nothing tragic happened today?"

"I have people to straighten out this mess if that's what you mean."

"People?"

"My publicist, my lawyer."

"Right, of course," Alfreah said exasperatingly. "I am sorry about your son. My last few questions regard your involvement with my son's building. You wouldn't know anything about that either?"

"Did I burn down his place of business? No, I didn't. Did my son? I'll never know the answer to that."

Alfreah nodded, wondering if anyone ever would.

"I've apologized a million times for the years I sought you, Alfreah, knowing you were committed to someone else. I lost my head then, I was young and foolish."

"Now? You're just old and foolish." Alfreah felt the bitterness on the back of her tongue ease to the front.

"I've made mistakes and now I guess I'll live my life alone."

"That was your choice, you could have had your pick of anyone, any woman you wanted . . ."

"But I only wanted one woman," Chauncey reminded her. "I'm guilty of having an unhealthy fixation on something that wasn't mine to have, and then I'm guilty of projecting those same unhealthy feelings on my stepson. It seems the Hardig men always wanted what a Jameson man had. Warren's feelings are . . . were much more ahead of my own. He took it to another level, one I can't evade responsibility for helping to foster, but if it's any consolation to you, your family is safe now. This Hardig won't bother you any further, and there aren't any more out there that will either. I'm guilty, yes, guilty because I held on to something, memories of you and me . . . I remember your passion, Free . . . Alfreah. That passion stirred me. Here even now as you question me, as it takes guts for you to even come here to see me at this hour, that boldness, that stirs me. Do you remember the passion we had for each other?"

"Don't go there. I've forgotten that. I replaced those

few, few times with memories of my husband, something you couldn't or wouldn't become at that time. I asked you if you could ever commit and I left because you said you didn't know. I always wanted to be married, to have a family, and that's what I sought after, that's what I got. Joe Jameson gave them to me and I've never regretted any of it, I never will regret the path that I've chosen."

"The struggle, you didn't regret that? Paying bills late, the time you asked for money to help your husband who nearly broke his back fixing other people's homes?"

"Asking someone I thought was a friend for money was a mistake! I made a mistake!"

"Don't you see that's what I did? That's what I'm saying now."

"It does not matter, it does not matter at all. I wanted to pay my respects, to say I'm sorry that your life, your pathetic life has come to this. I hope you're happy alone and without family to love you. You did this, you created this yourself. Your infidelity and your lies while we dated still hurt, but it compares nothing to what you'll feel when you finally take time to review your life: how lonely it is. To know the hurt you've brought to others by your take-all attitude. My son will recover, he will be all right. I now release you from our lives. I've lived my life, can now reap the benefits of raising children, or spoiling grandchildren . . . and you can live up here, work till all hours of the night, and burn in hell for all I care. You heartless, self-serving fool."

She felt better saying what she did, but that night her words would come back and she'd regret letting loose such hate. She wouldn't feel terrible for long though. She didn't truly wish for him the life he'd somehow created. She was sorry for him, sorry he couldn't have seemed to end up better than he did.

"I still love you, Alfreah, I've never stopped through all these—"

"I have, Chauncey," she said without hesitation. "Don't you get it? I let go many, many years ago. I have stopped and you've got to let go, there's still time for you to have more than just . . . this." She waved her hands about the space, quickly circling the room with her eyes. There was nothing left to say, and she turned, exiting through the door. She finally felt as if she'd closed a chapter in her life that had been left open far too long.

Chapter 33

His sisters looked at him as if he were crazy, but trying to play catch-up on the years would do that to any person. While Chyna slept for the next few days, only waking up sporadically to eat, drink, and use the bathroom, Dean Jameson was planning a wedding.

"You heard me correctly," he said, sipping a cup of coffee in a pair of jogging pants and a tattered sweatshirt. "I know how you guys like to plan things. I already talked to Angie, and she agreed to do the menu, but I still need help."

"There's no question we'll help you, it's just what's the rush?"

The sooner they got married, the sooner they could begin the rest of their lives together. After all, he kept reminding his sisters and everyone else like they'd kept reminding him, the entire production was more than fifteen years in the making. Hadn't he wasted enough time already?

"Shouldn't we wait until Lisa is apprehended?" Jina put in.

Dean nodded. That had crossed his mind, but what if it took forever to find her? She was nowhere to be found. She had dropped off the face of the earth, and as far as Dean was concerned, he wished she'd stay there. He expressed as much to them.

"Well, then," Jina said, "okay, just let us know what you want us to do, and we'll do it."

When the phone rang, he reached for it before it finished its first complete ring. Chyna had been in and out of sleep for the last seventy-two hours, and he still didn't want to interrupt her. Charlize had ordered her to take something Dean couldn't remember the name of, but it ran the makings of a slight cold from her body and also left her drowsy. But each time she awoke, she was looking, talking, and acting more and more like herself. The heaviest of the storm had passed. The Jamesons kept the television turned off until the story of their lives blew over, and another story about someone else's family took center stage.

Only Dean did read the paper. The entire story now read like a page out of a novel. A front-page, feature-length spread in the *Washington Post* about business tycoon Warren Hardig being found dead in his apartment. The story had been recounted in a handful of the most popular Washington magazines and then again and again in other business journals. Not one single advertisement interrupted the main story entitled "The Rise and Fall of Prominent Business Tycoon Warren G. Hardig."

The papers even a week later continued to fly off of newsstand shelves so quickly that production required a special edition and print run to compensate the need for additional copies.

"Yeah, she's fine. She's sleeping," Dean informed Jina, who was at the bridal shop selecting gowns for Chyna to try on when she was well again.

"I don't know but five seems like a good number to pick from. She's bound to like one of those . . . I mean don't you think so?" he asked, trying carefully to keep his voice low so as not to disturb Chyna. "Well, okay, just make sure they are something she would like."

Discussing a few more details with his sister about his

plan, Dean soon hung up, satisfied that things had already been set in motion.

When Chyna rolled over, she saw the most handsome face she'd ever laid eyes on. Dean leaned down to kiss her and she knew they were going to be all right. "Good morning," she whispered, still groggy from the antibiotic.

"Good day," Dean countered. "It's a little past noon," he said, showing her his watch.

"What's on the agenda for today? I can tell you've got something planned. You have this devilish look about yourself."

"Me? No!" Dean replied, but couldn't help the laughter and the excitement that oozed from his voice. "I do have a couple of things in mind, but only if you're feeling up to them. If not, they can wait until next week."

"Well, what are they?" Chyna asked, propping herself up onto her elbows. She managed her way out of the bed, looking at Dean all the while. Just from his face, she grew excited, knowing he was up to something. "Are you going to continue to sit there and look silly or are you going to tell me?"

"I am sworn to secrecy." Dean stood. Retrieving his coat from the end of the bed, he held it but thought better of leaving when Chyna's skimpy underwear caught his attention.

"How can you be sworn to secrecy? You're the one with the secret." Chyna was thoughtful a moment. "Aren't you?"

Dean nodded. "Yep, and I swore myself to secrecy."

They both laughed. Dean reached for her and his hands immediately traveled lower. "Are you all right?"

She nodded her confirmation. "Any word on Lisa?"

"No," Dean said. "But we can move on, Chyna. She won't hurt us, we can move on with our lives regardless of what she's planning, okay? Don't let things be on hold for us."

"I know, I just, I was just wondering."

He would wonder too until she was caught. It'd just have to be something they'd keep in the back of their mind. "Until then you stay here awhile."

"Are you sure? I don't want to crowd everyone. Are Chase and Tish going back soon?"

Dean shook his head. "They sent Thomas back to Georgia with my mom. Tish and Chase may stay through Christmas. If they do that they'll have Thomas fly up again."

"I missed you," Chyna said, growing serious.

"I've been here."

"No, I mean, I've really missed you," she whispered and gave him the kiss that woke all of his senses. "Do you think you're up to it? When do you go back to the doctor for a checkup?" She touched his side.

"Oh, I think I could manage," he said to answer her first question. Dean smiled devilishly and bent to remove his shirt, then his pants. The excitement, however, worked him up to a fevered pitch and he needed to slow down immediately.

"Are you all right? I'm sorry," Chyna said as she moved back from the bed.

"I'm okay, I'm all right. Just go slow." He smiled.

"Maybe we shouldn't. We can wait another week or so. We're in no rush."

"No," Dean protested, "there are advantages to going slow," he said, pulling her on top of him. "You'll just have to do the work."

Chyna laughed. Loving him wasn't work at all. She reached into the bedside nightstand, retrieving a small packet from the drawer. She opened the condom and rolled it down his length. "I'll go slow, okay?"

Dean nodded as she eased down onto him. "Oh God," he hissed through clenched teeth. Slow was one thing, torturous was something else. But he let her have her way. Knowing his injury didn't permit much thrusting action, this would have to do. He grabbed her hips, pulling her harder onto him so that they fit as close as they could.

"I think I like this, I think I have a lot of control over you," she said as she moved her hips in a slow circular motion while he glided her back and forth over him.

"Every time, Chyna, you're always in control," Dean whispered. And she was. No one made him lose his senses like she did. She was it, everything, and he couldn't hold on any longer. He let go, pulsing inside her, so glad to be there with her.

"I love you, Dean," she said, looking down at him.

"I love you, Chyna." She bent down to kiss him and his arms pulled her tight, thrusting so deeply into her, she couldn't help releasing her climax.

Chapter 34

Chyna sat patiently next to Jina and Tish on the comfy sofa of the Jameson living room. Whatever Dean had in mind, this hadn't been what she thought. First a woman with what looked like a rolling wardrobe came rushing into the room. Her assistant walked in behind her carrying boxes and boxes, each a different shape, size, and color. Some glossy gold foil and some stark white and each filled with a different wedding accessory.

The woman, a pale-skinned older lady with a high-pitched voice, was complete smiles, focusing most of her attention on Chyna. It took only moments for her to set up her show and when Chyna saw the dresses that came out of each bag, she was absolutely speechless. Today would be the day she picked out her wedding dress.

The first two gowns were less than desirable and did not meet Chyna's approval. They were not at all her style and she was beginning to doubt the woman's judgment until she was shown the third dress.

Slowly, Chyna's eyes moved along the flowing A-length skirt. It was like the first gown, but the material looked thicker. The sleeves were long and the neck wasn't dramatically dipping to the breast. It was square cut with definite lines and sleeves that tapered to a V that would stop in the center of her palm.

Chyna was on her feet moving toward the gown before she knew that's what she had done. Her hands ran lovingly over the fabric. She knew she'd wear that particular one. It was an absolute vision.

Closer she could see the tiny, handmade glasslike beading detailed and embellished over the chest and narrowing as it ran down the center. In each bead, Chyna saw visions of all her dreams dance in the reflections.

"Shall we try it on? No?" the woman asked crisply, and looked around the room for approval.

Chyna tried on the dress, and after much fussing from the woman, fluffing, primping, and all the other bothersome pinning and pulling she did, Chyna was finally permitted to turn around and see herself in the full-length mirror. It looked even better on than it did hanging from a rack. Chyna could only smile with elation. "It's beautiful," she whispered.

"Oh yes, beautiful," the woman said and clapped as if she'd just won the Nobel Peace Prize.

"We have alterations soon. The wedding is . . . No?"

Chyna noticed the woman stopped talking abruptly as Tish and Jina both shook their heads at once.

"Soon," Tish offered firmly, scooting herself as best her large stomach would allow off the couch to help the woman pack up their boxes. With the help of the assistant, Chyna removed the dress when the measurements were complete.

Tish and Jina all but shoved the poor startled woman and her assistant out of the door.

"Thank you so much for your time and all of your knowledgeable insight," said Tish hurriedly. "We will see you tomor . . . uh, soon."

She shut the door quickly behind the woman's back. Looking at Chyna, she smiled sweetly. "Get your purse, we're off to our next destination."

They made her dress warmly, then ushered her out the door too.

* * *

When Chyna had a moment of peace, she laid her head on the bed feeling absolutely exhausted. It had been a wonderful day and it seemed like every detail of her wedding was complete with her barely having to lift a finger. She'd chosen the invitations, though now that she had them picked out, she realized she hadn't had the faintest idea who to invite. Just Dean's family and her would be enough. She had no grandiose ideas of a marriage ceremony, just something sweet and intimate would be perfect.

Where was he anyway? she wondered silently to herself. Before she could get up to call him, sleepiness came and she drifted to sleep for the night.

Chyna blinked rapidly against the light and reached for the pillow beside her. Her hand landed on a thick piece of paper. She was up instantly, thinking whatever the card said was a message or note from Dean. She opened the envelope to find that sure enough, Dean had been by. She smiled knowing Dean had probably left the note to explain where he was. Ever since she'd become sick, he was hesitant to wake her while she slept. She hoped he'd also left a time of when he planned to return.

YOU'RE INVITED TO THE MARRIAGE OF CHYNA A. LOCKHART AND DEAN E. JAMESON, AT TWO P.M., TWO THOUSAND AND . . .

Chyna smiled. There were only five days left in the entire year and he wanted to somehow find the time to finish all the planning and marry her within them. She noticed the clock read eleven A.M. For a moment, she pretended that it was already her wedding day, meaning she had just over two hours to get ready. "Wouldn't that be something?" she said aloud.

She looked at the card again and saw it was the exact

invitation she had picked with the black embossed lettering, the tiny bow holding the reply card, the calligraphy with the exaggerated curls. The lettering for the C to her name and the D in Dean dipped and rounded to a fat curve lassoing the other letters as they met one another and closed. They looked as if they would take flight. She'd only chosen the invitations the day before. Chyna wondered how in the world they'd been able to do it so quickly.

She placed the card on the nightstand beside her bed, ensuring that it was upright and looking as if it was displayed. The previous day she had insisted to Dean that she spend the night at home despite his protests. He made her insist that she double-check the locks on the door before going to bed.

Chyna headed downstairs to find a small white bag containing a pleasant aroma that filled her nostrils. "Dean Jameson, you are the best!" she said, reaching into the bag for a scone that was still warm. Moving to the refrigerator for milk, Chyna noticed a folded paper with a picture of a piano with red roses on top of it. She did a double take as she read the caption under the picture. It read TODAY, I WILL MARRY THE ONE WHO HOLDS MY HEART.

Chyna dropped the card and covered her face with her hands. Tears immediately slid down her face. *It can't be today, not today. I'm not ready.*

Chyna continued to reread the card as she moved back upstairs to prepare her bathwater. With a new sense of energy and elation about her nuptials, whenever they might be, she ran up the steps.

In the bathroom, she found a garment bag. Silhouetted against the dark backdrop, for a spine-tingling moment, the bag gave the appearance of a person that loomed over her. Like Warren, she thought silently, her happiness dashing away. She quickly erased such thoughts. *Warren is dead!* she reminded herself silently.

After taking a quick bath, Chyna opened the bag to find a wedding dress. After looking it over once more, she discovered it indeed was *her* wedding dress.

She moved quickly to her room before the full-length mirror where she was able to see how perfectly it fit. How the puffiness of the lower gown portion flared out slightly. She turned and giggled, thinking back to Jina and the poor woman she'd traumatized.

The sleeves of the gown fit Chyna to a tee. How in the world were they able to make the alterations so quickly? Chyna wondered. She tried to remember the day she'd tried it on, the day before yesterday maybe? She couldn't be sure. Her days were so blurred they didn't make sense. Tish and Jina had planned one trip after another, leaving Chyna exhausted but excited about her upcoming wedding. It had been fun, and they'd probably had something planned for tonight, though she didn't know what could possibly be left.

Wedding cake samples, invitations, the groom's ring, the color of the bridesmaids' dresses, and basics had been taken care of in the last seventy-two hours. If Chyna had to pick what was left, she surmised that would simply be the guest list, the menu, the venue, and the groom's attire. Dean and his brother would handle what they were going to wear. As for people, Chyna's family was null. She wanted a small ceremony on an evening where they had dinner and just enough people that could sit around one large table comfortably. A small space for four to six couples to dance, she and Dean, Tish and Chase, Tony and Jina, Ms. Alfreah and . . . she put a mental question mark. She seemed happy alone, though it would be nice to have someone for her to talk to. Maybe Bubba would come by. Chyna knew he shunned the formal affairs if they required him to wear more than a nice shirt and a pair of his best jeans. That was fine with her, she wasn't picky and she wanted a friend of her mother's to be present at the biggest day in her life.

She moved on to her friends from high school, Cheyenne and Malcolm. Samson and Charlize. She'd have to find a single man and woman for them since they were sister and brother.

In such a good mood as she twitched and twirled before the mirror, Chyna thought she might even add Mrs. Jenkins's name to the list. Covering her mouth as she smiled into the mirror, Chyna laughed outright. Whether she invited the mean old woman or not, Loretta Jenkins would find a way to show up. Chyna laughed again, twirling around before the mirror and loving the way her gown swayed around her long legs. She looked down and snapped her fingers. "Shoes!" she said aloud. "We forgot the shoes!

"Well, we can get them today," she went on. "It's a good thing I'm not getting married today."

"Do or die, you are!"

"What?" Chyna turned to the voice that had startled her. Dean's sister appeared in the doorway, her wrapped hair hidden under a scarf, wearing a pair of faded jeans and an old sweater.

"Man," Jina said, "Dean said the notes would work. Look at you." Jina fanned the air, indicating for Chyna to parade in a twirl to show off her dress. Chyna obliged, and Jina continued, "All we have to do is your makeup and we'll make our two o'clock debut." She breezed her way into Chyna's closet.

Chyna watched in stupefaction as her friend moved hurriedly around the room talking a mile a minute like she always did.

Chyna shook her head in disbelief. "Two o'clock? J, please back up or I'm going to die if I think you're saying what I think you're saying." Smiling once again at her reflection, Chyna hiked up her dress and tried to follow Dean's sister as she exited the closet with one of Chyna's travel bags.

At Chyna's dresser, Jina slid the lotion bottles, perfumes, and different makeup compacts into the bag. Looking around, she reached for her deodorant, and grabbed that too. "You and your hypoallergens. Why can't you use Dial like most people?"

"Okay, stop . . . look and listen to me, over here." Chyna waved her hand. "Jina Nicole Jameson-King! Something is wrong. Someone sent you here for something, so spill it, and why and where are you taking all my stuff?"

"My brother . . . I've never," Jina said evasively, "I have never, ever seen him like this. . . . Oh, he is so romantic, I'd marry him if he asked me, of course, then I'd be on Jerry Springer." Jina laughed. "But Dean Emory Jameson, he's so in love, I can't stand it. I didn't think he had a sentimental bone in his body." Jina dropped the bags to fan her eyes when they filled with tears.

Chyna could only smile. Dean was sweet; his sisters, especially Jina, the one who swore she wasn't the touchy-feely type, never saw that side of him. Chyna looked over at her friend and future sister-in-law. "Okay, but that still doesn't explain why you're here, why you're taking my things. Where in the world are we going? Please sit down, you're making me nervous!"

"So many questions. Can't you just come along with me without questions for once? Where are we going? What are we going to do? Peck, peck, peck, peck. And don't look at me like that," Jina said as she removed an oversized robe from the garment bag she had brought in with her.

"My, aren't we touchy?" Chyna said, then laughed at her friend. Something was up but she didn't know what. She started to remove her gown when Jina looked at her and said, "Keep that on, and put this on, on top of it."

Chyna looked at Jina as if she'd lost her mind. She might not be able to get her to inform her where they were going but she was going to definitely find out why she needed to remain in her beautiful wedding dress. "Okay, J, why in the world would I stay in my wedding dress?" Chyna asked impatiently.

"We're going to be late for your wedding!" Jina exploded.

Chyna's mouth dropped in astonishment as she watched Jina pick up the tote bag as if she hadn't said anything alarming. She dropped the bag again, took a deep breath before she covered her face, and burst into tears. "I'm getting married? *Today?*"

"In an hour and forty-five minutes." Jina wiped her eyes and smiled. "Now come on!"

Chapter 35

"You know, you sent the wrong person to do the job. She will mess everything up, and you'll have one big nightmare on your hands," said Jojo.

"Thanks for the vote of confidence. I was hoping just one time she wouldn't spill the damn beans. She's gotta come through," Dean said.

Dean looked over at his brother, who heaved a garden torch into the ground like Paul Bunyan. "What was I supposed to do, send you over there? She would've known something was up for sure then. At least she's been with them all week picking out everything. Jina is just supposed to tell her that they're going out to take pictures, then bring her over here. If she could do that one simple task, then we're home free. If she agrees to marry me after all this, anything is possible."

"What the hell are you talking about?"

"I'm just saying that she probably is going to hate me for putting everything together so quickly. Don't women like to fuss over the details of just about everything?" Dean asked skeptically.

"Do I look like a woman to you? I guess they do, but hell, I don't know. I think that sometimes, though, they like it when we get all sappy and take over."

Dean nodded as if the logic his brother relayed was sound advice. He moved quickly to another subject. "I meant to thank you for what went down. I mean I know I got mad, I . . . we're cool?"

Jojo stood from clearing the pathway of the new brick patio. "We're cool, little bro. You were right to be mad, I'm trying to think more about the outcome of things, since Angie and I . . . I wouldn't want you to put her through something like that, no matter what. I'd probably kill you, you went easy on me. I'm sorry. I really am."

Dean nodded again. "So you and Angie, you sure about that?"

"Never been surer in all my years. It's weird, I kind of feel rushed, like now or never."

"That can't be good."

"It's not, but I won't analyze it to death."

Dean nodded again. That made sense. He knew about feeling rushed into getting through this wedding stuff so he could begin to truly live his life. "Casey and Cassie?"

"I realize they come along with the package, if that's what you mean. I know they won't say good-bye when we say I do. I think I love them too. I know, I know, my attitude . . ."

"Well, no, I mean what about Case?"

"Oh, you mean his talking?" Dean nodded. "Well," Jojo continued, "Angie's been working on some sign language with him. He's got some speech and hearing problems."

"What about school when it starts up?"

"He's had tests. He's going to have more over the summer and then they'll be presented to the school to see what's what. Angie, she's teaching them, on her own. They're as smart as a whip, both of them. But it's a long road ahead, I know."

Dean nodded again, hoping his brother did truly know what he was in for. Love was one thing, as he'd seen over the last few months; fighting for one's love over every obstacle possible was quite another. Dean was skeptical about his brother's ability to jump headfirst into long-term commitment. His brother's ability to deal with Casey's challenges and the work to maintain a relationship with Angie would put him to the ultimate test. Dean was skeptical, but he wasn't one to question it. Not yet, anyway. Only time would tell.

Somehow, through the tears, through all the commotion and excitement, Chyna managed her way over to the Jameson home. As silly as it was, she kept her dress on, used the large, oversized terry cloth robe Jina had had the forethought to bring over. Then she and Chyna, in her robe feeling silly and giddy at the same time, simply walked down the street to the house just a few doors down from her own. The entire situation was unbelievable. Unsure of what to do, Chyna stood in the kitchen, having just entered through the side door, while Jina ran back to the car claiming she'd forgotten something in the trunk.

A million thoughts ran through Chyna's mind: where to go and who in the world had orchestrated such a production. She would die from a fit of hysterical laugher if her heart would just slow down and let her. But it raced on regardless of what she did, said, or thought. Chyna placed a hand over her chest. In an hour and fifteen minutes she was getting married.

Chyna walked to the living room's terrace doors. The curtains were drawn and for the winter a more insulated drapery had been put up over Christmas to keep out the chilly weather. Just as Chyna was about to peek through them, the door swung open and Thomas—Tish, and Chase's son—bolted through. He waved quickly, not recognizing her at first, then slowly turned with a panicked, startled expression on his face to get a better look at her.

"Uh, hi, Aunt Chyna," Thomas said, thrusting his

hands into his pockets and looking repeatedly to the door.

"Hi, Thomas, you look so handsome. . . ." Chyna smiled, looking him over in his black tuxedo with a white shirt that peeked through. Chyna's eyes roamed down to his shiny patent leather shoes, and up again to the black bow tie.

"Uh, thanks, you might want to go upstairs. I think Mama is looking for you. And Grandma too."

"Well, all right, your grandmother and Tish are here. Aren't we going to a church? What were you doing out there?" Chyna pointed to the door.

"Oh, nothing, just playing outside."

"Are those playing clothes?" Chyna asked skeptically.

"Thomas, tell them to let me know when . . ." Dean peeked inside the door and looked up abruptly when he saw Chyna. He quickly stepped through the door, ensuring that none of the outside would be seen by Chyna's nosy peeking. He squeezed painfully through the opening he made.

"Hey!" Dean said and kissed Chyna on the cheek. "Are you, I mean you're ready?"

"I have to do my hair." She reached up and touched the hair that she now realized hadn't had a comb run through it at all. Chyna then touched her face. "And my makeup, but, but," she sputtered. "Dean, this is it. We're getting married today?" she whispered in disbelief.

"Yes, is that all right?"

"No, no, oh no," Chyna cried.

"Okay, okay, we can do it next week or next year," Dean said quickly.

"No, it's just that, you're seeing me before the wedding ceremony," she wailed louder.

"Listen to me!" Dean took Chyna's face between his hands and looked down over at Thomas, who watched as if he didn't know what to do, or say. "T, tell your mom and grandmom that Chyna is here, and that she'll be up in a minute."

He winked and Thomas was gone to do as he asked. "Look at me. Nothing can ruin this, ruin us. We've overcome every possible adversity to get to this point. Seeing you before the wedding, seeing me, it's some superstition someone made up. We have no room for such silly notions in our life."

Chyna nodded, then wiped her eyes. "You look so beautiful."

Dean only chuckled. "Thank you, but guys are handsome, okay? Handsome."

Chyna laughed. "What time is it?"

"Almost time," Dean said, pulling the sleeve to his coat, and checking his watch. Chyna nodded and turned to leave.

"Chyna, this is all right, right? I didn't take anything from you? You feel as if this is our wedding, not my sole production?"

"I don't feel that way at all, I'm just so surprised. I see everything within my grasp, everything you've given me, I'm just overwhelmed." Chyna reached out her hand to turn his face back to hers. "Delightfully overwhelmed, Dean. I'm so happy."

Dean visibly straightened and nodded, smiling. "Kiss me."

"After I say I do." Chyna turned and ran quickly up the stairs.

Alfreah Jameson, dressed in a creamy mint suit, stood from her seat on the bed. She'd been silent while Jina applied Chyna's makeup and Tish styled her hair. Chyna was so absorbed in her thoughts that she forgot Ms. Alfreah was there.

When Alfreah stood, everyone except Chyna left the room. "How are you doing?"

"I'm really excited," Chyna said. "I love your son so much."

"I know you do." Alfreah nodded. "I got this little story to tell you. One day, many, many years ago, I was looking out the window, my Joe by my side like he always was. All of my kids were playing outside, some kind of game. Then I saw my Dean, he pushed you and you skinned your knee and shed a few tears over the pain, scared you more than it hurt. Dean was right there seeing if you were okay. I told Joe."

Chyna watched as Ms. Alfreah stroked the air to her right side, and she wondered if the older woman missed her husband, or if she thought he was still very much spiritually present beside her now.

"I miss my Joe," Alfreah said as if reading Chyna's thoughts before continuing. "But I said to him then, 'Honey, did you see our boy, you see him out there, acting a fool for our new neighbor? And look how hard he pushed her. I think he really likes her.'"

Both Alfreah and Chyna laughed out loud.

"I know you don't believe it, but when you get my age your mind stops running around so much. The clutter up there"—Alfreah tapped an index finger to her temple—"clears up long enough to listen to what God whispers into your ear. I've already seen it, because He told me. Most things He keeps to Himself, lets us figure it out or just die waiting for Him to reveal it to us, but it does eventually come. I see you . . . some more children in my home, my grandbabies. For all my kids, more than my arms can hold, but they're coming. Believe, honey, believe and pray!"

Chyna nodded, wanting to believe and wondering if her future mother-in-law knew of the fate she had already met in the baby-bearing department. It didn't matter, Chyna surmised, she was getting married, and that was all that mattered to her at this time. She couldn't think of anything else, so she told herself while secretly she dreamed of children with Dean.

"Well, look, time's a-wastin', and I gotta get to what I have—blue, borrowed, new? Got all that," Ms. Alfreah continued as she ticked off the traditional items. "I told Dean to give this to you but he's still not convinced about my decision. . . .

"I have so many memories in this house, I don't want to lose it out of the family, and while I love it, I just don't think I can stay here. Now that Joe is gone, I think I want a nice small apartment, maybe nearby—though the transit here and the congestion, I don't like it. I'm growing into a small-town kind of girl even though I was raised in the city. As I age, I want quietness. Blessed quietness! For now, I'm going to live with my daughter and Chase a bit, about a year until the twins get a little older; then maybe I'll purchase something small down there. I haven't chartered all that yet, honey . . . someone's got to keep this place. . . ."

"No," Chyna whispered, shaking her head frantically when Mrs. Jameson removed a thick folded paper and pushed it toward Chyna's hand. "No, no," Chyna said more forcefully, her throat having turned as dry as the Sahara. She folded her hands so tightly she felt her recently manicured fingernails bite into the palm of her skin.

"Since you were a child, I know you wanted to live here and be a part of this family, and even though you didn't sleep here, Chyna, you were a part of this family. I love you like I would my own daughter. I know you had a rough time of it, your mama tried and did the best she could, but you do have her to thank. You get that caretaker stuff from looking after her. You did everything you could, spent a lot of time wishing she would just get up. I know about that. It takes a special person to go into people's homes, to whip the family into shape, not one of the duties you're supposed to have to take on, but you do it, with grace, and love, helping the family cope . . . not everyone can do that. Not everyone has the sensitivity the family needs, and what you did every day for your mother helped to foster that. I'm so far from what I'm trying to say, you did that for Joe, for me, you helped me and I want you to have this deed.

"This house is old and drafty, but I'd like to think it's got a lot of character, and a lot of memories for both of us. You can fix it up, make it yours and Dean's. I just would like for you to have it. It's my, Joe and my, gift to you.

"Let's not talk about it much more now. If you don't marry the man downstairs, he might die of a broken heart. One more thing: all that happened in the past? It's behind you now, let go, okay? One day, if you want, if you remind me, one day I'll tell you about the Hardigs, but not today. They won't mar your day and they won't interfere with your future either. They're gone, over and done with.

"I'll see you downstairs."

Chyna turned to face herself in the mirror. The tears ran profusely from her eyes and she hastily wiped them so as not to stain her dress with black from the mascara she wore. She couldn't believe it. She'd just been given a house, of all things. She'd expected a rope of pearls, a necklace, some antique piece; but property, a symbolism of family and a place to raise another generation of Jamesons? That she hadn't expected at all.

She placed the paper on the table and pushed it away as if it were some disease that would jump on her at any minute.

She closed her eyes and prayed as Alfreah Jameson had instructed her to do. She believed in God, but praying wasn't something she did every day. She would start today.

"Amen," she whispered aloud and looked up to see her reflection in the mirror, then higher up to stare at Lisa Stephens standing behind her.

Chapter 36

Chyna couldn't breathe. Lisa, a rope in her hand, had quickly leaned forward and wrapped it around Chyna's neck so tight it took the air from her lungs and permitted more from entering in. Lisa yanked once and the vanity bench Chyna sat on tilted with her weight until she was on the floor.

Their positions were quickly reversed, and Lisa was suddenly straddling her, applying each and every ounce of weight, of muscle the woman had to Chyna's chest, her thumb finishing what the rope hadn't. It pressed over Chyna's esophagus.

"Please," Chyna whispered. "Don't do this, Lisa."

"He is mine!" Lisa yelled, practically standing with her hands pressed on Chyna's throat.

Chyna blinked in and out. Her vision blurred and she was certain this was the end. Her hands couldn't get a hold of anything. If she could just hit her, punch her, she could get free. But her arms only flailed miserably through the air unable to coordinate anything properly. Finally it seemed her hand contracted into a fist and she landed it soundly against Lisa's cheek.

She tried to scramble away, but Lisa, only temporarily put off, was right back on her. When Chyna pushed her away, Lisa had grabbed a pair of scissors from her back pocket and now lunged at Chyna with her tool of destruction in hand.

Chyna couldn't get her vocal cords to work long enough to yell anything other than a harsh whisper of Dean's name. That clearly wasn't enough—it hurt just to inhale air let alone yell.

Chyna's head hurt, her chest felt heavy, and something sharp was on the verge of piercing the skin under her neck. Without turning her head, Chyna felt instinctively as if lowering her neck would cause the blade that pushed into her skin to slice a vital blood vessel and most likely end her life. Chyna lay very still, relaxing her entire body, and without moving any of her limbs she slowly rolled her eyes down to see the deranged woman that pressed most of her weight dead center on her chest, and held the scissors with precision. Chyna could only see the bright orange of the handle sticking out from Lisa's hand, but it didn't matter what she held, only that if she moved she'd never be married, she'd never have a chance to birth the children Mrs. Jameson had just told her she'd have. Why hadn't someone predicted this one last fight, why hadn't someone told Chyna she'd be in the fight of her life, for her life?

Downstairs, in the cool outside air, the sun was high, warming up the place where he stood. Dean couldn't have asked for a better day. It wasn't as cold as he thought it would be and the open-pit outdoor fireplaces he'd rented ensured that no one, even a beautiful woman in a wedding dress, got cold. Now if she would only come down the makeshift aisle he'd made by bringing in tall potted plants in golden pots that led the way to the edge of the space where Dean stood with the minister to his right and his brother at his back.

Growing antsy, he looked over again at this mother, who had been the last to come down. She'd said to give Chyna just ten minutes longer, only that was fifteen minutes ago.

He smiled to assure everyone gathered that everything was okay until he heard his name at the end of a scream. He looked up at the window and took off in a mad dash through the terrace doors and was up the stairs with his brother on his heels in a matter of seconds.

Seeing Lisa Stephens, a pair of scissors in her hand with Chyna's neck between the two blades, was enough to send him over the edge.

"Don't do this, Lisa. Please," Dean pleaded.

Chyna could barely make out what he said. Her head hurt and her vision blurred in and out of focus while the pain in her throat intensified from the little breath she was able to let in and out of her lungs.

Dean inched closer, his hands outstretched as if he could reach her.

"Why not?" Lisa said heatedly. "I love you, I did everything for you. You said you didn't care if your place burned down and I thought I did right, that you'd turn to me for comfort. That's what Warren said . . . that you'd feel despondent and need a shoulder to cry on, and then she came back to town." Lisa looked down with hateful eyes. She squeezed harder.

"This is not the way. I'm sorry, you need some help, and I'll . . . get it for you," Dean said, trying to sound sweet but realizing any falseness wouldn't help Chyna. He saw her eyes dazed and confused, somewhat cloudy, which wasn't good. She would pass out any moment.

"Lisa, I care," Dean said, trying a different route, "I care a lot about you, but this . . . this"—he gestured with a sweep of his hand to encompass what was before him—"this won't solve anything. I would never want you to hurt anyone. I'd never want you to . . . kill, that's just not the way, okay?" He saw her soften at his plea. Her hand relaxed just a little from its death grip on the scissors, and in a rush, Trent and Jojo moved forward to tackle Lisa and pull her off of Chyna.

For a moment, Chyna didn't know what happened. She felt the pressure on her chest ease abruptly, and then the carpet felt as if someone were snatching it from under her like a magician would a tablecloth. She was lifted, higher and higher, and heard Lisa Stephens's cries of unrequited love in the background. Just as suddenly, things went quiet. Dean had taken her to another room and closed the door.

"Chyna, look at me. Here, over here," Dean said, gently bringing her face around to meet his. He took his eyes from hers a moment, tilting her head to examine the tiny welts on her neck. They weren't bloody, and he thanked God that they rose only slightly with irritation.

"Dean."

"Yeah, babe. I'm here."

"She didn't kill herself, did she?" Chyna asked. No matter what, she didn't want another life to go, no matter how much it might have seemed appropriate. She thought back to Warren.

"No, no, she'll go to jail. She's still alive. Kicking and screaming but alive."

"Can we get married now?"

Dean smiled. Her fortitude astounded him. "Maybe in a bit. We've got a few more important things to take care of right now."

"Nothing is more important, Dean. You saw me before the wedding. You're seeing me again, this isn't right. Everything's ruined."

Dean rolled his eyes heavenward, thinking she'd almost been sliced up like a piece of paper and here she was thinking of silly superstitions. Dean sobered when he saw a tear snake from her eye. "Listen, that's a silly rule, it doesn't matter. We're going to get married, we are, but we have to make sure you're all right. Does anything hurt?"

"The minister is still here, we can still get married

now?" Chyna said, ignoring Dean's question and the pain in her head.

"Yes, everyone is downstairs, they've probably started on the lobster. Tish and Jina were eyeing it like a couple of malnourished children."

"We're having lobster?"

"And shrimp scampi and crab imperial; hot wings for men who don't like that fussy stuff. Now answer my question, Chyna. Where is your pain?"

"Dean, we could still get married," Chyna stated.

"We are going to still get married, but that is not what I asked you, Chyna. Please, please answer me."

"Dean," Chyna said, barely whispering. Her throat was scratchy and she was a bit shaken up, but more than that, she was frustrated, and hurt, that some crazy woman would ruin her wedding. "I'm hurt."

"Where?" Dean lifted her, ready to move to the door and down the steps.

"Where are we going?" Chyna grabbed her head when Dean moved so fast—lifting her as if she weighed less than a postage stamp—that her stomach was sent tumbling and her head spinning.

"You just said you're hurting. Damn it, we're going to the doctor, you could have a concussion."

"No, no, no. I'm hurt that she would—her, Lisa—try to ruin my wedding, and I feel so bad for her."

"You feel bad for her? Chyna, you astound me. She's an insane, satanic, crazy bit—"

"Don't say that, and sit down, we're not going to the hospital."

"Don't tell me where we are not going," Dean said, even as he sat down and smiled at Chyna. He took a deep breath. "About Lisa, she's going to go to jail if I have anything to say or do about it and I will, trust me. How you can still be so calm about her . . ." Dean shook his head, thinking back to what almost happened, what could have happened, and disbelieving all of it.

"You know, Dean, she loved . . . she loves you. There are all kinds of songs about love and how crazy it can make a person act, react, but she needs some help."

"So she should have pads in her cell and not just concrete walls?" Dean asked skeptically.

"No, I mean psychological."

"So do I. That's where the padding comes in," Dean said seriously.

Chyna couldn't help smiling. She rested her head where Dean had just placed a pillow. Waiting until he shrugged out of his coat and lay beside her, she started talking again. "What I mean is that, as children, Dean, coming up we were friends, not good friends, but we had similar home lives. . . . The difference was that I had a refuge. I could come here to find the most perfect example of what a family that loves and cares should be and do and how they should be toward one another. Lisa didn't have that."

"That's no excuse, Chyna. Some people, some children have been raised in the worst situations and still have been able to get along in society, to know what's wrong and what's right."

"I agree, and then there are some that still fall through the cracks. But while I have sympathy for her, it doesn't run so deep that I'll let her take the one thing I've waited so long for. There's something that you've planned, that I've unknowingly been preparing for these past two weeks: my wedding day, Dean. This is our wedding day. I've waited so long to get to this point, and I want it. I want you."

"You got me, Chyna. Make no mistake, I'm yours."

"Oh, I know." Chyna smiled devilishly and reached a hand around him. "Want to have the wedding night before the wedding?"

"Okay," Dean said, leaning in to kiss Chyna's lips.

"Stop it, I'm kidding," Chyna said. "I want our wedding, today, December twenty-eighth, the day you picked. For whatever reason, you picked it, and everything is in order."

"I picked it for no particular reason. I thought two weeks was enough time to get everything picked out, I thought it was enough time for you to recover from your cold and the other stuff, and I guess most importantly, I wanted to be married to you before the start of the new year, but there are still three days left, we can make it for the thirtieth or—" Dean stopped talking when Chyna placed her fingers over his lips.

"No, this is it. Now." Chyna sat up carefully. She knew if she exhibited any wobbliness, any sign that something was wrong, Dean would take her to the hospital without further argument. She really did feel fine, she just needed food and she could have all she wanted after she was married. Dean's eyes were upon her, scrutinizing her for anything out of order. She turned to him and smiled. "Will you carry me down the aisle?"

"No," Dean said. He stood, put his jacket back on, and reached for Chyna. "Bubba's here for that," he said.

"Oh," Chyna said, ready to cry again, so glad that her old friend would be such an important part of her special day. "You thought of everything," she said.

"I was highly motivated," Dean said and carried Chyna down the stairs to their wedding ceremony.

Epilogue

Chyna and Dean returned to her home after a long drive from Georgia and almost eight straight hours at a hospital. Lazily, they removed their clothes and climbed into bed. Chyna grabbed her notepad and quickly with the charcoal pencil set she'd received for Christmas sketched an idea as Dean sat in bed looking over her shoulder.

"Can you believe it? They're here," she said.

"I can't believe it. Chase was a wreck, I thought they were going to admit him in a bed next to my sister," Dean said.

Chyna laughed. "He was just so nervous."

"Yeah. What are you writing?"

"Their names. I'm going to make something, paint something, and add their names on it: Camille Sharon Alton, she came first, right? Then Karynn Sophie Alton. They were so precious, they looked like two little tubs of honey."

Chyna set aside her sketchpad, satisfied that she had at least jotted down a few ideas of whatever she eventually planned to make for the newborn Alton twins who had entered the world just hours ago.

"I'm so sorry I'm rambling on, honey." Chyna turned to snuggle closer to Dean, who lay beside her.

"It's all right. You're just happy. I am too. I am," Dean confirmed, knowing Chyna didn't totally believe him.

"But you're worried, too?" Chyna asked.

"Yeah." Dean nodded.

"About Jojo?"

"Yeah."

"What kind of military calls two days after the New Year, eight days after Christmas? That's insane."

"Yeah." Dean chuckled softly. "Eight days after Christmas?" And then, raising an eyebrow at Chyna's look of outrage, "Only you would think about it like that. I think it's going to be all right, I guess. I want to hope that it will anyway."

"It will, honey, it will. He's on special assignment, they're tying up some things overseas?" Chyna asked and moved farther down under the covers. She wrapped her arms around her husband.

"Yeah, something like that, he didn't seem to have a lot of details, or I guess he couldn't relay a lot of them."

"It would seem so," Chyna said.

"I think he asked Angie to marry him."

"What?" Chyna gasped. Dean nodded. "Wow. Well, we'll help out with the kids, whatever she needs. She's family."

"I love you, Chyna Jameson." Dean turned to look at her. He'd never cease to be amazed by how thoughtful she was, how she was always ready to do whatever she could for anyone. His heart would turn to mush, however, each time she said something just as she had to remind him how fortunate he was to have got it together enough to move on. He relegated the rest of his thoughts and whatever fate came to meet his brother to the powers that be. Dean turned his face, receiving more of Chyna's kisses. Wrapping his arms around her waist, he rolled both of them until she was pinned beneath him. Before he could speak his request, she nodded.

"Yes, right now," she whispered breathlessly.

Dean removed the covers and stood.

"Where are you going?" Chyna said, grabbing his arm and pulling him back to the bed.

"I'm going to get a . . ." Dean pointed over his shoulder to the bathroom but stopped talking when Chyna shook her head.

"I wanted to tell you before we rushed to the hospital earlier and before on our wedding night and I guess now is as good a time as any. Whatever happens, or doesn't happen, Dean, I want nothing between us. We are husband and wife."

"Are you sure, Chyna?"

Chyna nodded and Dean climbed fully onto the bed. He moved to be beside her, and eased his weight on top of her.

"Listen," Dean said, his voice hoarse when Chyna's cold fingers touched him, held him, stroked him a moment, before opening to guide him into her. "Chyna, baby, listen to me . . ." He breathed once inside her. Dean gritted his teeth, trying to keep his control and quickly relate the importance of what he wanted to tell her. Her nipples beaded to hardened pebbles against his chest and she held him close.

"A baby, Chyna?" Dean managed to whisper in her ear. He propped himself up on his arms to look at her. "I love you so much but a baby does not make or break us. We'll be okay without one, promise me, okay? Promise me you understand we can adopt. There are other options. We'll see doctors, have tests—"

"I do," Chyna interrupted him. "Dean? I really do," she said again, taking his face between her hands, imploring him to look into her eyes, see the sincerity, the contentedness that a family of three, five, and most importantly that a family of just two would be all right, that she would be all right with him, alone.

Dean nodded, kissing her again and again, until the need to stroke, to create their familiar rhythm, outweighed everything else.

Dear Reader,

I hope you have enjoyed Chyna and Dean's story and thank you for taking time to visit with them. I cannot begin to thank all of you enough for your support of my first full-length novel, *Come What May*. It has done well because of readers like you. I continue to meet, greet, and receive a word of praise and encouragement from each of you daily. Keep it coming. ☺ And thank you, again.

I hope that Jojo will have his own story soon. I am working on it. You can always read (if you haven't already) Tish and Chase's story in *Come What May* where Jojo and Angie and other special characters are first introduced.

Please drop me an e-mail, sign my guest book or send me a good old-fashioned handwritten or typed letter whenever you have time. I will always respond. Please use one of the methods below to correspond with me.

www.Teegarner.com

Teegarner@aol.com

Tracee Lydia Garner
P.O. Box 651362
Sterling, VA 20165-1362

Until next time, I wish the best to you and yours in every endeavor,

Tracee

ABOUT THE AUTHOR

Tracee Lydia Garner is a national best-selling and award-winning author. She is the grand-prize winner of BET's Annual First Time Writers Contest for her novella "Family Affairs," which appears in the *All That & Then Some* anthology. She has always written poetry and, a few years ago, found a great love when she explored longer genres and romance. A Virginia native, she currently resides in the northern Virginia area with her family. She is an advocate for persons with disabilities and often speaks to groups of persons with disabilities, youth and minorities. She tremendously enjoys writing, cooking and, of course, loves to read. Tracee is a member of the Mystery Writers of America (MWA), Sisters in Crime (SinC), Romance Writers of America (RWA National, Washington DC, and Virginia Chapters), The Writers Center and the Authors Supporting Authors Positively (ASAP) Organization.

More Sizzling Romance From
Francine Craft